Protecting Dakota

SEAL of Protection
Book 9

by Susan Stoker

Cover Design by Chris Mackey, AURA Design Group
Cover Model: Wander Aguiar
Edited by Kelli Collins & Missy Borucki

Manufactured in the United States

A Note to the Reader

This is a special book to me because for a couple of reasons.

It was a collaboration born over several glasses of wine at an author convention. The twelve of us decided we wanted to write books that were linked together, but still connected to our own series'. I loved the conception of a former commander who was tasked to covertly take down homegrown terrorists. I also loved that the books could be read in any order. I hope you'll check out the other books in the Sleeper SEAL series.

The other reason this book means a lot to me is because it's the last official book in the original SEAL of Protection Series. Protecting Caroline was my first indie published book, and it's only right that she kicks as much butt in this book as she did in her own.

BUT, this is not the end of the SEALs. You have been introduced to another team of SEALs in past books, but you'll get to meet Gumby, Rocco, Ace, Bubba, Rex, and Phantom once again here. Their series, SEAL of Protection: Legacy will debut soon.

And just because Wolf and the gang will be transitioned from an active SEAL team to a training role, doesn't mean that you won't see them again and get to catch up with their families.

Thank you for your support of my SEALs. Here's to many more missions, adventures, and love stories with the Legacy team!

Table of Contents

Prologue

RETIRED NAVY COMMANDER Greg Lambert leaned forward to rake in the pile of chips his full house had netted him. Tonight, he would leave the weekly gathering not only with his pockets full, but his pride intact.

The scowls he earned from his poker buddies at his unusual good luck were an added bonus.

They'd become too accustomed to him coming up on the losing side of Five Card Stud. It was about time he taught them to never underestimate him.

Vice President Warren Angelo downed the rest of his bourbon and stubbed out his Cuban cigar. "Looks like Lady Luck is on your side tonight, Commander."

After he neatly stacked his chips in a row at the rail in front of him, Greg glanced around at his friends. It occurred to him right then, this weekly meeting wasn't so different from the joint sessions they used to have at the Pentagon during his last five years of service.

While the location was now the Secretary of State's

basement, the gatherings still included top-ranking military brass, politicians, and the director of the CIA, who had been staring at him strangely all night long.

"It's about time the bitch smiled my way, don't you think? She usually just cleans out my pockets and gives you my money," Greg replied with a sharp laugh as his eyes roved over the spacious man cave with envy before they snagged on the wall clock.

It was well past midnight, their normal break-up time. He needed to get home, but what did he have to go home to? Four walls, and Karen's mean-as-hell Chihuahua who hated him.

Greg stood, scooted back his chair, and stretched his shoulders. The rest of his poker buddies quickly left, except for Vice President Angelo, Benedict Hughes with the CIA, and their host tonight, Percy Long, the Secretary of State.

Greg took the last swig of his bourbon, then set the glass on the table. When he took a step to leave, they moved to block his way to the door. "Something on your minds, gentlemen?" he asked, their cold, sober stares making the hair on the back of his neck stand up.

It wasn't a comfortable feeling, but one he was familiar with from his days as a Navy SEAL. That feeling usually didn't portend anything good was about to go down, but neither did the looks on these men's faces.

Warren cleared his throat and leaned against the

mahogany bar with its leather trimmings. "There's been a significant amount of chatter lately." He glanced at Ben. "We're concerned."

Greg backed up a few steps, putting some distance between himself and the men. "Why are you telling me this? I've been out of the loop for a while now." Greg was retired, and bored stiff, but not stiff enough to tackle all that was wrong in the United States at the moment or fight the politics involved in fixing things.

Ben let out a harsh breath then gulped down his glass of water. He set the empty glass down on the bar with a sigh and met Greg's eyes. "We need your help, and we're not going to beat around the bush," he said, making Greg's short hairs stand taller.

Greg put his hands in his pockets, rattling the change in his right pocket and his car keys in the left while he waited for the hammer. Nothing in Washington, D.C. was plain and simple anymore. Not that it ever had been.

"Spit it out, Ben," he said, eyeballing the younger man. "I'm all ears."

"Things have changed in the US. Terrorists are everywhere now," he started, and Greg bit back a laugh at the understatement of the century.

He'd gotten out before the recent INCONUS attacks started, but he was still in service on 9/11 for the ultimate attack. The day that replaced Pearl Harbor as the day that would go down in infamy.

"That's not news, Ben," Greg said, his frustration mounting in his tone. "What does that have to do with me, other than being a concerned citizen?"

"More cells are being identified every day," Ben replied, his five o'clock shadow standing in stark contrast to his now paler face. "The chatter about imminent threats, big jihad events that are in the works, is getting louder every day."

"You do understand that I'm no longer active service, right?" Greg shrugged. "I don't see how I can be of much help there."

"We want you to head a new division at the CIA," Warren interjected. "Ghost Ops, a sleeper cell of SEALs to help us combat the terrorist sleeper cells in the US…and whatever the hell else might pop up later."

Greg laughed. "And where do you think I'll find these SEALs to sign up? Most are deployed over—"

"We want *retired* SEALs like yourself. We've spent millions training these men, and letting them sit idle stateside while we fight this losing battle alone is just a waste." Ben huffed a breath. "I know they'd respect you when you ask them to join the contract team you'd be heading up. You'd have a much better chance of convincing them to help than we will."

"Most of those guys are like me, worn out to the bone or injured when they finally give up the teams.

Otherwise, they'd still be active. SEALs don't just quit." *Unless their wives were taken by cancer and their kids were off at college, leaving them alone in a rambling house when they were supposed to be traveling together and enjoying life.*

"What kind of threats are you talking about?" Greg asked, wondering why he was even entertaining such a stupid idea.

"There are many. More every day. Too many for us to fight alone," Ben started, but Warren held up his palm.

"The president is taking a lot of heat. He has three and a half years left in his term, and taking out these threats was a campaign promise. He wants the cells identified and the terror threats eradicated quickly."

These two, and the president, sat behind desks all day. They'd never been in a field op before, so they had no idea the planning and training that took place before a team ever made it to the field. Training a team of broken-down SEALs to work together would take double that time, because each knew better than the rest how things should be done, so there was no "quick" about it.

"That's a tall order. I can't possibly get a team of twelve men on the same page in under a year. Even if I can find them." Why in the hell was he getting excited, then? "Most are probably out enjoying life on a beach somewhere." Exactly where he would be with Karen if she hadn't fucking died on him as soon as he'd retired four years ago.

"We don't want a *team*, Greg," Percy Long corrected, unfolding his arms as he stepped toward him. "This has to be done stealthily because we don't want to panic the public. If word got out about the severity of the threats, people wouldn't leave their homes. The press would pump it up until they created a frenzy. You know how that works."

"So, let me get this straight. You want individual SEALs, sleeper guys who agree to be called up for special ops, to perform solo missions?" Greg asked, his eyebrows lifting. "That's not usually how they work."

"Unusual times call for unusual methods, Greg. They have the skills to get it done quickly and quietly," Warren replied, and Greg couldn't argue. That's exactly the way SEALs operated—they did whatever it took to get the job done.

Ben approached him, placed his hand on his shoulder as if this was a tag-team effort, and Greg had no doubt that it was just that. "Every terrorist or wannabe terror organization has roots here now. Al Qaeda, the Muslim Brotherhood, Isis, or the Taliban—you name it. They're not here looking for asylum. They're actively recruiting followers and planning events to create a caliphate on our home turf. We can't let that happen, Greg, or the United States will never be the same."

"You'll be a CIA contractor, and can name your

price," Warren inserted, and Greg's eyes swung to him. "You'll be on your own in the decision making. We need to have plausible deniability if anything goes wrong."

"Of course," Greg replied, shaking his head. If anything went south, they needed a fall guy, and that would be him in this scenario. Not much different from the dark ops his teams performed under his command when he was active duty.

God, why did this stupid idea suddenly sound so intriguing? Why did he think he might be able to make it work? And why in the hell did he suddenly think it was just what he needed to break out of the funk he'd been living in for four years?

"I can get you a list of potential hires, newly retired SEALs, and the president says *anything* else you need," Warren continued quickly. "All we need is your commitment."

The room went silent, and Greg looked deeply into each man's eyes as he pondered a decision. What the hell did he have to lose? If he didn't agree, he'd just die a slow, agonizing death in his recliner at home. At only forty-seven and still fit, that could be a lot of years spent in that chair.

"Get me the intel, the list, and the contract," he said, and a surge of adrenaline made his knees weak.

He was back in the game.

Chapter One

"HEY, WOLF, HOW'D it go?" Slade "Cutter" Cutsinger asked the SEAL as he entered the office on the Naval base.

"I'd tell ya, Cutter, but then I'd have to kill you," Wolf joked as he smiled at Slade.

It was a long-running joke between the two men. Slade was a retired SEAL himself, now working as a contractor for the Navy. He worked directly under Patrick Hurt, Wolf's commander. Slade probably knew more about the mission Wolf and his team had been on than Wolf did himself.

"The commander's waiting in his office for a de-brief," Slade told the other man with a chin lift, indicating the door to his right. "All good at home? Caroline okay?"

"She's good," Wolf told him. "Thanks for asking. And I should've said something before now, but I appreciate you checking on her during that last mission. She's used to them, as much as she *can* be used to her spouse leaving for who-knows-where for who-knows-how-long. She told me you helped make her and the others feel better about that mission. You know if you ever need anything, all you've got to do is ask."

"I do know, and it's appreciated," Slade told him.

He hadn't ever worked in the field with Wolf or the other guys on his team, but he respected the hell out of all of them. They were extremely successful on their missions, didn't take absurd chances, and most importantly to Slade, all took care of their families. And by "take care," Slade meant they realized how precious their women and children were and worked their asses off to make sure they knew it. They didn't sleep around on them. If they were running late on a mission, Wolf always made sure Slade checked up on their families. And they had tracking devices on their women, just in case.

Slade wasn't supposed to know about the trackers, but his friend, Tex, had let that little gem slip one night when they were shooting the shit on the phone. Slade had worked on a team with Tex before he'd been medically retired, and hadn't ever found another man for whom he had more respect. When he'd found out about Tex marrying, and then adopting a child from Iraq, he'd been almost as proud for the man as Tex probably was himself.

They'd been talking on the phone one night and

Tex had told him that his wife, Melody, had given birth to a little girl named Hope, then he'd told Slade that he'd be damned if any of their enemies got their hands on his baby. With his wife's approval and encouragement, he'd had a bracelet made for his daughter to wear with a tiny tracking device. That's when he'd let the cat out of the bag about the women who belonged to Wolf's team also voluntarily wearing similar jewelry.

Slade had felt a little melancholy that he hadn't ever found a woman he cared about enough to want to protect like that…and who would let him. His ex, Cynthia—not Cindy; God forbid someone call her Cindy—didn't have much interest in anything he did and by the end of their four-year marriage, the feeling was definitely mutual.

All his life, he'd wanted to feel a special connection with a woman. For some reason, he had a feeling he'd just know when he met her. In his twenties, he hadn't been too anxious to find her because he'd been young and eager to make a difference in the Navy. In his thirties, he was ready to settle down, even though he was neck deep working on the SEAL teams. And now, in his late forties, he felt way too old to try to start a serious relationship. He figured he'd lost his chance.

So now he was a confirmed bachelor who kept tabs on the families of the SEALs that worked for Commander Hurt instead.

Mentally shrugging, Slade tried to concentrate on the paperwork in front of him. He missed the action of being on a SEAL team, but he was definitely too old to do the work of the younger men anymore. He gladly left it to them.

The phone next to him rang, and Slade answered. "Cutsinger. How may I help you?"

"I'm looking for Slade Cutsinger. Is this he?"

Slade didn't recognize the voice, but he definitely recognized the authority behind the words.

"Yes, Sir. I'm Cutsinger."

"This is retired Navy Commander Greg Lambert. Is this line secure?"

Slade was taken aback. He didn't remember ever working with a Greg Lambert, and he had a good memory. "No, Sir, it is not. If you need to talk to Commander Hurt, I recommend—"

"It's you I need," Greg interrupted. "I'm going to give you a phone number. I expect you to call me tonight from a secure line. I have a proposition for you."

"No disrespect, Sir, but I don't know you," Slade said, having trouble keeping his tone professional. He didn't mind taking orders, but usually he knew the person who was giving those orders.

"You don't, but we have a mutual friend who speaks highly of you."

When he didn't continue, Slade asked, "A mutual

friend?"

"John Keegan."

Fuckin' A. Tex. What the hell had the man gotten him into now? "He's one of the best men I've ever met," Slade told Greg honestly.

"Ditto. Got a pen?"

"Yeah." Slade dutifully jotted down the number he was given.

"Needless to say, this is a highly sensitive matter. John assured me that you were discreet and would be extremely interested."

"At least he's half right," Slade mumbled, and ignored the chuckle on the other end of the line. "I'll call around nineteen hundred, if that's all right."

"I'll be waiting." And the former commander ended the call without another word.

Slade slowly hung up the phone on his end, lost in thought. He tried to quash the spark of interest that flared deep in his belly, but didn't quite succeed. Working as a contractor for the US Navy kept his toe dipped into the dangerous waters he used to swim in, but it wasn't the same. Somehow, he knew that whatever Lambert had to say to him tonight would change his life. Whether or not it was for the better remained to be seen.

"WHAT THE FUCK have you gotten me into now, Tex?" Slade asked as soon as his friend picked up the phone.

"Hello to you too, Cutter. How's the weather out there in California? Let me guess, you're sitting on the balcony of your apartment watching the ocean and wishing you weren't bored off your ass."

"Asshole," Slade said with a smile. Tex knew him too well. That's what happened when you worked side by side, getting shot at and saving each other's lives too many times to count. "I got a call from a former Commander Lambert today. He said you two talked about me."

"Not beating around the bush, I see," Tex said.

"I'm supposed to call him back in thirty on a secure line," Slade told his old teammate.

"Gotcha. Lambert is one of the good guys. Worked with him a few times. He has a new job, under the table, and wanted the names of some of the best of the best former SEALs I knew. You were at the top of that list."

"Under the table?" Slade asked. "Not sure I like the sound of that."

"Nothing we haven't been involved with before," Tex reassured him. "Hear him out."

"You been briefed on this job?"

"No. I know Lambert wanted to ask me to help out, but with Hope being so young and Akilah still settling in, I didn't want to do anything that would take me away from home," Tex told him.

Slade got that. If he had a wife and new baby, not to mention a recently adopted teenager, he wouldn't want to leave home either. Feeling restless, he got up and went into his apartment. "You have your hands full with all the teams you work with as well," Slade told his old friend.

"That I do. But I love it. I enjoy being involved in all aspects of our Armed Forces. But it's more than that. I do it to keep the men safe so they can get home to their families."

"It's more appreciated than you'll ever know," Slade told Tex.

As if uncomfortable with the turn in conversation, Tex replied, "That being said, even though I'm not the man for this job, you need anything, you better call. You know no one can find needles in haystacks better than me."

"I don't know, man. I hear there's a chick in Texas who's giving you a run for your money," Slade teased.

"I'll deny it if it comes up later, but that's no lie," Tex said immediately. "Beth is amazing, and she's been able to hack into some places I wouldn't even have tried."

Glancing at his watch, and seeing his time was up, Slade reluctantly said, "Gotta run. Appreciate the head's up and the confirmation that this is on the up and up."

"Anytime. I wasn't kidding, Cutter," Tex said in a hard voice. "You need *anything*, you call. I don't know what Lambert has up his sleeve, but I'm guessing since he didn't brief me when he called, he wants whatever he's asking to be on the down-low…meaning you working alone since you're retired, but nothing is ever fucking solo when it comes to my teams."

"I'll see what he has to say and make the decision whether or not to bring in anyone else," Cutter told Tex. "But I hear you. I'll call if I need you."

"Good. Later."

"Later," Slade echoed and clicked off the phone. He put his personal cell down on the arm of the chair he was sitting in and took a deep breath. Inhaling the scent of salt and sea drifting through the open balcony door, he took a moment to try to calm his mind and body. The pesky feeling that his life was about to change was relentless.

Slade thought about his life. He liked it…for the most part. His oceanside apartment was perfect for him. Not huge, not tiny. He'd saved up his money while he was active duty, and his retirement check wasn't anything to sneeze at. He had a fancy-ass 4K television in the living room behind him, good friends he worked with who he had drinks with every so often, and he could be in the ocean swimming in three minutes, if he was so inclined.

His family was good. His sister, Sabrina, was married with three kids, and his brother also had a wife and two kids. His siblings were both younger than he was, and lived on the other side of the country. He didn't see his nieces and nephews often, but when he did, it was as if no time at all had passed. He missed his parents, but he'd never had the kind of relationship with them where they'd communicated on a regular basis.

But Slade had to be honest with himself. He was lonely. He had a great apartment, a good job, but no one to share his life with. He'd tried online dating, *that* had been a disaster, and he was way too fucking old to pick up chicks at *Aces Bar and Grill,* the notorious hangout for current and former Navy SEALs. It had become less of a pick-up joint since it was now owned by Jessyka Sawyer, the wife of one of Wolf's teammates, but a bar would always be a bar and there would always be women trolling for a one-night stand or the chance to snag a military guy, and men hoping for a quick hook-up.

Without giving himself a chance to get any more morose than he already was, Slade picked up the secure cell phone he'd been issued by the Navy so he could talk to Commander Hurt and the SEALs under his command, and brought it back out to the balcony with him. He dialed the former Commander Lambert's number.

"Right on time," the commander said as a greeting.

"Bodes well for our working relationship."

"I'm not sure I *want* a working relationship with you," Slade told him honestly.

"This line is secure, correct?" Greg asked.

Irritated that he'd think for a second he'd call on one that wasn't when the man had made it more than clear he wouldn't talk otherwise, Slade bit out, "Yes."

Greg chuckled. "Had to ask. No offense intended. You talk to John?"

"Just hung up with him," Slade confirmed.

"Figured. I'm just going to get right down to it, if you don't mind."

"I prefer it, actually," Slade said, his body tensing with whatever he was about to hear.

"I'm in charge of a new initiative, a secret one, to take down sleeper cells of terrorists around the country. The fuckers are getting the drop on us, and it needs to stop. I've been authorized to mobilize my own brand of sleeper cells…retired SEALs."

Slade wasn't sure he understood. "And?"

"And I want *you*, Cutter. I've read your file. I know your strengths and weaknesses. I've spoken with John and some of your other teammates. You're levelheaded and you gather all the intel before jumping into anything. You're determined and have a love for your country that isn't matched by many people. But more importantly, you've been successful on your own."

"I was *never* on my own," Slade protested. "Not once. Even if I went in to get a hostage, my team was at my back."

"I know that." Greg backed off a bit. "What I meant was that when the shit hit the fan, you didn't panic. You simply changed to Plan B...or C, D, or E. I need you."

Slade took a deep breath and let it out slowly. He was curious. Dammit. "Tell me more," he demanded grumpily.

"Six months ago, there was a bombing at LAX."

When the other man didn't elaborate, Slade prompted, "Yeah? I remember it. There was one bomber, he took a handful of hostages. The building was in the process of being evacuated, but the fucker blew himself up, along with all of the hostages, before everyone was out. Ansar al-Shari'a took responsibility."

"Correct. That's what was reported in the news," Greg said.

The hair on the back of Slade's neck stood on end. "That's what was reported on the news?" he repeated.

"Yes. Internet chatter has been extremely active. The bomber was a college kid. He'd been recruited online. The leader's name is Aziz Fourati. Government believes he's Tunisian, and based on the success of the LAX bombing, he's actively recruiting more soldiers. He wants to duplicate his success...on a national level."

"Jesus," Slade swore. "If we thought 9/11 was bad, if

he's successful, he could cripple transportation in this country for months."

"Exactly. But that's not all."

"Fuck. What else?"

"He was there," Greg said flatly.

"Where?"

"At the bombing. He was one of the so-called hostages. Gave a speech and everything right before the kid pulled the trigger and blew everyone sky-high."

"How do you know?" Slade demanded.

"All security cameras at the airport were jammed right before everything went down. So there's no public video of anything that happened inside, but someone's been posting audio and video on the Dark Web of his speech on the Internet, and using it as a recruitment tool."

Slade knew there was more. "And? Jesus, spit it out."

"Besides Fourati, who slipped out right before the bomber let loose, there was one other survivor."

The words seemed to echo across the phone line. "What? *Who?*"

"Her name is Dakota James. She was supposed to be flying to a conference in Orlando that day."

"There wasn't ever anything in the newspaper," Slade protested. "How do you know for sure?"

"I've got copies of the propaganda videos Fourati has been sending to his minions. She's there, but her body wasn't one of those found when the pieces of that section of the airport were sorted. Lo and behold, she showed up at work the next week with a broken arm. Told her co-workers she'd fallen down a flight of stairs."

"So, what's the deal? What'd she say about the bombing?"

"That's just it," Greg told Slade. "She's in the wind."

"She's gone? What about her job?"

"Quit."

"Just like that?" Slade asked.

"Just like that," Greg confirmed.

"You think she's involved? That what you need me for?"

"No. We don't think she's involved, but we have nothing on Fourati. We have no photos, no videos that show his face. Nada. Zip. Zilch."

"But Dakota James saw him," Slade concluded.

"Exactly. We need her. Fourati has to be stopped before he can carry through with his plan. As far as we can tell, right now he only has a handful of men he's recruited, but the more he gets, the more his plan can snowball."

"You want me to find her."

"Yes. Find her. Get a description of Fourati, then track that asshole down and eliminate the threat."

Ah, there it was.

Slade had been waiting for confirmation that the former commander wanted him to kill for his country once again. The thought should've been repugnant. He'd left that part of his life behind. But then Slade remembered the pictures of the ruined section of the airport. Remembered the pictures and videos of the victims. A mother traveling with her three-month-old baby. The couple celebrating their fiftieth wedding anniversary by flying to Hawaii for a two-week vacation. The business men and women who were caught in the crosshairs of a terrorist.

The resolve to take down the asshole responsible solidified in his belly.

He opened his mouth to agree to take the job, when Greg spoke again. "There's one more thing…"

Ah, shit.

"Fourati has decided that Dakota James is his." Lambert's voice was matter-of-fact.

"What? How does he even know her?"

"Apparently, he saw her in the crowd at the airport, and whatever happened between them made him decide that he wants her for his own. This is why we think she ran."

"Fuckin' A," Slade swore. "She obviously didn't want to be a terrorist's plaything."

"Apparently not. From what we've been able to intercept and decode, he's on her trail."

"Where is she?" Slade demanded. The thought of the poor woman surviving a terrorist bombing, only to be on the run because said terrorist wanted her for his own, was too much for his psyche. His team had told him on more than one occasion that he had a knight-in-shining-armor complex, but Slade didn't care. He loved women. All kinds. Short, tall, fat, skinny, it didn't matter. When push came to shove on a mission, if it involved a woman, Slade was made point. He did whatever it took to protect the women and children.

"That's the thing. We don't know."

"What *do* you know?" he bit out impatiently. "From where I'm sitting, it's precious little. You know there was a woman, and her name, and that she quit her job, but that's about it."

Greg didn't even sound the least bit upset. "That's why we need you. Find Dakota. Get her to tell you what Fourati said before his soldier blew himself up. Figure out what that fucker looks like so we can find him, shut down his dot-com operation, and get one more terrorist off our streets. Yeah?"

"What backup do I have?" Slade asked, knowing he was going to say yes, but wanting as many details as he could get before he did.

"None," was Greg's answer. "Well, none officially. You can call me and I can get you information. But as far as the operation goes, you're on your own. This is an unsanctioned op. If you get caught, you're also on your own. The US government will not bail you out and, if asked, will deny any responsibility for anything."

Slade wasn't surprised in the least. He'd expected that. "Compensation?"

Greg named a figure that made Slade's eyebrows draw up in surprise. Apparently, the government wasn't fucking around.

"I'm in," Slade told him. He wasn't concerned about failing. He'd find Ms. James, get a description of Fourati, kill him, and continue on with his life. He was actually looking forward to the assignment. Not to kill someone, that wasn't something he ever enjoyed, but getting out into the field once more. Using his skills to eliminate a threat.

Once a SEAL, always a SEAL, apparently.

"Good. I've already arranged with Commander Hurt for you to take some time off. Starting tomorrow. There's a relatively new but vetted employee who will be transferred over to your job immediately. Even though he doesn't have your level of clearance, he can still help Hurt keep his head above water until you return. Your replacement has been briefed and your job is secure until you get back."

"Wow," Slade exclaimed. "I shouldn't be surprised, yet I still am. How'd you know I'd say yes?"

"John said you would. I trust him."

23

Slade mentally nodded. Yeah, he trusted Tex, too.

"Tomorrow at o-eight hundred, a folder will be delivered to your apartment with all the information I have on the terrorist group, Fourati, and, of course, Ms. James. Find her, get the intel, then stop Aziz Fourati once and for all."

"Is there a time limit?" Slade asked.

"Not per se. But time is always of the essence. As of right now, Fourati doesn't seem to have enough followers to be a viable threat. However, the more recruits he gets, the higher the possibility that someone will be able to take his place and carry out the threat if he's killed."

Slade understood that. So while Greg said there was no time limit, there was.

"Oh, and not only that, Fourati has said that he wants his new wife by his side before the new year hits."

"Fuck," Slade swore quietly. It was almost the end of November. That meant Fourati was getting impatient, and could have a lead on where Dakota was hiding. The urgency of the case just got ramped up. "I'll look for that folder," Slade informed him.

"Thank you, Cutter," Greg said, using Slade's SEAL nickname once again, proving he really did know a lot about him. "Your country will never know about this, but they're in your debt nevertheless."

"Is this the number I should contact you at if I have questions?" Slade asked. He knew the deal. He knew no one would ever know how many times he'd killed for the sake of national security. He'd long ago gotten over that.

"Yes. I'll be waiting for updates." And with that, Greg hung up.

Slade clicked off the phone and put his head back on the seat. A million things were racing through his brain. Details about the weapons he'd need, how best to take down Fourati without causing a panic, and how in the world he'd pull it all off on his own.

But the one thing that wouldn't let go, that he kept coming back to, was Dakota James. Where was she?

Chapter Two

"HELLO, MR. JAMES. My name is Slade Cutsinger. May I speak with you for a moment?"

Slade waited patiently a respectable distance away from the door he was standing in front of. He'd received the information folder the morning after his phone call with the former commander and had read every word, twice.

It wasn't a lot of information to go off of—it was no wonder Greg had called him—but the picture of Dakota James had made his teeth clench and his hands curl into fists.

He'd never had as visceral a reaction to seeing someone before in his life as he'd had when he'd gazed into her green eyes. They seemed to grab him around the throat from the paper. She wasn't classically beautiful, her facial symmetry was a bit off for that, but it was the happiness and glee he saw in her eyes that made him want to know everything about her.

The picture was from the latest yearbook from Sunset Heights Elementary School where she was the principal…or *had been*. She was wearing a dark blue suit jacket with a white blouse underneath. She had earrings in the shape of apples in her ears, and her dark blonde hair was in a bun at her neck. Her makeup was minimal, but still, her eyes were her best feature and needed no enhancement.

Slade had stared at her picture for a full ten minutes, shock holding him immobile as he memorized her facial features. He wanted to see more of her. Wanted to see her body, see how tall she was when she was standing next to him, talk to her—was her voice low or high?—touch her. He'd had a sudden and unmistakable reaction to her photo. What would it be like to actually be in her presence?

Thinking about what Dakota had been through made him growl low in his throat, which shocked him back into awareness of where he was and what he was doing.

He wanted her. It wasn't rational, it wasn't normal by any stretch of the imagination, but there it was. Slade wanted to see her smile at him. Wanted to see her eyes twinkle with joy as she looked at him. Wanted to see her eating across a table from him, and most definitely wanted to see her green eyes open and look sleepily at him from the other side of his bed.

Slade had looked at hundreds of dossiers, seen hundreds of targets, and not once had any ever affected him like Dakota James. He would make her safe if it was the last thing he did.

Intel about Dakota's father had been included in the file he'd received from Lambert. He was in his upper seventies and living in a house just north of San Diego. Not sure if the man would give him any information about his daughter—he actually hoped he wouldn't, that he was being extremely cautious about Dakota's whereabouts—Slade had packed his saddlebags on his Harley just in case, and headed out.

Feeling as if time truly was running out for Dakota and she was in extreme danger, his only goal was to get to her as soon as he could. He couldn't explain the feeling, and if he tried, knew he'd sound insane, but Slade's intuition had served him well for his career on the teams. He wasn't going to ignore it now.

"What are you selling?" Dakota's dad barked from behind the screen. "I don't need no cookies, I'm fat enough, the election's over, and I don't need my lawn mowed."

"I'm a friend of Dakota's," Slade said.

"Bullshit," he responded immediately. "Dakota wouldn't have a friend like you. No way."

Offended, but also somewhat amused, Slade asked, "Why not?"

"You're too good lookin'," her dad said. "Her

friends all wear fucking sweaters and khaki pants. And no way in hell they'd be ridin' a Harley like you've got parked in my driveway."

"My leather jacket gave it away, huh?" Slade asked, trying to keep a straight face. He respected this man. He said it like it was.

"Just a bit. Want to try again and tell me why you're here, askin' about my Dakota?"

"Your daughter's in danger and I'm probably the only person who can get her out of it."

The older man was silent for a long moment, but Slade stood still and let him look his fill. Finally, after what seemed like hours, but was in reality only a minute or so, Mr. James flipped up the little hook holding the screen door shut and said, "It's cold out there. Don't know what you're thinkin', ridin' around on a motorcycle. Come on in."

Letting out a relieved sigh, Slade followed the gray-haired man into the house and stood back as he closed and locked the front door. He shuffled slowly into a small living room toward a beat-up chocolate-brown recliner that had seen better days. The television was on and a show about female killers was playing. Dakota's father lowered the volume, but didn't turn it off, and gestured to the sofa nearby. "Go on. Sit. Don't got any refreshments to offer. I don't snack much and the Meals on Wheels lady hasn't come by yet. Thought you were her, honestly. You want to know where my Dakota is, don't ya?"

"Why do you say that?"

"Because I'm old, not stupid," was his response. "Look, you're not the first person to come knocking on my door asking if I know where my daughter is. I'll tell you the same thing I told them, I don't know where she is. And I wouldn't tell you even if I did."

"Who else has been here asking about her?" Slade questioned, his brows drawn down in concern.

The older man waved his hand in the air. "Government types, police types, people from work…you know, the usual."

Slade wasn't sure about that, but he let it go for now. "Mr. James, I—"

"Finnegan."

"I'm sorry, what?"

"My name's Finnegan. Finn."

"Right. Finn, I think you know that Dakota's in danger."

Slade sat still even though Finn narrowed his eyes and stared at him for a long moment before saying, "Why would I know that?"

Taking a chance that Dakota was close with her father, Slade laid it out for him…well, as much as he could. "You and I both know she's the only survivor of that bombing at LAX. She not only saw things she shouldn't have, she probably heard them too. If I was a terrorist who wanted to make sure my future plans went off without a hitch, I'd want to ensure all ends were tied up in a nice fancy bow."

The silence in the room was deafening.

Finally, Finn asked quietly, "Who did you say you were again?"

"My name is Slade Cutsinger. I'm a retired Navy SEAL. I know Dakota has to be scared. I don't blame her. And Finn, she has reason to be. I'm not bullshitting you about that. I can't tell you much, but I *can* say that Dakota has *nothing* to be worried about with me. My only goal is to help her put this behind her so she can move on with her life. Safely."

"You got ID?"

His lips twitched. Hell if he didn't like this old man. Slade slowly reached for his wallet. He slid out his driver's license and government ID, then leaned over to hand them to Finn.

After several moments of scrutiny, Finn returned them and reclined back into his chair. "See that box on the floor next to the television?"

Slade turned his head and nodded when he saw the beat-up old shoebox sitting under a stack of at least a week's worth of newspapers.

"Get it for me."

Doing as he was told, Slade retrieved it and handed

SUSAN STOKER

it to Finn.

The old man fingered the top of the box lovingly as he said, "Dakota is all I have. My wife died ten years ago, and me and my girl have taken care of each other. She pays for someone to look in on me every day. Pays for the Meals on Wheels people to bring me lunch and dinner. She even makes sure my bills and mortgage are paid. She's a good girl, and doesn't deserve any of this. All she did was go about her daily business and get thrust into a situation neither of us understand."

"I know," Slade said softly.

"She's not here," Finn continued. "Not in San Diego or LA, and probably not even California. She was real shook up after that airport thing. Didn't say much about it, but told me enough that I put two and two together. Then something happened at her school, though she wouldn't tell me what. A couple of days later, her apartment complex burned to the ground. Newspapers said it was some idiot burning candles in an apartment, but I'm not sure what to believe."

"When was this?" Slade asked.

"September. She was so excited for the new school year, but said she had to quit. That someone was following her and she didn't want to endanger the kids at the school."

"You haven't heard from her at all?" Slade doubted that. Someone who obviously loved her dad enough to make sure he was taken care of wouldn't just completely cut off communication.

"She sends postcards," Finn told Slade as he ran his wrinkled palm over the box once more. "Not often, but sometimes."

"Can I see them?" Slade asked, wanting to grab the box out of the old man's lap and get to work finding Dakota.

"If you hurt her, I swear to God I'll kill you," Finn threatened.

"I'm not going to hurt her."

Dakota's dad continued as if he hadn't spoken. "I don't care who you are or where you hide. I'll find you and put a bullet through your heart. It doesn't matter if I go to jail for it either. I'm old, I'm gonna die soon anyway, but it'd be worth it to kill you if you dare do anything that will make my baby suffer more than she already has."

"I've spent my life fighting for the underdog. I've gone where I've been sent and seen and done things that no one should ever have to," Slade told Finn, looking him straight in the eyes. "But one look at a picture of your daughter, and I knew I'd do whatever it took to make her safe."

Finn held his gaze for a moment, then looked down. He cleared his throat twice, as if trying to compose himself, then held out the box. "They're not signed, but

I know they're from Dakota."

Slade took the shoebox from Finn and sat back on the couch. He eased the top off and picked up the first postcard. It was from Australia and had a kangaroo on the front. He flipped it over and saw Finn's address written in a womanly script. As the man had said, it wasn't signed, but there was one word written. "Peace." The postmark was from Las Vegas.

He picked up another. It was a picture of the Statue of Liberty, and once again Finn's address was on the back in the same handwriting as the first. This one said "love." It was appropriately postmarked from New York City.

Slade flipped through the rest; there weren't a lot, about ten or so. Each had a different postmark and only one word written on it.

"Do you think she's really traveling all over the country?" Slade looked down at the cards in his hand. "From New York to Florida to Seattle?"

"No," Finn said without any hesitation. "She's getting others to mail them for her."

"But she could be," Slade insisted.

"Me and my girl would watch TV when she came to visit," Finn said, gesturing to the television set older than Slade. "The ID Channel. Mystery, forensic, and murder shows. We used to talk about how people could get away with killing for years before they were caught, without even really trying. Not long after the airport thing, she was here and we were watching one of them murder shows. I could tell something was wrong, but didn't want to pry. She flat-out told me she might have to to lie low for a while. I told her she could stay with me, but she shook her head and said the last thing she was going to do was put her daddy in danger…"

Slade sat patiently, waiting for the older man to regain his composure.

Finally, he cleared his throat and said, "She told me she didn't know how safe it would be to call, and was leery of writing letters with any information in them that could lead anyone to her."

"Postcards," Slade said softly.

Finn nodded. "Postcards," he confirmed. "I don't know where she is, but she's gotten her hands on them postcards from all over. Then she has others mail them when they get home from wherever they're visiting when they meet her."

"And the messages on them? Do they mean anything?" Slade asked.

"It's not code, if that's what you're asking," Finn said. "It's just Dakota's way of letting me know she's fine. Love. Peace. Contentment. Happy. She's trying to reassure me she's okay. But she's *not* okay," Finn said. "Look at that last one. The one with the Grand Canyon on it."

Slade pulled it out and turned it over.

"Fucking ink ran. She was cryin' when she wrote it. My baby was cryin' and I can't do anything about it," Finn said bitterly.

"This one's postmarked Las Vegas," Slade mused. "There was another one from Vegas as well."

Finn simply shrugged. "Told her a father would instinctively know if his little girl was alive. What an idiot I was." The old man pinned Slade with a hard gaze. "I *don't* know if she's alive, if she's in pain, if whoever she thought was following her has caught up to her and is hurting her. She could be hungry, or cold, and I'm sitting here snug and happy in my house and can't do a damn thing about it."

"But I can," Slade said firmly.

"If she's in danger, don't bring her back here," Finn replied. "Just let her know her old man loves her and is thinkin' about her."

"I will, but I have a feeling she already knows." Slade put the items back in the box and ran his finger over the mark on the last postcard where one of Dakota's tears had fallen and smeared the ink. Simply touching the same piece of paper she had somehow made her all the more real to him. He'd fallen hard for the woman in the photograph, but seeing how much she loved her dad, and was loved in return, really struck home for him.

He returned the lid to the box and stood, placing it back by the television stand and replacing the newspapers on top.

Finn pushed himself up and out of the chair and the two men stood toe to toe. Slade was at least five or six inches taller, but Finn didn't let Slade's size intimidate him. "Remember what I said," he ordered gruffly.

"I'll remember," Slade told him. "But I'll say it again, you and your daughter have nothing to fear from me."

A knock sounded and Slade's head whipped around to stare at the front door.

"Meals on Wheels," Finn reminded him. "She's right on time."

Slade nodded, but kept close to Finn as he opened the door just in case. As he'd said, a woman wearing a company jacket stood on the other side. "Hello, Mr. James, it's good to see you today."

"You too, Eve," Finn said and unlocked the screen, letting the woman inside. "I'll be right in, give me a second to say goodbye to my guest."

"No problem. I'll just get this served up," Eve said as she breezed past them, obviously having been inside the house before.

Finn put his hand on Slade's leather-covered arm. "She means the world to me," he said seriously.

"I don't even know her, and I think she means the

world to me too," Slade responded, dryly.

Finn laughed then. A dry, rough chuckle that sounded like it hurt. "That's my Dakota," he said, smiling.

Slade's lips curled up in response and he nodded at the man. He was about to leave when Finn said softly, "She's not going to trust you. You're going to have to prove that you've talked to me. That *I* trust you."

Finn had all his attention now. Slade's lips pressed together as he waited.

"Dakota loves Starbucks. Their peppermint mocha was always her preferred choice this time of year. And donuts. Glazed with that maple frosting shit on top. She won't eat no other kind. You bring those with you when you find her, and tell her I told you they were her favorites. The rest is up to you."

Knowing the old man was right, and that he did need a way to convince Dakota to at least hear him out before she ran, he nodded in appreciation. "Thanks. I'll remember. Can I ask something?"

"Sure."

"Why did you let me in? Tell me all that about Dakota?"

Finn looked at Slade for a long time before he said, "My daughter told me the bad guys might come here pretendin' to be good guys. She warned me not to trust anyone, no matter what they looked like." The old man paused. "Several have tried to get me to talk. Reporters pretending to be Dakota's friends, people sayin' they're government employees who just have her best interests at heart. Bah—liars, all of them. But you...you weren't lyin' to me."

Slade's lips twitched. His former team members would get a kick out of Finn's assessment of him, especially considering he was always the best liar of the bunch.

"Man ridin' around on a Harley, leather jacket, bags packed...you can't exactly kidnap a woman on a motorcycle. Besides...your eyes told me what I needed to know."

"My eyes?"

"Yeah. You took one look at my Dakota's picture and that was it for you." Finn nodded. "Love is a weird thing. When it hits you, it hits you. I knew the second I saw my late wife that I wanted to spend the rest of my life with her. Take care of my girl, Slade. I've worried about her since she was born. The one thing I want is to see her protected and taken care of when I'm gone. Oh, I know, she can take care of herself, but as self-sufficient as she is, she needs someone who will make sure she eats when she gets busy, give her a backrub when she's had a hard day, and will be there for her when she needs to talk."

Finn's words struck Slade hard. Yes. That's what

he'd wanted all his life. To have a woman by his side and to be the one someone else leaned on.

"Am I wrong?"

"You're not wrong," Slade said "I'm not going to stand here and tell you that your daughter and I will get married and all your worries are over, but I *am* telling you that I'll do everything in my power to make her safe and allow her to return to her normal life. After that?" He shrugged. "It's up to her. But, if my reaction to her picture was any indication, I'm going to do what I can to convince her to let me be a part of her life."

"That's why I let you in. Why I told you what I did," Finn said, then stuck out his hand. "Good luck. Make my baby safe."

After a final handshake, Slade strode toward his Harley in the driveway, knowing Mr. James was watching him as he did so. He swung a leg over the leather seat and grabbed his helmet.

He began to buckle it when Finn said loudly from the doorway, "You got two of those? Because if you plan to have a passenger, I expect her head to be protected."

Slade grinned, despite the seriousness of the situation. Without a word, he twisted his body and unsnapped one of the saddlebags. He pulled out an identical helmet to the one he was wearing, except a size smaller, and held it up for Finn's inspection.

"Good," was all Finn said, before backing into his

house and closing the door.

Slade stowed the extra helmet he'd bought specifically with the intention of having Dakota James on the back of his bike and turned to face the front. He backed out of the drive and headed for the highway. He'd call Tex as soon as he could and let him know he was on his way to Vegas, but first he needed to beat the LA traffic out of town. I-15 to the Nevada border was always a crapshoot this time of year. Starting his search in Las Vegas was a given, as there were two postcards with that postmark.

Whether or not Dakota was there wasn't quite as certain, but one thing was clear...Slade was more determined than ever to find her and keep her safe. Any woman who cared enough about her father to try to reassure him she was all right while on the run from terrorists was someone he wanted to know. But because it was *Dakota* who'd done it...she'd just blown away any doubts he'd had about her. He'd find her, make her safe, then hopefully convince her to give an old retired SEAL like him a chance.

Chapter Three

"**H**AVE YOU EVER seen an alien out here?"

Dakota James forced a smile and turned to face the tourist. She was working the afternoon shift at the Little A'Le'Inn in Rachel, Nevada, and got asked this exact same question at least once a day. But she really couldn't blame them. They *were*, after all, right outside Area 51 in the Nevada desert, and the small diner she worked at had gone out of its way to put every kitschy piece of alien crap on sale that it could find.

"Nope. Just lots of hungry tourists," she told the teenager, then shrugged in apology for the lame answer and hurried to bring a platter with three plates of hamburgers and fries to the group sitting at a small circular table in the middle of the room.

She smiled and left them hungrily tucking into the food she'd brought them.

Working as a waitress and sales clerk wasn't what she'd had in mind for a life plan when she'd gotten her master's degree in higher education, but life had a funny way of making sure you never got too big for your britches.

Wiping her hands on her apron, Dakota rang up a T-shirt with an alien head on it, a bumper sticker and mug with the A'Le'Inn logo, and an inflatable plastic green alien, then collected money from the pair standing at the register.

She'd been working at the small restaurant/bar for quite a while now and knew it was about time for her to move on. She was grateful that Pat and her daughter, Connie, had hired her. They'd obviously seen the desperation in her eyes when she'd shown up all those weeks ago.

Rachel, Nevada, population around fifty-four, wasn't exactly on the beaten path. People didn't accidentally end up there, and Dakota was no exception. She'd hidden out in Las Vegas for a week, but hadn't liked how dirty the city seemed. Not only that, she always felt as if she was being watched…and since there were so many people, she couldn't figure out if she was *really* being watched, or if it was only in her head.

So she'd left, deciding to make her way across the US, away from California and *him*. She'd stopped for gas just east of Vegas and started chatting with a happy-go-lucky group from Indiana. They'd said they were geocachers, and were headed to the ET Highway. Dakota had no idea what they were talking about, but she'd gotten a crash course soon enough.

Apparently geocaching was kind of like treasure hunting with a GPS. The players downloaded coordinates from a website and followed them to the "treasure." It could be a Tupperware container, film canister, or even a large ammo box. Sometimes there were toys inside, and others only enough room for a log book, which the players were required to sign.

The group was on its way to the ET Highway because there were literally thousands of geocaches alongside the ninety-eight-mile road. They'd talked about the black mailbox, Area 51, the town of Rachel, and the Little A'Le'Inn as if anyone who didn't see them once in their life was absolutely missing out.

So off she'd gone. Instead of heading out of Nevada along Interstate 15, she'd turned north on Route 93 to Highway 375—also known as the ET Highway.

It'd actually been fun. She'd stopped at the black mailbox, which was now painted white. Enjoyed the desert vistas, mooed at some random cows, and waved at clusters of people she now knew were geocachers who'd randomly stopped along the road searching for the elusive little containers.

Rachel certainly wasn't what she'd been expecting. She thought it would be a typical little town, with a gas station, hotel, and fast food restaurants…but it wasn't. It was literally a pit stop in the middle of nowhere.

There were no businesses, other than the A'Le'Inn bar and restaurant. No other places to eat and, more importantly, no gas stations.

She'd planned on seeing what the fuss regarding Rachel was all about, then continuing north to Reno and eventually up into Idaho. Since she'd coasted into town on fumes, she was temporarily stuck. But the second she'd seen the tiny town, she'd decided it was actually a good place to lie low for a while.

Pat and Connie, the owners of the Little A'Le'Inn, had agreed to let her work as a waitress in the restaurant/bar and as a maid for the rooms they rented out—mostly to geocachers on their way through—in the trailers behind the bar. The pay wasn't huge, but it was enough to slowly increase her meager cash reserves before she headed off again.

She'd rented a small room from a local resident, but didn't stay there often. The owner was a smoker who didn't get out much. Dakota had slept in her car most nights, preferring that to being cooped up in a trailer home full of cigarette smoke. Pat caught her one morning and, after hearing why she was sleeping in her car, offered to let her stay in one of the motel's trailers when it wasn't booked.

Working at the motel/bar/restaurant also allowed her to see most of the people who came to town. It wasn't foolproof; if *he* walked in and found her, he wouldn't hesitate to hurt anyone who came to her aid. But the little town suited her. She much preferred the genuine caring nature of most of the people of Rachel to the city folks she'd come into contact with in Vegas.

She'd changed her name to Dallas, thinking it was close enough to her own that she might actually remember to answer to it. The work was monotonous, but the people she met kept the job from being absolutely horrible.

She'd also admitted to Connie that she'd run out of gas, and the other woman had volunteered to bring back enough to allow her to get to either Tonopah or Warm Springs. Dakota had taken her up on the offer, and felt good knowing she wasn't trapped in the small town. She could leave at any time.

Until now, she'd been enjoying working for cash; it kept her from using credit cards and being tracked through them. Though recently, she felt itchy and nervous. As if someone was watching her again. As much as she hated to just up and leave the quirky little town, it was looking like the time was coming when she'd need to do just that.

"Hey, Dallas, order up," George called from the back. He was the line cook who worked from one to seven. Pat or Connie usually had the morning shift, serving breakfast and early lunch, and after seven, tourists who stopped in could choose from pre-packaged snacks and drinks.

Dakota shook herself and smiled at the older man. Rachel, Nevada, might literally be in the middle of nowhere, but the people who lived and worked there were some of the friendliest she'd ever met. It was too bad she'd be leaving soon.

"HEY, TEX," SLADE said when his old friend picked up the phone.

"'Bout time you called, Cutter," Tex complained. "I figured you were glued to the slot machines or something. Leaving a message telling me where you're going isn't the same as actually talking to me, you know."

"Yeah, well, I was a bit busy," Slade told him. He'd called two days ago when he'd reached Primm, the border town between California and Nevada. Tex hadn't answered, so he'd left a message about what he'd found out and where he was headed. He'd waited until now to call again because he'd wanted to have some concrete information to share, not simply conjecture.

"I did some checking while waiting for you to call back, and there's been a lot of chatter on the Net about picking up a certain package and preparing for a ceremony," Tex told him.

"Fuck," Slade murmured.

"You got any ideas where she might be?" Tex asked.

"I've been all over this city in the last couple of days. I've shown her picture to everyone, and I might have a lead."

"Yeah?"

"Yeah. You ever been out to Area 51?" Slade asked Tex.

"Nope. Is there anything out there other than desert?"

"Not much. But I'm at a gas station just northeast of Vegas and a clerk says she thinks she remembers someone matching Dakota's description asking about the infamous ET Highway a couple months ago. Said she remembered her because she specifically asked if they had any peppermint flavor for her coffee, and picked up a flier about the road on her way out. I could use your help checking traffic cams for any more recent signs of her in the city, in case this lead is bogus. I thought I'd check out Rachel, Nevada, midway point of the ET Highway, and see if she's been there."

"Already on it," Tex told him. "Started my search right after you left your message. So far, I haven't found anything from the last day and a half, but I'll keep on it. If I find she's been in Vegas recently, I'll let you know."

"Appreciate it."

"You be careful," Tex warned. "With the increased chatter, it certainly sounds as if Fourati has intel on where Dakota might be hiding and could be moving in."

"I will."

"Eyes on your six, Cutter," Tex told him. "If anything feels off, get the hell out of dodge. And don't hesitate to live up to that nickname of yours. Hear me? I'll cover your ass if it comes to it."

"Got it." Slade didn't like the fact that Tex was feeling nervous. If he thought Fourati had a lock on where Dakota was, and had sent some of his minions after her, he was probably right. And Tex telling him not to hesitate to slit someone's throat was telling.

It was Tex who had come up with the moniker during one of their first missions together. Slade had cut the throat of a terrorist who'd had no idea his position had been compromised. It wasn't the first person he'd killed that way, and certainly wasn't the last. Tex had congratulated him on the kill and that was that. The story Slade usually told people, however, was that he was called Cutter because of his last name. It was a bit more politically correct than airing his SEAL kills to polite society.

"I'll call when I can," Slade told Tex.

"You do that. Later."

"Later." Slade hung up and sighed in frustration. The fact that Fourati was one step behind him wasn't comforting, but at least he was *behind* him, and not *ahead* of him.

Slade slipped the phone back into his pocket and headed into the gas station. If he was going out into the desert, he wanted to top off his tank. He got great gas mileage with his Harley, but had no idea what he'd find when he hit Area 51 and wanted to be ready for anything.

An hour later, Slade turned onto the ET Highway and grimaced. He was suddenly very glad he'd let the gas station attendant talk him into the extra four gallons strapped to the seat behind him. The weather was chilly, but he knew he'd actually lucked out. It could be a lot worse, and he hoped the weather would hold out until he made it to Rachel and, if he was lucky, found Dakota.

The chatty gas station attendant had told him all about how Rachel was the only town along the ET Highway, and they didn't have any services there, only a bar, which seemed wrong to Slade, but nobody asked him. This long desert road wasn't the place to be driving drunk, that was for sure. Not only would it be extremely easy to drive right off the road, it was actually active grazing land for hundreds of cows. The attendant took great delight in telling him two gory stories about motorists who'd hit cows that were standing in the road, minding their own business in the middle of the night.

Taking a deep breath, Slade gave the Harley some throttle as he continued down the long stretch of highway. The faster he found Dakota and got her to safety, the better.

DAKOTA GRIMACED WHEN the bell over the door to the bar tinkled. She was tired and ready to get out of there. She'd been playing bartender for a while now. Doug and Alex, two brothers who worked at the Tonopah Test Range, had come in at the tail end of the day and asked for a couple of beers. They'd said they didn't want any food as they'd grabbed sandwiches at home before heading up to the bar. That had been hours ago, and they weren't acting like they wanted to leave anytime soon.

It was Dakota's responsibility to make sure people got what they wanted to drink, paid, and to try to talk them out of driving if they were out-of-towners. She'd shot the shit with the brothers for a while, but she was bored, tired, and wanted nothing more than to head to the open room in one of the trailers for the night. Luckily, there had been a cancelation that day, which meant she got to sleep in a real bed.

The stress of constantly being on the lookout was getting to her. It was definitely time to head out and find a new place to settle for a while. One more populated than Rachel this time. She'd talk to Pat and Connie tomorrow and let them know she would be moving on.

She smiled in the direction of the doorway—and froze when she saw the man who'd just walked in. He was probably a couple years older than she was. His black hair was graying, but instead of making him look old, it only made him sexier. He had a short beard that was well trimmed and brought attention to his full lips. He had on a leather jacket and an old, worn pair of jeans with black boots. His nose looked like it'd been broken at least once and his cheeks were rosy from the cold, dry air.

He was tall, really tall, at least half a foot taller than her own five-eight. He wasn't skinny, but he wasn't fat either. He was…built. Muscular.

She should've been scared. He could easily overpower and hurt her, but somehow, she knew he wouldn't. How she knew that, Dakota had no idea, but for just a moment, the thought that she knew him flashed through her mind.

That was crazy. She'd never seen this man before in her life, she would've remembered if she had. But the spark of recognition was there, nevertheless.

The man lifted his chin at her in greeting, and Dakota's knees wobbled. How in the hell he could make her want him with a mere chin lift she had no idea, but suddenly, having a wild fling with a stranger sounded like the best idea she'd ever had. It had been a long time since she'd had any sexual feelings about anyone, especially in the last couple of months, but all her worries seemed to drain away simply by looking into his dark eyes.

"Welcome to the Little A'Le'Inn," she said automatically. Business was business, and she didn't want to be the reason the bar got a bad review online. "Grill's closed, but we've got snacks and liquid refreshments. Although if you're continuing on your way to Tonopah, I don't recommend drinking anything alcoholic. It'd be dangerous." Dakota smiled as she said the last, wanting to seem friendly instead of preachy. It would be an absolute shame for this man to come to any harm, that was for sure.

The man's eyes seemed to pierce right into her soul, as if with one look he knew all her secrets. The scariest thing was that it wasn't an altogether unpleasant thought. She'd never had someone she could lean on to help with troubles in her life. She'd been okay with that, modern woman and all, but in that moment, all she could think was that *this* man would keep her safe. He'd never let anyone do her harm.

Dakota turned her back on him, pretending to wipe off the counter to try to regain her equilibrium.

Out of the corner of her eye, she saw the man saunter into the dimly lit building and gaze around. She'd seen many reactions from tourists who'd wandered into the eclectic bar, but this man had absolutely no reaction whatsoever. It was...odd.

"Nice place," he said, and Dakota's toes curled in her sneakers. His voice was low and growly and she felt it all the way to her tummy. She had no idea why she was reacting to this man's obvious maleness, but she was.

"Yeah. The owners have worked hard to make it...unique."

"Slade," the man said, holding his hand out to her in greeting.

"Oh...uh...I'm Dallas," Dakota said shakily, almost forgetting her fake name, and tentatively put her hand in his own.

She was half afraid he'd crush hers with his brute strength, but he merely smiled and grasped her palm with a firm, but not bruising grip and said, "It's good to meet you."

Dakota gave him a half smile. "You too."

They stood still for a beat, each looking at the other without blinking, before Dakota reluctantly pulled her hand back. He let go without complaint, but she swore she could feel his touch long after they'd dropped their hands. He had calluses, which made her think about what his hands would feel like on her bare skin. Damn, she had to get it together.

"So, what's it gonna be?" Dakota asked.

"Just a Coke, I think," Slade said.

"What kind?"

"What kind of Coke?"

Dakota chuckled and shook her head in self-deprecation. "Sorry. Habit. I call all soda, 'Coke.' I use it generically. I can get you one," she finished quickly, knowing she was beat red with embarrassment.

"So if someone asks for a Coke, you ask what kind, and they say a Pepsi. Or Dr. Pepper, or something else?" Slade asked with a friendly smile. He leaned his forearms on the scratched wooden bar top in front of him.

For a moment, Dakota wished that it was summer and Slade was wearing a short-sleeved T-shirt. She'd pay just about any amount of money to see his biceps and forearms. She'd bet they were muscular as hell. When he tipped his head and raised his eyebrows as she continued to stare at him, she blushed even harder. "Sorry. Yeah, that's how it works. So you really do want a Coke, right?"

"Yes, please. If it's not too much trouble," Slade said with a smile.

"Of course not. It's my job," Dakota told him, glad to have a reason to go into the back room for a moment. There were a few cans under the bar, but she wanted to get him a cold drink from the refrigerator in the back.

She used the few moments alone to give herself a stern talk. *He's just passing through, Dakota. The last thing you need right now is to get involved with a guy, even if it's only for the night. No matter how sexy he is and how badly you want him. Get ahold of yourself.*

Satisfied that she had her head on straight, Dakota went back into the bar area with a smile on her face and held up the can. "Got it!" Instead of drooling over the fine specimen of a man who was sitting at the bar, she got busy grabbing a glass and filling it with ice. She poured the cola into the glass, concentrating so hard on what she was doing, she jumped when Doug pounded on the bar top down by the cash register.

"We're gonna get out of your hair, Dallas."

Dakota looked up and nodded, putting down the half-empty can because her hands were shaking too hard to finish. She glanced around and met Slade's concerned eyes.

"You okay?" he asked quietly.

Dakota nodded quickly and pushed the glass and can of soda over to him. "Here ya go. Excuse me."

He nodded and she took the few steps to the register. She made small talk with Doug and Alex while she rang up their drinks. After they left, the room seemed to shrink. Being alone with Slade made her extremely nervous for some reason. She tucked a stray piece of hair behind her ear and smiled awkwardly at him.

"You worked here long?" he asked.

Dakota shrugged. She'd learned to keep her answers

vague. "Not really."

"It's a long way from civilization, isn't it?"

She shrugged again. "It is what it is. I've met some of the nicest people around. You on your way north or south?"

It was his turn to shrug. "I came up from Crystal Springs, but I'm not sure if I'm going to go back that way or carry on. Anything worth looking at if I go up to Tonopah?"

"Depends on what you like to look at," Dakota told him. "I've heard Goldfield is really interesting, with the history of being haunted and all, but there's not much out here in either direction, if I'm being honest."

"Hmmm. Any place to stay the night around here?" Slade asked.

Dakota swallowed hard. Damn. There went her bed for the night. But she smiled brightly and told him the truth. "You're in luck. There was a cancelation tonight so there's a room available. It's not fancy, you actually share a trailer with another couple, but they checked in about an hour ago and I think they're planning on being up early, so they won't be a bother. The middle is a common space, and the two bedrooms are on either side and have locking doors. It really is private."

Dakota knew she was babbling, but couldn't stop. "It's only forty-five bucks for the night, which is a really great deal. There's hot water and you can use the wi-fi here at the restaurant for free. Breakfast is included. Nothing gourmet, just cinnamon rolls and juice, but again, it's safer to stay than to try to make it all the way up to Tonopah in the dark."

Slade chuckled, and Dakota's womanly parts spasmed at the sound. Jesus, he was beautiful. "I'll take it. How could I not after that wonderful sales pitch?"

"Sorry. People just tend to turn up their noses because it's a trailer and they have to share it, but I promise it's clean, safe, and totally worth the money."

Slade tipped his head back and chugged the rest of the Coke in the glass. He pulled out a five-dollar bill and slid it over to her. "Sounds good. I'm beat."

"Let me get your change."

Slade waved her off. "Keep it."

"Oh, okay, thanks. If you're ready, I can walk you over to your room."

He looked at his watch. "You're closing?"

Dakota nodded. "Yeah, we're not expecting anyone else tonight and it's dark. The locals know we close up around now."

"Don't want any aliens to wander in when the sun goes down, huh?" Slade joked.

Dakota chuckled even though she'd heard it before. "Yeah, something like that. If you want, I'll meet you outside in five minutes or so? I need to finish up in here." Actually, she needed to give herself another talking to, but he didn't need to know that.

"Sure. I'll be out by my bike."

Dakota nodded. Her eyes were glued to his ass as he walked out the door. He was definitely a fine specimen of a man. And it figured he'd have a motorcycle, just to amp up the sexiness. She'd never ridden on one, but once upon a time, before she'd gotten old enough to have given up on many of her dreams, she'd imagined what it would be like to sit behind a man, her arms wrapped around him, her chin on his shoulder as the wind blew in her hair and they flew down the highway.

Shaking her head in disgust at herself, she mumbled, "Get ahold of yourself. Jesus, you'd think you weren't on the run from a psycho crazy terrorist or something. You've got no time for mooning over a man. No matter how sexy he is or how much you want to know if his beard is soft or scratchy."

Satisfied with her pep talk, Dakota quickly washed the dirty glasses and locked the ancient cash register. There wasn't a bank in Rachel to take the cash to, and besides, most people paid by credit card anyway.

She hung up her apron and smoothed her hair, securing it back into a bun at the nape of her neck, and walked out the door.

Slade was leaning against his Harley with one ankle resting on the other. His arms were crossed on his chest and he was frowning. Dakota quickly turned and locked the door, making sure the closed sign was clearly visible to anyone who might pull up later. Taking a deep breath, she turned to Slade. "Everything okay?"

He shook his head. "There's no cell service."

"Yeah, sorry. Once upon a time the residents petitioned the big phone companies to put a tower out here, but it wasn't worth the money. And if you ask me, the government put the kibosh on that as well. It's in their best interest to keep things on the down low out here, if you know what I mean. Area 51 and all. If it's any consolation, once you get up to Warm Springs and past the big mountain up there, you'll be in range again. If you really need to get ahold of someone, I could ask Pat—she owns this place with her daughter—if she'll call someone for you. There are a few residents who have satellite phones out here."

Slade shook his head. "No, it's okay. I can wait. I was just hoping to get ahold of my friend and let him know I made it safely and that I'd be spending the night."

"Sorry," Dakota apologized again. "You could probably send him an email later if you wanted. I'll make sure you have the password for the wi-fi. Ready to see where you'll be staying?"

"Don't I need to pay for the room?" he asked.

She waved her hand. "Don't worry about it. You can pay Pat or Connie in the morning. They man the restaurant until I come on in the afternoon."

"Trusting," Slade observed.

Dakota smiled at that. "Yes, they are. Come on, it's around back."

He straightened and turned to grab the handlebars of his motorcycle. He pushed the bike as they walked silently around the front of the iconic restaurant, past the giant metal spaceship announcing to anyone who passed by that they'd reached the A'Le'Inn, to one of the trailers off to the side of the parking lot.

"Here it is. And I know it doesn't look like much, but I promise it's clean."

"I believe you," Slade told her, holding out his hand for the key Dakota had been playing with.

"Oh yeah, here ya go." She inhaled when her finger-tips brushed Slade's palm. He was warm, and she was quickly getting chilly in the desert air. "Right, so there's the entrance, just turn to the right when you enter and that's your room. Sleep well."

"See you later," Slade said as he nodded at her.

"Yeah, okay," Dakota mumbled, knowing he wouldn't. She did her best to avoid the restaurant in the mornings, not wanting to interact with the people who stayed the night, and needing the time to herself. Connie let her use her computer in the mornings, and Dakota used the time to search the Internet for mentions of her name, and to try to see if she could figure out the name of the asshole who was following her. So far, she hadn't had any luck, but it didn't really matter. She knew she was in trouble; the guy had practically told her straight up she would be his. She shuddered at the memory.

Turning and heading for her car, which was behind Pat's trailer, Dakota mentally reminded herself once more to talk to the other woman soon. It was time to go.

THREE HOURS LATER, Slade walked silently past the trailers that were rented out to tourists and headed for where he'd last seen Dakota. She looked exactly like her picture, right down to the bun at the back of her head. At least she'd altered her name a bit; it wasn't much, but it was something. She hadn't tried to disguise herself at all.

But then again, why would she think anyone would follow her to Rachel, Nevada?

The town seemed like it was at the end of the world. Strangers stood out like sore thumbs and she knew exactly who was sleeping where each night. Slade had used the wi-fi to kill time and find out more information on the small town. He knew Dakota wasn't going anywhere, she didn't seem to be suspicious of him at all.

And if he wasn't mistaken, she'd been struck by the same thing he had when she'd lain eyes on him the first time. Slade recognized the look of interest and lust in her eyes, because he knew it was the same look on *his* face when he'd first seen her photo. And as he thought she would be, she was even more beautiful in person. She was curvy, and he estimated her to be around five-eight or nine; her head came to about his chin. Slade knew she'd fit against him perfectly.

She was funny and endearing when she got nervous. He could absolutely see her as an elementary school teacher and principal. It was the uncertainty and uneasiness behind her eyes that really struck him, though. He hated that she was scared, and wanted to hold her tightly and reassure her that he'd make sure Aziz Fourati didn't get anywhere near her. He needed to be smart, but didn't have the luxury of time to let her get comfortable with him. He needed to talk to her about her situation, get her to trust him, and get the hell out of Rachel, Nevada.

The bottom line was that Dakota James was no longer merely a face on a piece of paper. She was a flesh-and-blood woman, and Slade wanted her more than he wanted his next breath. But he wanted to keep her safe more than he wanted, or needed, to have her under him…for now.

He'd been planning to break out the bribe he'd

picked up for her in Vegas when they'd been alone at the bar, but she'd seemed too uneasy around him. And he was afraid she'd bolt if he spooked her. So, he was biding his time, and he'd catch up with her in the morning.

Slade really wished he could get ahold of Tex and find out if he had any information about Fourati, and if he or his cronies were on their way to Rachel, but for now, he was winging it. He didn't trust email to be secure and decided he'd wait.

When enough time had passed, Slade had eased out of the plain and simple room in the trailer and was now looking for Dakota.

The wind blew in from the north and he shivered in the cool night air. Winter was definitely arriving in the valley, and Slade wouldn't be surprised if there was snow in the forecast. Peering around one of the trailers, he grinned. Bingo.

Tex had given him the details on Dakota's car...a two thousand and eight Subaru Impreza. Gray. And it was parked in front of him. She hadn't even taken off her California plates. Slade inwardly grimaced. She didn't have the first clue how to hide. It was both endearing and frightening at the same time. It was a good thing it was *him* there looking for her and not Fourati.

Slade walked silently up to the car and peered in,

not expecting to see anything worth his time. He stopped short and stared through the window.

Dakota was wrapped up in a blanket in the driver's seat, only the top of her head and blonde hair showing. She was sleeping in her car.

She was *sleeping* in her fucking *car*.

Slade wanted to hit something. Wanted to bang on the glass and wake her up and read her the riot act. It was cold out there, but honestly that was the least of her worries. What if he'd been Fourati? Or a drunk resident who'd decided she was free game? Yeah, Dakota was tall, but she wouldn't be any match for a drunk, horny guy.

Swearing under his breath at the entire situation and hating himself for not confronting her earlier that evening, Slade turned around and headed back to his room. If he was going to watch over one Miss Dakota James, he needed warmer clothing.

She might not have asked for it, but starting right now, she had a protector. Seeing her sleeping, vulnerable, and probably cold, had ramped up his interest in her from warm to red hot. Dakota needed protecting, and he'd be the man to do so.

And when she no longer needed protecting, he'd still be the man in her life.

Chapter Four

DAKOTA CAME AWAKE slowly. The morning sky was just beginning to lighten and was casting a purplish hue over the valley. She shifted in her seat and grimaced. Every muscle in her body was stiff, and it was cold. Surprised her windshield wasn't iced over, she bent her neck to the left, then the right to stretch it out.

Something moved out of the corner of her eye and she glanced to the side—and squeaked in terror.

Sitting next to her, *right* next to her, inside her car, was the man from the night before.

Slade.

He was propped against the passenger door, his arms crossed over his chest, one leg bent at the knee and resting on the seat, and he was scowling. At her.

"What the heck?" Dakota breathed, and immediately reached for the door handle, her breaths coming out in quick pants, the cold air making it obvious how freaked she was.

"You're sleeping in your car," Slade said in a flat

tone.

Dakota nodded and cursed under her breath. She didn't want to take her eyes from Slade's, but she couldn't find the stupid handle.

"I told you last night, but my name is Slade Cutsinger. I'm a retired Navy SEAL and I'm here to keep you safe."

"Uh huh," Dakota murmured, only partly listening. She found the handle, finally, and pulled, planning on getting the hell away from the huge man currently glaring at her.

"I talked to your dad the other day. I saw the post-cards. It's how I found you."

Dakota froze with one foot on the hard dirt outside her vehicle and spun back around to face Slade. "He has nothing to do with this. Leave him alone," she whispered shakily.

"I know he doesn't," Slade reassured her. "The post-cards were a good idea, by the way. Your dad was sure you were doing okay, as was your intention. Unfortunately, a few people you gave them to got lazy and instead of waiting until they got home, mailed them from Vegas."

"Darn," Dakota said. She figured she might as well listen to what Slade had to say. Since he knew about the postcards, he most likely *had* seen her dad. She might be stupid, but she wasn't getting scary vibes from Slade, so hopefully her dad was in his house secure in the knowledge his daughter was okay…even if she *was* on the run from a terrorist.

"I know all about the bombing in the airport, Dakota," Slade said softly, bringing her out of her musings.

Dakota's stomach cramped. He'd used her real name.

Of course he had. If he'd seen her dad, he had to know who she really was.

"I know you were the only survivor. I know that you saw Aziz Fourati, and I also know that you're the only one in the world right now who can identify him. He *also* knows this, and not only wants to make sure you keep that information to yourself, but wants you for his own. To be his wife."

Dakota shut her car door and shivered. Damn, it was cold. She tried to clear her foggy morning brain. She never functioned well before she'd had a cup of coffee. "His name is Aziz?"

She'd surprised him. Slade's eyebrows went up and he tilted his head as he asked, "You didn't know his name?"

"No. He never said it. What's his last name again?" She was trying really hard not to freak out. Oh, she was leaving today for sure, but she needed to know what Slade knew before she bolted. Information was power.

"Fourati."

"That sounds foreign," Dakota observed, proud of herself for how calm she sounded.

"It is. Best guess is that he's Tunisian."

"Tunisian?" she asked, really confused now.

"Yeah, Tunisian. The country between Algeria and Libya in Northern Africa."

"I know where Tunisia is," Dakota answered grumpily. "I just…" She paused for a moment, realizing that she should definitely not be talking to Slade about anything. She didn't know him. He could be one of Aziz Fourati's goons. She was happy to have a name for the guy who was making her life a living hell, but she needed to be smart…no matter how much her intuition was screaming that she could trust the man next to her.

Slade leaned over and grabbed something off the floor at his feet. It was a metal travel cup. He offered it to her without a word.

Dakota stared at the cup, then back at him. If he thought she was going to drink something he gave her, he was insane. "No thank you," she said politely.

"You don't know what it is," Slade said evenly.

"I don't know who *you* are," she returned a bit snarkily. "The only reason I'm still sitting in here right now is because it's cold outside, and there's nowhere for me to go. I'm sure if you wanted to, you could catch me in two-point-three seconds and slit my throat. Call me a glutton for punishment, but I'd like to get as much information as I can about why my life is in the crapper before I die."

"You don't swear."

"What?"

"You don't swear," he repeated patiently.

Dakota shrugged. "I'm an elementary school principal. Or I was. I can't exactly go around saying fuck, shit, and damn all the time."

"True. I like it."

"I can die happy," Dakota grumped.

His voice lowered further, if that was even possible, and as much as she hated it, goosebumps broke out on her arms at his tone. "I'm one of the good guys, Dakota," he told her. "The short story is that the government knows Fourati is behind the airport bombing and they want to make sure he's punished for what he did. But now he's gathering soldiers online. Trying to convert them to his cause. He wants to do it again, but on a grander scale this time."

"I'm aware," Dakota whispered, and she was. Aziz had bragged about his plans while she and the other hostages had huddled together, scared out of their minds in the airport.

"Then you know how important it is to stop him."

"I almost died that day." Dakota told him something he probably already knew.

He confirmed it by saying simply, "I know."

"You can't just show up out of the blue, tell me you've been looking for me, and expect me to trust you are who you say you are."

"Why not?"

"What do you mean, why not?" Dakota asked, confused.

He continued to hold the cup out to her, but said, "I told you that I'd been to see your dad. I saw the postcards. I *am* a retired Navy SEAL. I'm not Tunisian and couldn't pass for an Arabic terrorist on a good day. If I had cell reception, I'd call one of my best friends in the world and let him vouch for me. But that will have to wait until we're back in civilization. I'm one of the good guys, Dakota. Swear to God."

"That's what *a terrorist* would say," she informed him, not swayed in the least. "Besides, calling someone in order to vouch for your trustworthiness isn't going to make me believe them."

"Take the cup," Slade ordered gently.

Without thought, Dakota obeyed his urgent words. She reached out and took the stainless-steel travel mug from him. Her fingers brushed his, and she swore she could feel the heat from his fingers shoot up her arm.

But no, it wasn't his fingers that caused the heat, it was the mug. It was warm. She looked up in question.

"I stopped by the restaurant before coming here and asked Pat to warm up the contents for me." He looked

71

sheepish for a moment before saying, "I'm sure it doesn't taste the best after two days, but your dad told me what you liked. He said you'd know I was telling the truth about talking to him if I brought this."

Dakota slowly and carefully turned the plastic lid— and immediately the smell of peppermint wafted up to her nose. She closed her eyes in ecstasy and brought the mug closer to her face. She inhaled the delicious scent of her absolute favorite coffee in the world, and thought about all the times she and her dad had shared a cup of coffee like this while sitting in his small living room. She fought the tears that sprang to her eyes.

"And this," Slade said softly, interrupting the memory.

Dakota opened her eyes and saw he was holding out a small white paper bag. She knew what was inside without having to look.

"A maple-iced donut," she said.

"That's right. Although I'm afraid it's probably a bit worse for wear after being in my saddlebag on the back of my bike."

Dakota reached out and snagged the bag from his fingertips, being careful not to touch him this time, and peered inside. Sure enough, the donut was mushed on one side and the maple icing was mostly stuck to the bag rather than on the pastry itself, but again, the memories that assailed her were almost overwhelming.

"You really did go see my dad."

"I did."

"And you *swear* you didn't hurt him?"

Slade made a weird sound and Dakota's gaze went to his. He looked pissed now. "No, I didn't hurt him," Slade growled. "I'm exactly who I've told you I am."

Dakota studied Slade for a long moment. The heat from the metal cup seeped into her palm, warming her cold hand. The paper from the bag crinkled as she shifted in her seat. Would a terrorist haul a cup of peppermint mocha coffee all the way from Vegas? Would he sit in a car next to her for who knows how long waiting for her to wake up without hurting her? Aziz certainly wouldn't. She was well aware of what *he* would do if he was in Slade's shoes.

Aziz Fourati wanted her. Dakota knew that without a doubt. But he wouldn't have his men treat her like this. Friendly. Respectful. Cautious. She knew exactly how they would treat her, *had* treated her that day back in the airport.

"You said that you couldn't pass for an Arabic terrorist on a good day," Dakota said softly.

"That's right," Slade agreed. "Once upon a time, I took pride in being able to move amongst people in the Middle East and blend in, but those days are over. This is the real me...graying beard and all." He gestured to his face as he said the last.

73

Dakota paused to take a small sip of the ambrosia she held in her hands and sighed as the peppermint flavor exploded on her tongue. The coffee was luke-warm, and a bit stale, but was still the best thing she'd tasted in a very long time. She looked up into Slade's eyes. She might be signing her death warrant by confiding in the man, but even in the short amount of time she'd spent with him...she trusted him. There was just something about him that she felt down in her soul. That he was meant to find her.

She'd never been very religious in her life, but she did believe in souls. And reincarnation. Her parents had been soul mates; of that she was sure. She'd hoped to find the man meant to be hers in this lifetime, but had just about given up...until Slade had walked into the Little A'Le'Inn last night.

So far, Slade had been patient and protective of her...but more than that, she could see the honesty in his eyes. Aziz and his friends had cold, dead eyes. Slade's were a warm dark brown, and while she was well aware that he could probably kill her with his bare hands—he was a retired SEAL, after all—she knew he wouldn't.

When she didn't say anything else, Slade suggested, "How about we get out of the cold and grab something other than caffeine and sugar for you?"

"You came all the way out here because you wanted to know what Aziz looks like so you could catch him,"

Dakota said in confusion. "Why are you being so nice to me?"

"You're right, I did come all the way out here to find you and get more information on Fourati. But that's not the only reason. Sweetheart, you're shivering from cold, you have to be stiff from sitting here all night. I'm more concerned with taking care of *you* right now than getting information about Fourati."

Dakota licked her lips nervously, tasting the lingering peppermint that clung there, and asked, "Don't you need to report back to your superiors or whatever they're called and track him down? It's why you're here," she insisted again.

Slade immediately shook his head. "No. I won't lie, that's the original reason, yes. But the second I saw your picture in the mission folder, I knew I had to find you for a different reason."

He didn't elaborate, and Dakota asked, "Why?"

Slade's hand moved again. His fingers brushed her cheek, but then the heavy weight of his palm eased around and rested against the back of her neck. Dakota felt the goosebumps rise again and shoot all the way down both arms this time. With her hands full of the mug and paper bag, she couldn't do anything but lean on him when he put pressure on his hand and slowly tugged her forward.

His other hand went under her chin and he raised

her head so she had no choice but to look him in the eye. She felt surrounded by him. His warmth. His caring. His passion.

"I'm not a young man, Dakota. I'm forty-eight years old. And not once in all that time have I been so affected by a photo as I was yours. I've seen hundreds of pictures of women who were in need of protection and rescue. Not one made me lose my breath and feel as if I was smacked on the back of the head. It was as if you reached out and snagged a piece of my heart. But that was nothing compared to seeing you in person. When I walked into the bar last night, I felt as if I had finally found what I've been looking for my entire life. You."

Holy crap. Was he serious? Did he really think that? Could he truly be the man she'd been looking for all *her* life? Dakota shook her head in weak denial. "That's not possible. You're just saying that to get me to tell you what I know."

"I don't give a shit what you know," Slade returned immediately. "I don't care if you never tell me what Fourati looks like. I'll just tell my boss you don't know anything."

"But you'll get in trouble," Dakota told him.

"I won't get in trouble because this isn't a government-sanctioned op. Besides, I'm retired. Dakota, I don't give a shit what the person who hired me thinks. The point is, *you* are my main concern. I found you, and so can Fourati. I'd be surprised if he and his goons weren't already on their way here. In fact, I'm fairly certain they *are* on their way here. It's only a matter of time...how much, I don't know. I believe I have a couple days lead on them, but can't be sure. But whatever happens, know that my main mission from this moment forward is keeping you safe. Not capturing Fourati."

Dakota had no idea how to respond. On one hand, she absolutely knew what Slade was talking about because from the second she'd lain eyes on him she'd felt...calm. As though she could finally take a deep breath and relax the hyper alertness she'd had for the last couple of months. He would stand between her and the rest of the world. But on the other hand, that was crazy talk. Insane. She didn't know the first thing about the man sitting next to her practically holding her in his embrace.

Luckily, he didn't give her a chance to say anything. He gently bent her head down, kissed the top, then straightened and said, "Come on. Let's get you inside and warmed up. Then we can discuss where we're going from here."

Feeling docile and mellow, Dakota simply nodded and sat back. It felt good for someone else to make the decisions for once. They looked at each other for a long moment, then Slade turned and opened his door.

Shaking off her lassitude, Dakota followed suit after twisting to grab her backpack from the backseat. As soon as she was standing, Slade was there. He took the paper bag from her and tucked her hand into the crook of his arm, protecting her fingers from the chilly morning air.

"You have your car keys?"

"Why?"

"So we can lock it."

Dakota laughed. "Nobody is going to steal my car out here. The key's been in the ignition since I parked it. With my luck, I'd lose the stupid thing otherwise."

Slade shook his head as if exasperated, but didn't say anything else. He shut her car door and began to lead them to the trailer where he'd spent the night.

"I thought we were going to the restaurant?" Dakota asked as they approached.

"I figured you might want to shower to warm up first. And it's more private for us to talk in the trailer. The other occupants left already, like you said they probably would."

It was considerate of him. Dakota stopped suddenly, forcing him to as well.

It was considerate, but it was also conniving and potentially dangerous. The last thing she wanted to do was get naked with him nearby. She'd be vulnerable and—

"While you're showering, I'll head over to the restaurant. Give you some privacy."

"Thank you," she told him. Even though she didn't one hundred percent trust him, she still felt bad for thinking the worst.

Slade unlocked the door and led them inside. Dakota glanced into the bedroom and came to an abrupt stop.

Then she found herself staring at Slade's muscular back as he forced her backwards away from the bedroom, even as he was asking, "What? What did you see?"

"Nothing, I...the bed's still made."

As if realizing she wasn't in mortal danger, Slade slowly turned around and took a deep breath. "Yeah, and?"

"You made the bed before you left this morning?" she asked, knowing the answer before he said it.

"No. I didn't sleep there. I wanted to make sure you were safe last night, and when I saw you were sleeping in your car, I kept watch."

"You kept watch," Dakota said woodenly.

"Yeah."

"Over me."

"Yeah, Dakota. I wasn't going to fucking let you sleep in your car in the middle of nowhere when a fucking terrorist is after you. No fucking way."

She wasn't about to comment on the fact that he'd

said "fuck" three times in two sentences. The precisely made bed in the other room did more for making her believe he was exactly who he said he was, a retired Navy SEAL, and that he was there to keep her safe, than anything he could've said.

Still holding the mug with both hands now, Dakota didn't even think. She leaned forward and rested her forehead against the cool leather of his jacket on his chest.

His arms immediately folded around her, resting on the small of her back, gathering her close. She couldn't hug him in return with her hands full, but it didn't seem to matter.

This time when he spoke, the anger was gone and all that was left was concern...for her. "You were going to sleep *here* before I showed up, weren't you?"

She nodded against him. "Pat and Connie let me stay in the trailers when they aren't rented."

"I'm sorry I took your bed."

"But you didn't," she said in a voice muffled because she was still facing his chest. "You didn't use it. You slept...I don't know where. But you didn't take my bed."

"Mmmm," was his only response. His hands slowly caressed her back, and with each stroke, she melted farther into him until she didn't think she could stand of her own volition anymore. He was the only thing holding her up.

"I'm scared," Dakota admitted in a barely audible voice.

Slade's arms tightened around her and Dakota finally turned her head, resting her cheek against his chest.

"You're not alone anymore," Slade told her confidently. "No one is going to get their hands on you."

"Promise?" She knew she shouldn't have asked. It wasn't like he could actually promise something like that, but the word came out before she could call it back.

"I fucking promise." It was a vow, and they both knew it.

They stood together for another long moment before Slade pulled back, kissed her on the forehead this time, and ordered, "Shower. Change. I'll be back in twenty minutes to walk you to the bar."

"I thought we were talking here?"

"We are. But you need some breakfast first. Real food, not just that," he said, indicating the cup she still held.

"You don't have to come back. I'll just meet you over there."

Slade lifted her chin with his index finger and said softly, "I'll be back to walk you over. I'm not taking any chances. I promised to keep you safe until Fourati is either captured or dead. You're going to have to get used to me being by your side twenty-four seven."

Dakota nodded. Right now, that sounded perfect. Oh, she knew in reality it would probably be a pain in the ass, but remembering what he'd said about only having a couple days lead on whoever Aziz sent to get her and bring her back to him, it was heavenly.

"Okay," she told him.

"Okay. Have a good shower. Drink your coffee. I'll be back."

Dakota watched as Slade turned and walked out of the trailer.

Her life had completely changed when she'd had the bad luck to be caught in the middle of a terrorist act, but she had a feeling it'd just done another one-eighty.

Chapter Five

EXACTLY TWENTY MINUTES later, Slade knocked on the door of the trailer. Even being apart from her that long was somehow painful. He kept imagining someone sneaking in through the other door and taking Dakota away from him. He might have been upset at his thoughts, except there was every reason for him to believe someone *might* do just that.

Until he could get Dakota out of Rachel and back where he had cell phone reception to call Tex and make sure they were still in the clear, he wasn't going to take any chances.

Instead of returning to the bar, Slade leaned against the side of the A'Le'Inn and kept watch over the trailer while Dakota showered. He might be going overboard, but he didn't think so. She'd been dead to the world when he'd opened the passenger door to her car that morning. She hadn't even twitched when he'd shut it, either. If he could sneak up on her that easily, so could anyone else. And the thought of Fourati or any of his followers getting their hands on her made him want to hit something.

"I'm ready," Dakota called out in response to his knock. "Come in."

Slade turned the knob and entered the small but cozy trailer. As far as accommodations went, it wouldn't win any traveler awards, but for this town it was down-right palatial.

"I saved part of my donut for you," Dakota told him somewhat shyly.

If he hadn't already been halfway in love with her, that would've sent him over the edge. He knew how much she treasured those maple-frosted pastries…her dad had made it more than clear that no one touched her donuts. "You go ahead, sweetheart. It's been a while since you've had a treat."

She eyed him for a long moment and he thought she was going to either comment on the use of the endearment, or refuse to eat the pastry he could tell she wanted by the look in her eyes, but she finally shrugged and gave him a small smile.

"Thanks. And for the record, I was going to let you have it, but I'm happier that I can eat it all myself."

Slade chuckled. "I can see that." And he could. Her green eyes sparkled in the low light in the trailer and she'd already reached into the bag to grab the rest of the sticky donut.

"You ready to talk?" he asked her, pulling out one of the chairs to the small square table sitting next to the communal kitchen. "It's a pretty full house over at the restaurant."

"Yeah, people tend to get going early around here. At least the tourists. And while I really like Pat and Connie, they're the worst gossips. I guess it comes with not much to do or see out here," Dakota said matter-of-factly, and sat in the chair he'd pulled out for her.

They made small talk as she finished eating and when she licked the maple frosting off her fingers, Slade had to shift in his chair to give his dick room. He'd grown hard at the look of satisfaction on her face as she'd finished the donut, but when she began to use her tongue to catch every last speck of the sugary confection, he almost came in his pants.

"You said something earlier that I've been thinking on," Dakota said quietly, interrupting his inappropriate sexual thoughts.

"What's that?"

"You said that Aziz is foreign. Tunisian. What did you mean by that?"

Slade was puzzled for a moment. "What do you mean, what did I mean? I meant exactly what I said."

"But he's American," Dakota told him.

"Aziz Fourati is the leader of the Tunisian faction of the Ansar al-Shari'a terrorist group," Slade said firmly.

Dakota's eyebrows drew down in confusion. "Okay, then who was the guy at the airport?"

"Hang on, let's back up a second," Slade said, and he stood to go to the sink. As he pulled off a paper towel and wet it in the sink, he continued. "I'm part of a top secret task force assigned to find out all I could on Fourati and take him down. He's gaining followers online. Quickly. I told you he's trying to replicate the LAX bombing all over the country in simultaneous attacks. No one is sure where he's getting the money to fund such an operation, but at the moment that isn't important. He's sneaky. He's good at staying under the radar, and the fact of the matter is that the government can't find him, partly because there are no known pictures of the man. Absolutely none."

He squeezed out the paper towel and came back to the table. As he continued to talk, he picked up each of Dakota's hands and gently cleaned them of the sugary mess the donut had left behind.

"Part of my goal, other than making sure you're safe, is to get a description of the man, maybe even a sketch, so the government knows who they're looking for and can put it into the facial recognition program. That way, if he ever steps foot inside an airport again, they can stop him."

Dakota put her hand over his, halting his movements. She looked into his eyes. "The man who pretended to be a hostage, and then ranted and raved for twenty minutes before he ordered the other guy to blow himself up, is American, Slade."

Slade's fingers gripped her own. "Are you sure?"

She nodded. "Positive. He had blue eyes and blondish hair. He also had what I'd say was a New York accent. I know people can fake accents and change their looks, but at no time did I *ever* think he was anything but American when I was around him."

"Did he ever call himself Aziz?"

"No. I didn't know his name until you said it, remember?"

"Then it might not be the same guy," Slade said more to himself than Dakota. "Tell me about LAX," he ordered gently.

"I was in the security line waiting just like everyone else. I heard yelling and screaming and turned to see what was happening. There were two men waving rifles around and shouting. They pointed their guns at a group of us in line and ordered us to follow them. We were herded through a door that said 'employees only,' I guess one of them had the code or a swipey thing to get in. I have no idea. Anyway, we all were marched down a hall and through another door into some sort of room. Maybe a break room or something for the employees?

"Everyone was scared and crying. One of the guys had explosives strapped to his chest. He handed that

Aziz guy a pistol. He pulled me to my feet by my hair and held the gun to my head as he spoke. He had one arm around my chest and jammed the muzzle of that gun to my temple. He said that America was broken. That no one understood the meaning of spirituality anymore and that the Quran was the answer. He said it would take a grand act to make everyone face their mortality and turn to the revelations of God according to the Quran."

She was whispering now, and while Slade hated the fear on her face as she recalled the awful experience she'd been through, he let her continue to speak. He needed to hear what happened in that airport, and she needed to get it out so she could begin to heal.

"There was a younger hostage there, I hate that I don't even know his name, but he stood up and challenged the guy I now know was Aziz. And he just shot him. Took the pistol away from my temple, shot the guy who stood up for me, then pressed it right back against my head. The barrel was still hot and it hurt. Everyone began to scream and cry even louder as the man lay on the floor bleeding. Dying. And Aziz didn't care. He started talking about how every leader needed a woman at his side, supporting him. Having his babies to continue the dynasty."

Slade couldn't stand it anymore. He pushed his chair back a few inches, then grabbed Dakota's hand.

He pulled her up and into his lap. She snuggled into him as if they'd done this exact thing hundreds of times. He was tall; at six-five, most furniture didn't fit him well, but he didn't give a shit at the moment if he was uncomfortable. He'd sit there and hold Dakota in his arms as long as she needed him to.

He put one of his big hands on the back of her head and held her tightly to him as she continued.

"I knew he was talking about me, that he wasn't going to martyr himself for his cause like I first thought. He rambled on a bit more and continually checked his watch as if he was waiting for a specific amount of time to pass. Then he nodded at the guy with the explosives, fired in the air, I think to make everyone scared of what was going to happen, then pulled me behind him as he quickly walked away. I knew if I didn't get away from him, he'd make me his sex slave and keep me locked up. So as soon as we exited the room, I attacked him."

"Good for you," Slade murmured, interrupting her for the first time.

"Not so good," she said with what he hoped was amusement. "I kicked him and he went down, but I didn't incapacitate him. I started to run toward the door that led back into the terminal, but he caught and tackled me. He kneeled above me and whispered, 'Good to know my future wife has courage. You're going to need it.' Then he bent down as if he was going to kiss me, but that's when the explosives went off. I don't know if the guy set them off too early or not, but I saw surprise and anger in the man's eyes before the ceiling fell in on us."

"His body protected you from the debris," Slade guessed.

She nodded against him. "Most of it, yeah. Knocked him out cold. Something hit my arm and broke it. I was so scared and the guy was deadweight on top of me, but I wiggled out from under him, hoping he was dead, and made my way out to the terminal. It was chaos, and no one realized that I'd come from the room the men with guns had entered. I was just another frantic person trying to get away from the building. I blended right in."

She fell silent then and Slade let her have the moment. A couple minutes and a few deep breaths later, she continued. "I thought I was good. That I'd gotten away. But I figured out pretty quickly that he didn't die."

"How did you know?" Slade asked.

"Because a week or so after I went back to work, I started to get presents delivered to my office. They were delivered anonymously, but I knew. Each one was addressed to 'My Future Bride.' There wasn't anyone else who would do that sort of thing. I'm not the kind of woman who has secret admirers. I quit the day one of the second-graders in my school brought me a box tied with a red bow. She said a man had given it to her outside the front doors and told her to bring it to me."

"What was it?" Slade prompted when she didn't continue.

"A plastic grenade," Dakota told him as she sat up a little straighter on his lap. "The bastard was not only threatening me, but all my kids as well. I called the cops, they took the threat seriously, but there wasn't much they could do. There weren't any prints and the little girl couldn't really describe the person who gave her the box."

"So you quit."

"I quit," she confirmed. "I didn't want to. But what else could I do? He wasn't going to leave me alone, I knew it. Hell, he *told* me. Then it got worse. My apartment complex burned to the ground. I know it was him. He wanted me scared out of my mind with no place to go and ready to agree to anything he wanted."

"But you're too tough for that."

She chuckled then. A sad sound that conveyed her hopelessness. "I don't know about that. I went to my dad's, said goodbye and told him to be careful, not to trust anyone who came to the door, then left. My first plan was to go to the East Coast, as far away from California as I could get, but I only made it to Vegas. And now here I am."

"Why Rachel?" Slade asked, genuinely curious.

"I wasn't planning on staying. I met some people who told me all about the area and how cool it was. I thought it sounded like a good place to hole up for a while, figure out what my next move was going to be. But I didn't take into account that when I got here, there wouldn't be any gas stations, and I didn't have enough fuel to get me to one." Dakota shrugged.

The chuckle began softly enough, but when she looked up at him and her own lips quirked into a grin, he couldn't hold it back. He threw his head back and laughed. She joined in and soon they were laughing at the randomness of life.

Through chuckles, she elaborated, "I quickly got that sorted out, but the more I thought about it, the more I realized that Rachel was a great place to hide. I'm paid in cash and can save up some money while not using my credit cards, and there aren't a lot of people out here, so I can keep watch on who comes and goes pretty easily."

Slade finally got himself under control and said, "I think staying out here was a really good idea. It's like you've been hiding in plain sight."

"I guess."

"I'm sorry you lost all your belongings in the fire."

"Don't be. It was just stuff. My dad still has pictures of my mom, so I don't even feel that bad about losing mine. I feel worse for the families and other residents who lost everything because some asshole thinks he can take whatever he wants. If you ask me, he's less a terrorist than a big baby."

"Can you describe him for me?"

"He's about my height. Five-nine or so. He's got short blond hair, at least he did a few months ago. Blue eyes. Pale skin. He was dressed really nice in the airport…slacks, polo shirt, and he was carrying a briefcase. I don't know if it was just a prop or not. He was fairly young. Probably mid- to late-twenties, if I had to guess. He was muscular and honestly looked like any other businessman on his way to a meeting." Dakota sat up straight on Slade's lap and looked him in the eyes.

"He looked like the boy next door, Slade. Completely harmless, which is what made what happened so scary. When he was on top of me in the airport and looking down at me, I swear to God I saw nothing but blackness in his eyes. I don't think he cares about religion at all. He just wants to kill people. He gets off on it."

Slade closed his eyes in both relief that Dakota had gotten away from him, and frustration that the search for the terrorist just got tougher. A man with his description could blend in anywhere in America.

"You aren't going to be able to find him, are you?" Dakota asked, obviously more attuned to him than he'd thought.

Slade opened his eyes and looked directly at her as he swore, "We're going to find him."

"But how? He—"

"Sweetheart, you're not going to have to worry about this guy for the rest of your life. I know people who know people who know people. They'll find him. Can I change the subject for a second?"

"Oh…well…yeah, I guess so," she said uncertainly, obviously not really wanting to drop the subject of Aziz.

Slade tightened his arms around her waist and asked, "You feel this?"

She hesitated for a moment, then nodded shyly, not asking what he meant.

"Yeah. I've been in your presence for less than twelve hours and I can tell you without a doubt that you've somehow become the most precious thing in my life. I've been married and divorced, I have nieces and nephew and I love my family. But *nothing* has ever made me feel like I do right this moment with you in my arms."

"We don't know each other," she protested.

"I know."

"And we're too old for this kind of insta-lust."

"Speak for yourself," Slade said with a grin. "I might be forty-eight, but I'm not dead, sweetheart. I spent four years married to my ex, and not once did I ever feel this way about her."

"What way?"

"Like if I take my eyes off you, I'll lose something precious. Like I want to hold you so tightly against me, until I can't ever remember what it feels like to not have you in my arms. Like if I don't kiss you right this second, I'll die."

He held his breath, hoping he hadn't just scared her away.

Instead of answering him or laughing at his words, Dakota slowly leaned toward him. Her eyes dropped to his lips, and the erection Slade had been controlling with sheer stubbornness sprang to life at the desire he saw there.

One of her hands came up between them and landed on the side his neck. Her fingers brushed against the sensitive skin behind his ear, and her thumb rested on the side of his face and caressed his beard.

"I've never kissed a man who had a beard before."

"Then I think it's about time you did," Slade told her, not moving an inch. He wanted her to take what she wanted. He wanted to make sure this was something *she* wanted to do.

Dakota pulled him toward her and kissed him.

She kissed *him*.

The second her lips touched his, however, Slade took over. It was enough that she'd made the first move, he couldn't hold back any longer. His head slanted, his hands came up to frame her face and he devoured her. This was no tentative first kiss, this was a claiming.

Slade's tongue pushed past her barely parted lips as though if he didn't get inside her in the next second, he'd die. Their tongues tangled together as they kissed. When Dakota pulled back to take a breath, Slade followed her, not giving her more than a second's respite before claiming her mouth again.

For what seemed like hours, he drank from her. She tasted like sugar and peppermint. It was a taste he knew he'd crave for the rest of his life. Slade learned that she enjoyed a little roughness, but melted into him when he lightly nipped and sucked on her lower lip. He brushed his cheek against hers, smiling when she made a whimpering sound deep in her throat as his beard made contact with her sensitive skin.

Sometime in the midst of their kiss, she'd turned into him and straddled his hips on the small chair. His cock was now flush against the cleft between her legs, and she was rubbing herself against his hardness in the same rhythm he was using to suck on her tongue.

When he finally allowed her room to breathe, he rested his forehead on hers and held her hips tightly against him as they both fought to catch their breaths.

"I think it's safe to say I like you back," she said with a small smile.

His lips twitched, but he remained serious when he said, "Good."

"I thought your beard would be scratchy. But it's really soft. It feels good."

"I'm glad you don't hate it. I've gotten kinda used to it."

"I don't hate it," she told him firmly. They sat still for a moment, then Dakota asked softly, "Should I be embarrassed about this?" She motioned to their laps with her head.

"Embarrassed that I can feel how hot and wet you are from only the touch of my mouth on yours? Fuck no. You can see and feel how much *I* liked it."

At his words, her hips nudged his hard-as-nails dick once more and he smiled at her.

"This is the beginning of us," he declared firmly. "I don't care what the future holds. I'm not giving this up. I'm not giving *you* up."

"It's probably the danger thing," Dakota told him. "You'll feel differently when it's all over."

"Wanna bet?" Slade asked.

"What?"

"A bet. I bet you fifty peppermint mochas and maple-iced donuts that when Fourati is dead, I'll still want you just as much, or more, than I do right this moment."

"Oh...uh...okay. And if it's just the heat of the

moment?"

"It's not."

"But it's not a bet if you don't bet on both sides, Slade."

He smirked. "Fine. If, after Fourati is out of your life for good, I don't feel exactly how I do right now, like I want inside you more than I want my next breath, then I'll give you enough gift cards to set you up for life with your coffees and pastries. And if I do, then I'll personally deliver a coffee and donut to you in our bed every morning for the rest of our lives."

Dakota opened her mouth to speak—but Slade quickly covered it with his hand.

It was as if a switch had been turned on inside him. He lost the relaxed, teasing vibe he'd had when they were talking about the bet, and was suddenly all business.

"Shhh," he ordered urgently, easing them to their feet at the same time.

Dakota nodded and he took his hand away from her face, running his thumb over her lips in apology for how hard he'd been, even as his eyes swept the interior of the small space.

The soft noise came again at the other door of the trailer.

Slade didn't waste any time. He pushed her into the room she'd showered in, grabbing her backpack as he went. Closing the door silently, then locking it, he turned to Dakota and slipped the backpack over her shoulders without a word.

He stalked silently to the window and pried the top of the blinds apart a minuscule amount so he could see out. Seeing nothing alarming, he quietly pulled the cord to open them and pushed the window up. Thank God there was no screen.

Holding out his hand to Dakota, he said softly, "We need to go, sweetheart. Looks like our time has run out."

"Aziz?" Dakota asked in a whisper.

"Or his goons. But we're not going to wait around to find out."

Glad to see determination on her face rather than fear, Slade took hold of her hand and squeezed. "I'm going out first, then I'll help you. You need anything from your car that isn't in that backpack?"

Dakota shook her head and whispered, "I keep my stuff with me as much as possible. I always have a couple changes of clothes and a few personal items. Just in case."

"Good. My bike is parked to the side of the restaurant. I filled the tank with the gas I brought with me after we parted last night, so it's ready to go. We've got enough to get back to civilization. There's not much cover between here and my bike though, so we're going to have to make a break for it. You ready?"

She nodded, but pulled on his hand when he went to climb out of the window. "I've never ridden a motorcycle before, Slade."

He took precious seconds he wasn't sure he had to lean down and kiss her lips hard. "All you gotta do is hold on, sweetheart. I'm not going to let anything happen to you. Trust me."

"I do."

"Good. Then let's get out of here." Slade let go of her hand and quickly eased out of the window. Because he was so tall, his feet hit the ground before he was all the way out. He grabbed hold of Dakota as she began to climb out, and had her standing next to him in seconds.

Without letting go of her hand, Slade quietly moved to the side of the trailer and peered around the corner. Standing at the far door was a Middle Eastern man fiddling with the lock. Obviously not Fourati, if Dakota's description was correct, but certainly one of his flock. He briefly wondered how the man had found them, but didn't have time to ponder it. It wasn't relevant anyway. It didn't matter if this was the last trailer he'd checked, or the first, he was here now, and it was time for them to *not* be here.

He turned to Dakota and pulled her back the way they'd come. He cautiously peeked around the corner of the trailer and saw nobody. "New plan. See that truck?"

He pointed to the rusted hulk of what used to be a truck sitting about twenty feet away from the trailer.

She nodded.

"Go and hide behind it. Do not come out no matter what you hear. Got me?"

"But—"

"Dakota. I was a SEAL. I got this. But I need you to help me. If I'm worried about you, I won't be able to do what I need to do. Please. I need you to hide. Hunker down and wait for me to come get you."

"Okay, but don't get dead," she whispered fearfully.

His lips twitched. She was kinda funny even when she wasn't trying to be. "I won't. Now go on. You'll hear me coming. Be ready."

"Am I supposed to leap on the back of your bike while it's moving like they used to do to horses in the wild west?"

He couldn't hold back his smile this time. Funny. "No, smartass. I'll stop. If we have time, you'll also put on the helmet I bought for you."

"You bought me a helmet?"

Slade rolled his yes. "Yes. Now go."

Without hesitation, she stood on her tiptoes, kissed him, then took off running for the rusted truck. Slade felt his lips tingling where she'd touched him, and licked them as he watched her disappear behind the dubious safety of the rusted vehicle.

Forcing himself to leave her, Slade headed back toward the front of the trailer. He waited until the man had entered to make his move. He had no idea if the guy was by himself—not likely—so he couldn't dick around.

Looking around to make sure no one witnessed him entering the trailer, and not seeing anyone lurking nearby, Slade slipped in behind the man silently. He needed to get Dakota out of town, but he couldn't just leave this asshole walking around free and clear. It wouldn't sit well on his conscience if he blew up the A'Le'Inn or killed anyone in town while looking for Dakota.

Five minutes later, the man was unconscious and tied up in the trailer, and Slade headed for the bar. He needed to warn Pat and Connie that there might be more terrorists lurking about and get them to call the police. It would probably take a while for help to arrive, but at least the asshole in the trailer wouldn't hurt anyone in the meantime.

Slade figured the man had a partner, or partners, somewhere, but couldn't take any more time to try to track them down. He'd warn the owners and make sure they were safe before getting the hell out of dodge.

The second the guy's partners realized he'd been compromised, they'd be hot on Slade and Dakota's trail. If they were going to escape, they needed a head start. It wasn't as if they could disappear in the small town, and there was only one road leading into and out of Rachel, with absolutely no cover whatsoever. As much as he didn't like it, his best option at the moment was to bolt, not track down an unknown number of terrorists.

He made one other quick stop before hurrying to his motorcycle. They needed to be far out of sight before the man, or men, knew which way they'd gone. His actions might buy them some time, but Slade had a feeling things were just getting interesting.

Chapter Six

DAKOTA HEARD SLADE before she saw him. She had stuffed herself as far under the rusted-out old truck as she could and hoped she couldn't be seen from the other side.

Her heart was beating wildly and she had to constantly force herself to stay where she was and not peek around the truck to look for Slade. He said he'd come and get her, so she had to stay in place until he did.

The morning had been intense, there was no doubt about that. But whatever weird connection she felt for Slade was obviously returned. She'd never felt as strongly about a man as she did him. She'd been scared for so long, it felt good to have someone care whether or not she lived or died.

Besides the physical attraction she and Slade had for each other, there was something more. Something almost divine. It was if her soul recognized him from the second their eyes met.

Dakota was a romantic. She knew it and didn't try

to hide it. She read romances, watched sappy movies, and cried at the end of *Cinderella* every time. But she hadn't ever had that ah-ha moment she'd always felt so sure she'd experience when she met the man destined to be hers. At forty-three, she figured she never would. She'd been to sixty-seven weddings in her lifetime. Sixty-freaking-seven. When teachers in her school got married, they'd inevitably invite her and she'd go. To every one. And each time, it felt more and more like a stake in the heart as she watched her friends and colleagues tie themselves to their soul mates. Knowing she'd probably never have that, hurt.

But now here she was. On the run from a terrorist who wanted to make her his love slave, in danger, not knowing what her future would bring, and it had finally happened. Slade Cutsinger had walked through the door last night and she'd known he was hers with one glance.

The amazing thing was that apparently, he felt the same. But he was in danger while she hid like a coward. Suddenly staying put didn't seem like the best plan after all.

She sat up and began to brush off the sand from her legs, determined to do more than hide like a coward, when she heard a loud engine approaching.

Dakota held her breath and sighed in relief when Slade pulled up next to her on his Harley.

"Climb on, sweetheart. No time for a helmet right

now. We'll stop in a few and get you all set. That's it, put your left foot there on the peg and swing your right leg around. Good. Watch the engine, it gets hot, don't let your calf touch it. It'll burn the shit out of your leg. Hold on. No…hold *on*. Good. Here we go."

And with that short intro to riding a motorcycle, he gunned the engine, sand spewed behind the tire, and they fishtailed for a few yards before Slade gained control of the huge machine between his legs and they shot forward.

Dakota squeezed her eyes shut and held on to Slade for dear life. She guessed that her fingers were probably white with the pressure she was exerting on his belly. Her chest was flush against his back and the wind blew her hair crazily around her head. The bun she'd put her hair in after her shower was quickly torn out as they raced down the road at what seemed like an insane speed.

She kept her eyes closed as Slade raced away from Rachel. Dakota had no idea which direction they were even going, but at the moment it didn't matter. Slade would take care of her…she had no doubt.

It could've been hours later, but was probably only fifteen minutes or so, when Dakota felt the bike slow. She waited until they were completely stopped before opening her eyes. Slade had turned his head and was watching her.

"You okay?"

She nodded shakily.

He put his hand around her fingers still clutched together at his belly. "Come on, sweetheart. We can't stop for long, but I need to take care of you before we continue. Let go."

Dakota forced her fingers to uncurl, surprised at how stiff and cold they were.

"I've got a pair of gloves for your hands. I'm sorry I had to wait so long to pull over. I would've picked you up faster, but I had to take care of something."

"Take care of something?" she asked with a tilt of her head.

"I couldn't in good conscience let the asshole who broke into the trailer possibly take out his frustration at finding you gone on the residents of Rachel."

"Did you kill him?"

"No. But he certainly won't feel like doing much anytime soon. Come on, stand up, let me get you outfitted properly."

"Outfitted properly" included a leather jacket exactly her size, a pair of gloves, and a helmet. "I'm sorry I can't fit your backpack in my saddlebags. Are you okay wearing it?"

"Of course. It's no problem," she told him. "Were you that sure you were going to find me?"

"What do you mean?"

"You have a jacket for me…which fits perfectly, by the way. And a pair of gloves in my size. And the helmet."

Slade put his hands on her shoulders and turned her so her back was to him. He began to gently finger comb her long, tangled hair. "I was that sure I was going to find you," he confirmed. "Because I wasn't going to stop until you were safe."

Dakota swallowed hard at the feeling of his hands in her hair and said simply, "Okay."

"Okay," he agreed, then began to braid her hair.

"Why are you doing that?" she asked softly.

"Because we have a while to go. And it'll just continue to get tangled if I don't. And…" He paused dramatically and she felt him lean into her. "It gives me an excuse to run my hands through your hair."

She chuckled, but didn't protest. He quickly finished the simple braid and tied it off with her hair elastic. Then he turned her to face him and picked up her helmet. He gently placed it on her head and wiggled it a bit. "How's this feel? Too tight? Too loose?"

"No, it seems okay. Not that I'd know how a motorcycle helmet is supposed to fit though."

"Let me know if it pinches in any way when we get started." And with that, Slade buckled the strap under her chin and stared down at her for a long moment.

"What?" she asked nervously. "Does it look stupid?"

"No, Dakota. It doesn't look stupid. It looks great. *You* look great. I just can't believe you're here. On the back of my bike. I know the situation sucks, but I can't be sorry. I'm so happy to be here with you."

"I'm glad you're here with me too," she told him softly.

Then he tapped her on the end of her nose with his finger and smiled down at her. "We gotta get going. This time you need to open your eyes," he teased, then threw his leg over the Harley and settled in, looking back at her expectantly.

Ignoring his jibe about her eyes, she said, "Are you sure we won't be followed?" Dakota settled in behind him as she asked. Her arms tentatively circled his waist. Now that they weren't moving, she wasn't sure where she should put them.

Not even hesitating, Slade reached down and took a hand in each of his own and wrapped them tighter around his waist once more. He linked her fingers together, then pressed them against his stomach, giving her a nonverbal command to keep them there.

She was plastered against him once again, but now that she was wearing a leather jacket, she was warmer and could appreciate how his muscles moved under her hands and chest more.

He started the motorcycle and turned his head so she could hear him over the motor. "Followed by the guy I knocked out, no. But I'm not sure about any of his buddies. I did stop and pierce the gas tank of the only other car that hadn't been there when we entered the trailer though," he said matter-of-factly. "If there was more than one of them, they aren't going to be going anywhere for long in their piece-of-shit car. I bought us some time to get back to San Diego ahead of them."

Dakota's arms tightened involuntarily. "Back to California? Is that a good idea?"

Slade's eyes met hers, and the reassurance she saw there made her relax before he even said a word. "I want you on my turf. I've got people there who will have our backs. I can communicate with my friend, Tex, who will give me a head's up on what's happening with Fourati. I know it's scary, but I can end this faster if we're there."

"You won't use me as bait, will you?" Dakota asked quietly, her voice barely audible over the roar of the engine. It was a concern. She figured it was cowardly of her, but she wasn't exactly GI Jane. She was an elementary school principal, for goodness sake. The last thing she wanted to do was see Aziz Fourati again, even if Slade and his friends were watching over her. He scared the crap out of her.

"Fuck no," Slade bit out with a shake of his head. "There's no way I'd allow you to put yourself in danger like that. If there's even a one percent chance that something could go wrong, I won't do it. And since this Fourati guy is obviously off his fucking rocker, there's no telling what he'd do if he got his hands on you. So no, you won't be fucking bait."

Dakota thought it was somewhat amusing that the more emotional Slade felt, the more he used the f-word. Wanting to soothe him, she ran her hands up and down his stomach. "Okay, Slade. Good."

"Good," he agreed, and turned around to face forward once again.

But before he grabbed hold of the handlebars, he reached down and picked up her right hand. He kissed the palm before placing it back on his stomach.

Dakota's own stomach tightened at the tender gesture. She couldn't feel his lips since she was wearing gloves, but somehow her hand still seemed to warm.

As they took off, Dakota realized she still wasn't sure which way they were headed, but assumed north. They could take Route 95 down through Goldfield and into Vegas, then get back on Interstate 15. But at that moment it didn't matter. She was on the back of a motorcycle with a man she trusted down to the very marrow of her bones, and she felt safer with him than she'd felt in a very long time.

Ten minutes later, Dakota felt the motorcycle slowing. It was still early morning, but the the sun had come up, warming the chilly air enough so she wasn't freezing.

Slade's body heat, the leather jacket, and the helmet went a long way toward keeping her body heat in as well.

"Why are we stopping?" she asked in a loud voice to be heard over the engine.

Slade was bent over a piece of electronics and didn't answer her immediately.

Giving him time, Dakota looked around. There was a mountain range in the distance ahead of them. She had no idea how far away it was because distance was skewed out here in the desert. It could've been two miles or twenty. Spatial reasoning wasn't her forte.

There were big puffy clouds in the sky, and it would've been beautiful if it wasn't for the fact they were trying to outrun goons who wanted to do her harm.

"How're you holding up?" Slade asked.

"I'm okay," Dakota said immediately.

"No. How are you holding up?" Slade repeated firmly.

Her brows drew down in confusion. "I don't know what you're really asking."

"You haven't ridden a bike before. It's chilly. You've been tense the entire ride. The morning has been stressful and I'd like to do whatever I can to keep that stress at a minimum for as long as I can. I'm sure your legs are probably beginning to get sore from straddling the seat and the vibrations of the bike. I'm asking how you're feeling so I can determine which route we're going to take to Tonopah."

"What are our choices?" Dakota ignored his incredibly accurate rundown of the morning. She would be sore later, no doubt about it. Slade's Harley was big…he was a big man, after all. The vibrations had started out feeling good, like a large erotic massager, but as they'd ridden on, they began to get irritating. Her teeth felt like they were still rattling even though they weren't moving. And forget about her girly parts being aroused, numb was more like it.

But she was beginning to understand Slade a little more. It was crazy, it wasn't as if she'd known him all that long. But she knew without a doubt that he'd put her comfort first…even if it wasn't the best tactical decision. She might not be the strongest woman in the world, but she refused to be a burden.

"We can continue on the blacktop road. It's probably another forty miles or so to Tonopah. The road heads north, then turns west directly to the small town. It's a straight shot. With no cover."

Dakota understood his concern. The desert was beautiful, but if she could see for miles, so could the people who were after her. If they managed to somehow catch up with them, there would be absolutely nowhere for them to hide.

"And our other option?" she asked.

Appreciating that Slade didn't treat her like a child, he laid it out. He pointed to his left. "This dirt road leads to the Tonopah Test Range Airport. It continues on to Tonopah itself. It's rough. *Really* rough. We won't be able to drive very fast because of the likely condition of the road."

"But it's safer," Dakota concluded.

"Yeah. Definitely. There's no way anyone could follow us…not in a regular car. They'd have to go the long way around," Slade told her.

"But they could go faster, right? Beat us to Tonopah?"

"It's a possibility," Slade agreed. "They won't be able to fix their gas tank, I put a big-ass hole in it. But if they were able to obtain another vehicle, they could drive like a bat out of hell and get there before us. But, it'll be much easier to hide, if we need to, once we hit ninety-five. There are small towns all along the way down to Vegas."

"Let's take the dirt road," Dakota said firmly. "If it's safer, we should do it."

Slade twisted around so he could see her better. "It's not going to be comfortable," he warned. "It'll be really dusty and I can guarantee before we're twenty miles down this piece-of-shit thing called a road, you'll be wishing we'd stayed on the blacktop."

"Probably," she agreed. "But there are a lot of things I've wished in the last couple of months. I wish I woke up late and didn't make it to the airport on time. I wish there was a longer line to check in so I wasn't in the right place at the right time to catch Aziz's eye. I wish I'd stopped to check to make sure he was dead before I ran. Taking the shorter road here seems like a no-brainer to me. The last thing I want is for us to be caught in the middle of the desert, with nowhere to go and no way to protect ourselves."

"I never said I couldn't protect you, Dakota," Slade said quietly. "I will always protect you."

She swallowed hard before saying, "I'm looking at this as an adventure. I've never ridden a motorcycle, and now's my chance. Just like I'd never kissed a man with a beard before...and that turned out okay."

"Just okay?" Slade asked with a smile.

"Maybe a bit better. I need more data to make a definitive decision," she teased.

He smiled at her response, then leaned in. "You need a break, don't hesitate to let me know. We have the time. We can stop. Let you walk around."

"I'll be fine," she told him, not sure she would, but trying to be strong. "Slade?"

"Yeah, sweetheart?"

"Do you think we might be able to find a hotel that has a Jacuzzi? If I'm going to be sore, it might be nice to have a warm soak."

"I'll make it happen," Slade vowed.

And somehow, she knew he would. Even if they were in the middle of nowhere, Nevada, somehow Slade would find the one hotel that had a Jacuzzi so she could soak her sore muscles.

"Here," Slade said, interrupting her thoughts. "Wrap this around your face. It'll help keep the dust out of your nose and mouth." He held out a handkerchief.

Dakota didn't know where he'd pulled it out of, but it didn't matter. She unbuckled her helmet and tied the cloth around her face. It smelled good. Like Slade. She might be uncomfortable and miserable, but she'd have Slade's scent in her nose. She could deal with that. As she buckled her helmet again, she noticed that Slade had donned a bandana around his face too, and, even though she couldn't see his mouth anymore, knew he was smiling at her by the wrinkles around his eyes.

"I'll make a biker babe out of you yet," he teased, then ran his gloved fingers down her cheek and turned to face forward again. "Ready?"

"Yup," Dakota chirped, trying to hide her trepidation. "Drive on, James."

Slade pulled her arms around him again, taking the time to lift her hand once more, pull down his bandana, and place a kiss in the middle of her palm. Once more, she couldn't feel his lips through her glove, but the tender gesture made her shiver anyway.

"Here we go," he told her as he gave the engine some gas. "Hold on."

An hour later, Dakota thought she was going to die, but she held on, determined not to be a wuss. Slade had warned her, had said it was going to be tough. She thought she'd be able to hack it, but it had become clear about ten minutes down the dirt road that she'd overstated her "hack it" ability.

She didn't want to be weak. Didn't want Slade to see how pathetic she was. But this riding-a-motorcycle thing was for the birds. She wanted off. At this point, she'd be willing to walk the rest of the way to San Diego if it meant not having to straddle the beast anymore.

Her inner thighs hurt from gripping the seat. Her head hurt from the noise of the engine. Her fingers hurt from clutching each other. Her arms hurt from squeezing Slade's sides. And finally, even her eyes hurt from squinting and trying to keep the dust and wind out of them.

She was miserable and ready for Aziz to find her and have his way with her just to put her out of her current suffering.

Dakota didn't even realize Slade was slowing down until he cut the engine and the silence of the desert washed over her. Picking her head up from his shoulder, where she'd rested it miles ago, she blinked and looked around in confusion.

"Are we there?"

"No, sweetheart. But you need a break."

"But we need to keep going."

He'd climbed off the bike, unbuckled his helmet, and had removed the bandana around his face. He spoke as he did the same for her. "You've held up wonderfully, but if we're going to make it to Goldfield tonight, you need to walk around. Take a break."

"I can keep going," Dakota protested, even though the thought made her wince.

Slade pulled her bandana to rest around her neck and hung her helmet next to his on the handlebars then leaned into her. "I have a feeling you could do anything you put your mind to. But you don't have to lie to me. In fact, I'd prefer you didn't. I appreciate your stubbornness, but I know without a doubt you need to stop for a while."

"How?" She hated that she was so easy to read.

"You were flinching after every pothole. You were gripping me so tight, I know you've got to be sore as hell…and we haven't even gotten halfway to Tonopah. You're wincing, so it's obvious your head hurts, and your legs are shaking as you're sitting there."

"Darn," Dakota murmured, looking down at her lap. Sure enough, her legs were trembling as her feet rested on the pegs on the back of the bike.

"Throw your right leg over the front of the bike and turn toward me. Then you can slide off the seat and have both feet on the ground at the same time. Hold on to me. I won't let you fall."

"This is gonna suck, isn't it?" Dakota asked rhetorically under her breath as she followed his orders. She went to scoot off the seat, but Slade stopped her by putting both hands on either side of her neck and tilting her head up toward him.

"I'm proud of you, sweetheart."

"Why? Because I can't ride more than an hour without wanting to cry like a baby? Because I feel so weak I know I'm not going to be able to stand by myself? Or because the thought of having to get back on this monster and continue makes me want to lie down right here in the dirt and cry?"

"Because you're feeling all those things, but you won't let any of them hold you back. You aren't the first newbie to be sore after riding, but I daresay others haven't been on the run from assholes nor ridden for an hour over the worst excuse for a road that they've ever seen. You don't have to worry about standing by yourself, because I'm right here and won't let you fall. And you might not want to get back on the bike, but you will. And that right there is why, with just one glance at your picture, I knew I wanted you for myself."

Feeling flustered and hot, Dakota joked, "And the

crying?"

"You go right ahead," Slade told her. "I'm not afraid of a few tears. I hate that you'll shed them because that means you're hurting, but if they'll help release your emotions, then go for it."

Dakota closed her eyes tightly and took a few deep breaths. She didn't feel very strong at the moment, but Slade thinking she was went a long way toward making her feel better.

He moved his hands from her neck to her waist and gently lifted her off the seat to stand in front of him. As soon as her feet hit the dusty ground, her knees buckled. She would've fallen if he hadn't been holding her up.

"Easy, Dakota. Just stand there for a moment. Let the blood work its way back to your feet."

"I can't believe you do this for fun," she bitched as her legs tingled from the increased blood flow to her toes.

He chuckled in her ear. "I wouldn't say driving my Harley on roads like this is fun. This is more something I'd do on my dirt bike."

"Oh lord. Don't tell me. You've got a garage full of motorcycles at your house."

"Nope."

"Thank God."

"I live in an apartment. They're in a buddy's garage," Slade told her, grinning.

"Evil," Dakota told him, easing back a little, trying to stand on her own.

"Come on," Slade said, putting an arm around her waist and turning them to the side. "Walking will do you good. Get your blood pumping and your muscles working again."

"I think sitting would be better, or maybe lying down and never moving again," Dakota told him, wrinkling her nose at the pain when she began to move. She knew she was walking completely bowlegged, but Slade didn't say anything or make fun of her. She was going to call that a win in her book.

He helped her limp up the side of a small rise. It seemed more like a mountain when they were walking up it, but when they got to the top, Dakota saw that it really was just a tiny hill compared to the mountain range that stretched in front of them.

Slade helped her sit, then settled in behind her, pulling her back to his front and taking her weight. Dakota bent her legs up and put her feet flat on the ground in front of her, relaxing into Slade.

He pointed toward the mountains. "The highest point there is Kawich Peak. It's about ninety-five hundred feet high."

"Do people climb it?" Dakota asked, not really caring, but needing to talk about something to keep her mind off of how much her body hurt.

"Not much. It *is* out here in the middle of no-where," he deadpanned.

Dakota chuckled. "True."

"But more than that, see all these scrub bushes around?"

Dakota nodded.

"I've heard the brush gets horrible the higher you go. It gets to a point that it's a pain in the ass to contin-ue."

"You've talked to someone who climbed it?" Dakota asked, surprised.

"No, but I researched the area before I came out here. I wanted to know what my options were in case we needed to hide."

She craned her neck and gave him an incredulous look. "You were going to have us climb that mountain?"

He smiled back. "I'm not saying it would've been fun, but I'd be an idiot to follow you to the middle of the nowhere and not have a plan in case things went south."

"So you knew this road was here."

"I knew this road was here," he confirmed, then pulled her back against him.

Dakota relaxed as she looked out at the beautiful landscape in front of her. "It feels as if we're the only people in the world. It's so quiet and peaceful."

"Mmmm," Slade responded.

"You know, at night, the stars look so much brighter out here. I've never seen anything as gorgeous in my life."

"I've been in some pretty remote places myself, and I agree."

"I used to lie on the hood of my car at night, when it was warmer, and look up at the stars and marvel at the fact that we're so inconsequential. So small. But more than that, I was comforted by the fact my dad could be looking up at the exact same stars at the same time I was. It made me feel closer to him."

"I've done that," Slade admitted. "When me and my team were in the middle of some desert in the Middle East, I've looked up at the stars and wondered who was looking up at them at the exact same time. No one but the government knew where we were, but somehow those stars made me feel not so alone."

"Yeah, that's it," Dakota agreed. "Even though they're millions of miles away, they somehow bring me closer to my dad. To my old life."

Slade kissed the top of her head in response to her words.

After several minutes, Dakota asked softly, "What's going to happen when we get back home? I don't have any place to go. I literally only have the clothes on my back, no food. Hell, I don't even have my car anymore. I feel lost, Slade."

He squeezed her tightly, then ran his hands up and down her arms. "I can't imagine how you're feeling," he told her honestly. "But you said so yourself…things can be replaced. My plan, at the moment, is to stay with my friend, Wolf. He's a Navy SEAL himself, and he and his wife don't have any children. They have an apartment set up in their basement that's mostly private."

"Will you call and let me know what's going on?" Dakota asked, strangely disappointed that Slade wouldn't be taking her back to his place with him.

"You think I'm going to drop you off at a stranger's house and go about my business?" Slade bit out.

"Oh, well, I—"

"Dakota, I'll be there with you. I'd take you back to my place in a heartbeat, but I've been compromised. After this morning, they know you're not alone and most likely have someone who knows what he's doing helping you. It won't take long for them to figure out who I am and where I live."

"True," Dakota muttered.

"There's nothing I want more than you in my space. Cooking in my kitchen. Eating at my table. Sleeping in my bed. Watching the waves while we sit on my balcony together. But I won't knowingly put you in danger. We talked about you not being bait, and taking you to my place would definitely fall in that category. Caroline and Wolf will be happy to let us crash at their place."

"Won't that be dangerous for them?" she asked.

"No."

"Why not?"

"Because Wolf is in charge of a SEAL team. One of the best teams I've ever known. No matter what the danger is, he'll protect his wife and I'll protect you."

Dakota closed her eyes and took a deep breath. She heard the wind blowing through the scrub bushes surrounding them, but that was about it. There was literally nothing out there with them, nature, and the sky.

"I feel as if I'm a burden to everyone I meet."

"You're not a burden."

He sounded so certain. "What would you be doing right now if you weren't chasing me down?" she asked.

"I'd be sitting at my desk at the Naval base looking at boring-ass reports and trying to reconcile expenses for the government. I'd go home at the end of the night, make myself dinner, then eat by myself. Maybe watch a movie, or sit on my balcony and watch the surfers or the stars for a while. Then I'd go to sleep in my big bed by myself. If I felt like it, I might think about the woman I hoped was out there somewhere waiting for me and get myself off. Then I'd clean up, go to sleep, and get up the next morning and do it all over again. My life is good, but since I've retired from the teams, it's boring. That was nice at first, but now, quite frankly, I'm lonely."

Dakota tried to ignore the bolt of lust that swept through her body at the image of Slade lying on a bed stroking himself until he exploded…but she was having a hard time, especially since she was practically sitting in his lap. "You were married, though, right?"

"If you want to call it that, yeah. I met Cynthia at the grocery store, of all places. We got along. But she absolutely couldn't take what I did for a living."

"What do you mean?" Dakota asked. "She knew you were a SEAL when she married you, right?"

"Yeah, but that doesn't mean she really understood what it meant to be married to one. I think she liked the *idea* of it better than the reality. I was gone on missions a lot. And I couldn't talk about what I did with her. Most of them were top secret. I guess she thought she'd be able to brag to her friends about how I was off saving the world or something, but instead all she could say was that I was at an undisclosed location for an indeterminate period of time doing something top secret."

"How'd it end? If you don't mind me asking."

"I don't mind at all. In fact, I love that you want to know more about me. It wasn't all that dramatic, really. I came home from a mission. She'd packed all her shit, and told me she didn't love me anymore and was moving on."

"Ouch," Dakota said, wincing. "What a bitch."

"No, we just weren't compatible," Slade told her,

not seeming at all affected by the actions of his ex-wife. "I'd fallen out of love with her years before. I was just going through the motions. She married a guy who worked in IT for a local university within a year. Last I heard, they had two kids and had moved to Seattle."

"Do you miss her?"

"Not like you're thinking. I miss having someone to talk to. I miss the simple joy of making dinner with another human being. Of sitting on the couch, holding hands, watching TV."

"Yeah," Dakota said, knowing exactly what he meant.

"What about you?" Slade asked.

"What about me, what?"

"You haven't been married, right?"

"No." Dakota wasn't sure she wanted to talk about this. But fair was fair. "I dated a few men I thought I could be happy with, but ultimately decided that wasn't what I wanted."

"To be happy?" Slade asked.

"To settle," she said. "I enjoyed being with them, but didn't feel a bone-deep need to see them. I didn't think about them in the middle of the day. I wanted a relationship like my parents had. Even though it grossed me out, my dad was always hugging and kissing my mom. They held hands wherever they went. All the time. They weren't afraid to say 'I love you' to each other."

"What happened to your mom?"

Dakota shrugged. "Cancer. By the time they found it, it was too late to do anything other than give her drugs to make her comfortable. She was gone almost four months to the day she got the diagnosis. It's been about ten years now."

"I'm sorry, sweetheart."

Dakota swallowed hard. "Me too, but I'm sorrier for my dad. He lost the love of his life. His soul mate. He told me once, not long after Mom died, that they truly believed they'd been together in a past life."

"He believes in reincarnation?" Slade asked.

"I guess so, yeah. I can't say I don't believe. It was uncanny the things they knew about each other when they met. Mom would sometimes say stuff out of the blue that she literally shouldn't have known about him. It was really cool. My dad has been so strong since she died, but I can tell there's a part of him that's missing. Every day is a struggle for him." She turned in Slade's embrace and looked up at him. "That's what I want, and I didn't feel that with any of the men I dated. I didn't want to settle."

"You shouldn't settle," Slade told her softly, running his fingers over her cheek lightly. "My parents are still together, and even though I know they love each other, I don't think they have the passion that you've described your folks having."

"It's so rare, most people never find it."

Slade's eyes seemed to pierce into her soul as he gazed down at her. "I've seen that kind of passion with my friends and their wives. I want it. I'm willing to give up everything I have to get it too. I'd fight and kill for it."

"Slade," Dakota whispered, shaken by the truth she saw in his eyes.

He ignored her unspoken plea and continued. "I see and feel that same passion with you, Dakota. I don't know what's going to happen tomorrow, or even later today. But I know without a doubt that time is precious. Every second I get to spend with you is a second that I'm a better man because of it. Your arms around me as we drive down this fucking excuse for a road are what keep me going. Wanting to find Fourati and end the threat to you is what's driving me. Not the love of my country. Not wanting to keep random strangers safe. I'm an intense guy, I get that, but I haven't waited almost half a century for you to come along to waste time now."

He stopped speaking, but didn't drop his eyes from hers. The look on his face was both tender and fierce. Dakota knew without a doubt he meant every single word. There was nothing she could say that would come close to telling him how she felt, so she showed him instead.

Licking her lips nervously, she rose stiffly to her knees and turned to face him. The ground was dusty and small pebbles dug into her skin through her jeans, but she ignored the pain. She leaned toward him, suppressing a groan as her muscles complained, and kissed him.

Slade immediately wrapped his arms around her waist and hauled her into his body, easing them backwards until he was flat on the ground and she was lying on top of him. Dakota could feel every muscle move and flex under her as she settled over him. His legs spread and her own fell between them. She felt surrounded and protected.

She kissed him with all the fierce passion pent up in her soul. The passion she'd never felt for any other man poured out of her as if she'd turned a faucet on high. She couldn't get enough of his taste, his mouth on hers, the way his facial hair felt against her own smooth cheeks. She wanted to inhale him and burrow herself into his chest at the same time.

Slade let her take control of their kiss. He lay still under her as her hands roamed his chest, as she nibbled on his bottom lip, even as she moved to his neck and began to suck on the tender skin there. It wasn't until her hands began to wander south toward the button on his jeans that he moved.

Grasping her fingers in his own, he stopped her, then sat up, manhandling her until she was straddling his lap. His hands went to her ass and he hauled her against him so there wasn't an inch of space between them. Then his hands eased upward, under her jacket and shirt, until his chilly fingers touched her warm skin at her waist.

He didn't stop when she giggled and flinched from his cool touch, nor when she breathed in sharply as he skimmed the undersides of her breasts. One hand went to her chest, where he cupped a breast in his large hand, and the other pressed against her spine, encouraging her to arch into him.

Dakota tried to breathe, but was finding it difficult. She couldn't tear her eyes away from Slade's. She felt his thumb brush over her nipple in a gentle caress. She pressed both her pelvis and breast into him at the same time. Wanting more. Needing more.

"Fucking beautiful," Slade said softly. "I knew you'd be like this."

Dakota closed her eyes then, lost in the joy of his hands on her.

"Did you mark me?" he asked.

Her eyes flew open. "What?"

"Did you mark me?" he asked again calmly. "When you sucked on my neck. Did you give me a hickey?"

Dakota giggled and glanced down at the collar of his

shirt. Sure enough, there was a small bruise on the side of his neck, right where everyone could see it. "No," she told him in a tone that she knew he'd be able to tell she was lying.

He smiled and his hand moved down the front of her body and came to rest at her waist. He leaned in and ran his nose up the side of her neck. Dakota tilted her head, giving him room. "You smell so good," he told her, before latching onto her neck and sucking…hard.

Dakota moaned at the sensation, then giggled at what he was doing. She should be appalled. They were acting like teenagers, but she couldn't deny that she wanted Slade to mark her just as she'd done to him. As he sucked, his tongue licked and caressed her skin, once again leaving goosebumps in its wake. When he finally pulled back, Dakota rolled her eyes at the look of satisfaction on his face.

She wrinkled her nose at him. "It's huge, isn't it?"

"Yup," he said immediately. The look on his face was smug and proud.

"I can't believe we just did that."

The hand that had been at her back came up and he tenderly smoothed it over her head. "I can. And I'm hoping for more when we get to Goldfield tonight."

At the reminder of how far they still had to go, Dakota groaned.

"How about this?" Slade asked. "As incentive for you, when we get to Tonopah, you get another kiss.

When we get to Goldfield, you get more of my hands."

Dakota's eyes glittered. Now he was talking. He was great incentive, that was for sure. "And when we get to San Diego?" she asked.

"You get whatever you want," Slade returned.

"I want it all," Dakota whispered. "I'm scared, but I want it all."

"It's yours," he said, all trace of teasing gone. "Anything you want. Everything I've got. It's all yours."

"I'm ready to continue," Dakota told him, still whispering.

"Okay." But instead of standing, Slade wrapped his arms around her and crushed her to him. They sat on the ground for several moments, soaking up the residual feelings of passion, respect, and trust that had been garnered over the short time they'd known each other.

Finally, Slade pulled back, kissed her lips hard, and stood. He helped Dakota stand on wobbly legs, and they walked hand in hand down the short incline back to his bike.

As they set off once more, Dakota hardly felt the bumps and aching muscles anymore. She'd made a decision on that small hill in the middle of nowhere, Nevada. She was going to take a chance with Slade Cutsinger. The biggest chance of her life. If they could make it through whatever Aziz had planned for her, she might just be rewarded with a love like her parents had.

She smiled all the way to Goldfield.

Chapter Seven

"IT DOESN'T LOOK like much," Slade told Dakota honestly. They were standing in front of the old Goldfield Hotel in downtown Goldfield, Nevada. He'd thought the small town was going to be bigger. There was literally only one place to stay, the Sante Fe Motel and Saloon. He considered driving back up to Tonopah, but knew Dakota was done.

She'd held up better than he could've hoped after their short break. He'd pushed through to Tonopah, where they'd grabbed a quick lunch. She'd told him she was going to wait for her reward until they reached Goldfield.

As they'd driven south toward the infamous mining town, Slade didn't see hide nor hair of anyone suspicious. He was going to call Tex when they were settled for the night. He was cautiously optimistic that they were safe for the time being.

Dakota had been talking in his ear for the last thirty minutes about the haunted Goldfield Hotel. He hadn't even heard of the place before, but because of Dakota, he was now an expert.

"Come on, let's go look inside," Dakota urged, tugging on his hand.

He'd parked his Harley around the corner, trying to keep their location on the down-low for as long as possible. Slade grinned as he allowed Dakota to "lead" him toward the large glass windows at the front of the building. She wasn't so much leading him as he was holding her up as she walked.

She was hobbling along, and every step looked like it pained her something awful, but she still had a beautiful smile on her face and did her best to pretend nothing was wrong. She might not think she was tough, but Slade knew differently. The more time he spent with her, the more she reminded him of Caroline. Understated beauty, thinking of others first, and a spine of steel.

He'd been on plenty of missions in his lifetime where the women they'd been sent to rescue had completely fallen apart at the slightest hint of danger. Others had been so traumatized they couldn't even walk. It wasn't fair to compare some of the situations he'd been in to what Dakota was going through, but he had no doubt if the shit hit the fan, she'd stand tall and firm and claw her way out.

They stopped at one of the large windows on the front of the building and Dakota dropped his hand, limped to the glass, and cupped her hands to peer inside. Her voice was muffled as she excitedly reported on what she was seeing.

"Oh my gosh, Slade. It's amazing! It's like time stood still. There are two black leather circle couch things. I can just picture people sitting around and waiting for loved ones. And the front desk is still there. There are little mailbox slots behind it where I imagine the keys would sit. Oh! And a staircase with red carpet leading upward to something. I can't see what. And a set of double doors with what look like pineapples etched in the glass. It's dusty, yeah, but it's like the place is just waiting for the front doors to be thrown open and guests to stream through."

She picked up her head and smiled at him. "Wanna see?"

"Yeah, sweetheart, I do," Slade told her. He walked up behind her and leaned forward, trapping her body between his own and the glass window in front of them. He felt every inch of her body against his as he peered inside. To him, it looked like an old, rundown abandoned room, but he wasn't going to burst Dakota's bubble.

When he leaned back, she grabbed his hand again and headed down the sidewalk toward another window. She repeated the same routine, peering inside, giving him a rundown of what she saw. This time she included some other information as well.

"The owner won't let anyone inside because he's afraid the ghosts will hurt them. The *Ghost Adventures* crew went in there in two thousand seven or eight, and had a brick thrown at their heads! They even got it on film. It was creepy, but so cool. Man, I wish we could go inside!"

"You're kidding, right?" Slade asked her.

"What? No! That would be awesome!" Dakota gushed. "There's supposed to be a ghost of a woman named Elizabeth who was handcuffed to a radiator, and she had a baby and the father of the child killed them both. And there have been a few people who've committed suicide in there, and they're supposed to haunt the place too."

"Only you would be on the run from terrorists, but not scared of ghosts," Slade said, shaking his head.

Dakota turned to him with her hands on her hips and demanded, "Look me in the eye and tell me you wouldn't be fascinated to see proof of ghostly activity."

Slade leaned forward until she took a step back, trapping her against the glass window. He put his hands on either side of her head and got close enough that their noses were almost touching. "I've seen my share of ghostly activity, sweetheart. I can't say any of them were great experiences."

"You've seen ghosts?" she breathed, her eyes wide.

Her hands came up to clutch his sides. "Seriously?"

"Unfortunately, yeah. You don't spend as much time as I have overseas and avoid it. Although the ones I saw were mostly women and children. I don't know how they were killed. Maybe it was their husbands, maybe it was by bombs. Regardless, seeing them wandering the streets at o-three-hundred, lost and calling for their loved ones, isn't something I'll ever forget or want to experience again."

"Wow, I guess not," Dakota said, petting his sides unconsciously.

"You seen enough? Ready to check into the hotel, rest for a while, then grab something to eat?"

She grimaced and nodded. "Thank you for indulging me. I've wanted to see this place for myself ever since I saw Zak and Nick experience that brick flying across the room. Hey, maybe we can watch that episode together when we get home...err...sometime."

Turning and wrapping his arm around Dakota's waist and helping her walk back toward his Harley, Slade smiled. "I'd love to watch it with you when we get home," he told her, purposely using the word home. He loved the thought of them having a home together.

They made it back to the motorcycle without encountering any specters, much to Dakota's disappointment and Slade's relief. He loved spending time with her but hated to see the pain cross her face as she gamely climbed on the back of his bike again. He needed to take care of that for her.

"Hang on, sweetheart. I'll have you in a tub full of hot water as soon as I can."

She squeezed his waist and Slade smiled as he drove the short distance to the motel. He would miss having her arms around him twenty-four seven when they got to San Diego and he parked his bike in favor of his car. It was amazing how quickly he'd gotten used to her weight and heat at his back and her arms locked around him.

The motel had eight rooms, which weren't any more impressive than the trailers in Rachel. But they were clean, and had bathtubs, which were Slade's most pressing requirements. He wanted to get Dakota soaking as soon as he could. She'd held up better than he thought she would, but that didn't mean she wasn't hurting.

He requested a room on the end, and parked his Harley around the corner where it'd be harder to be seen from the street. He opened the door and peeked in, making sure it was clear before gesturing for Dakota to enter.

"Why'd you do that?" she asked.

"Do what?"

"Look into the room. I thought for a second were going to push me out of the way to get inside first," she teased.

Slade didn't even crack a smile. He shut the door behind them and turned to her. "I know people have been conditioned to think it's the gentlemanly thing to do to open doors and let ladies enter first, but that doesn't fly in my world."

"But *isn't* it the polite thing to do?" Dakota asked, dropping her backpack on the bed and tilting her head at him in question.

"It might be polite, but it's not safe," Slade told her. "If there's someone waiting in the room for us, I absolutely don't want *you* to be the first one through the door. I'll always be the one to check out the room before I deem it safe for you to enter. On missions, I saw way too many times where men shoved women and children through doors before they entered. If there was danger, they'd either use them as shields or run when they were shot as they walked inside. So no, sweetheart, I don't care if it makes me impolite. I won't allow you to go first in any situation where there could be the smallest chance you could get hurt or caught in any kind of crossfire."

"I hadn't ever thought about it that way," Dakota said, limping toward him. Then she put her arms around him and hugged him. Hard.

Automatically wrapping his own arms around her, Slade asked as they stood together in the small motel room, "What's this for?"

"For all those women and children you had to watch get hurt," she told him softly. "I'm sorry."

Slade's throat closed up and he pressed his lips together hard. The things he'd seen and done for his country while overseas were a part of his past. He'd dealt with them, talked with counselors and hadn't thought about them much after retiring. But he definitely could've used Dakota's sweet sympathy and concern for him when he'd returned from a few of those awful missions. "Thank you," he finally croaked.

They stood together for a long moment before Dakota said, "If I don't move, I'm gonna fall asleep right here standing up."

Appreciating her attempt at lightening the situation, Slade chuckled and pulled back, keeping his hands on her waist in support. "Come on. Let's get you in the tub. I'll get some pizza, since that's apparently the only choice at the bar, and we can eat when you're done. Yeah?"

"Sounds heavenly. You think this place has hot water?" Dakota joked.

"If it doesn't, we're heading back to Tonopah," Slade returned immediately.

"I was kidding."

"I wasn't," Slade told her. "I promised you a Jacuzzi, and while I have to renege on that, I'm not budging on the hot bath. You need it. We've got a long day of riding tomorrow and I want to make sure you'll be able to make it."

"I'll make it," Dakota told him stubbornly.

He ran his hand over her hair and said softly, "Let me rephrase then. I want to make sure you'll make it with the least amount of difficulty possible. And that'll happen easier if you can soak your muscles tonight. I've got some painkillers in my bag and between those and the hot water, you should be okay for tomorrow. So if this place doesn't have hot water, I'm hauling your ass back up to Tonopah to one of the chain hotels where I know there will be some."

He saw the tears form in her eyes and frowned. "What did I say to make you cry?" he asked.

"Nothing. It's just that…it's been a really long time since anyone has cared about me like that. When I'm sick, I deal with it myself. I once tripped in my apartment and hit my head on the counter. I passed out and woke up about fifteen minutes later with a pool of blood under my head. I just…it's nice not to be alone."

Slade's teeth ground together at the thought of her lying unconscious and bleeding and no one knowing she was hurt. He took in a big breath through his nose and kissed her forehead. "Get used to it," he ordered, before helping her sit on the side of the bed.

He went into the small bathroom and turned on the

taps. Fortunately for them both, hot water immediately began filling the tub. Trying to gauge the temperature and making it as hot as he thought she could stand, Slade returned to the room to see Dakota lying on her back on the bed. Her legs were still hanging off the end of the mattress and she seemed to be asleep.

"You awake?"

"Yeah," she mumbled.

Slade had gotten a room with two beds, not wanting to be presumptuous, and Dakota hadn't even commented on the fact that he'd rented only one room or the number of beds. He'd been prepared to argue against them sleeping in different rooms because of the danger, but as it turned out, he didn't need to. She accepted the arrangements as if they didn't even bother her. And it was obvious they didn't.

"Come on, up you go," Slade said as he grabbed her hand and pulled her to a sitting position.

She groaned and twisted her head back and forth as if working out the kinks. "I take it the water is hot?" she asked.

"Yup. And it's calling your name."

"Is that what I hear? I thought the mumbling I heard was the water mocking me for overdoing it today."

Slade chuckled, but didn't respond. He merely pulled her upright and helped her into the bathroom. He left her sitting on the toilet seat and went back out to get her backpack. She hadn't moved by the time he'd returned. "You need help?"

She looked up then and asked coyly, "In taking off my clothes? Definitely."

He smiled at her teasing, but said seriously, "You shouldn't tease about something like that."

"Who said I was teasing?" she returned softly.

Taking another deep breath, which he found himself doing a lot lately, Slade said, "If I thought you were up to it, I'd have you naked and under me before you could blink. But as much as I want to see, and hold, your naked body, you need hot water more. And food. And I need to call my friend, find out what's been happening while I've been offline."

Dakota nodded. "You're right."

"Of course I am."

"But that doesn't mean I've forgotten what you promised me if I made it to Goldfield," she said with a grin.

"And what are you gonna take as your reward?" Slade asked, not able to help himself.

"I want to sleep with you."

He about choked, but she hurried to finish her thought, as if he might protest.

"I know you got two beds, and that was sweet of you. But what I want as my reward is to sleep next to you. I haven't felt as safe as I did today with you in a long time. I'm not saying I want to have sex...but I've been snuggled up to you all day. I just...I want that tonight, too."

"Then you'll have it," Slade told her, knowing he had a full night of torture ahead of him. Lying next to Dakota, holding her in his arms, was going to kill him. But it would be the sweetest kind of hell he could ever imagine. "Bathe. I'll be back with pizza. Take as much time as you want. I'll call Tex after we eat."

"Why don't you use the time away from me to call him? I'm sure you want your privacy."

"I've got nothing to hide from you, Dakota," Slade said. "You've got just as much right to know what's going on as I do...more so. Besides, I want to introduce you to him."

"You're going to tell him about us?"

"If you mean am I going to tell him that you're important to me and that I see us having a relationship when the threat against you is neutralized...the answer is yes."

"Oh...um...okay."

She was cute when she was flustered. Slade leaned down and kissed her on the lips before straightening. "Make sure you check the temperature before you get in. I don't want you burning yourself." Then he turned and left the small bathroom before he took her up on her offer to help remove her clothes. He shut the door behind him and headed for the exit to go see about getting them some dinner.

Chapter Eight

I T WAS AN hour and a half later. Slade was lying on the
bed, Dakota snuggled up against him. Her head was
resting on his shoulder, one arm flung across his belly,
the other bent up against her body, and she was finger-
ing the sleeve of his T-shirt. She'd rested in the tub until
she was a prune—her words—then pulled on a pair of
sweatpants and a T-shirt. They'd eaten the meat lover's
pizza Slade had gotten from the small bar/restaurant at
the motel, and now it was time to talk to Tex.

"Are you sure that line is secure?" she asked when he
picked up his phone.

"What do you know about secure phones?" Slade
asked with a teasing glint in his eye.

Dakota rolled her own. "It's the twenty-first century, Slade, anyone who's ever watched TV or gone to the
movies knows about secure phone lines."

He chuckled. "Right. And to answer your question,
yes. My phone is definitely secure. It was issued by the
Navy, and I guarantee Tex's lines are all more than

safe."

"Can I ask something?"

"Of course."

"What makes a line secure? I mean, I know abstractly what it is, but not how it works."

"A secure line has end-to-end encryption. It prevents someone from tapping into the line and listening. As long as both speakers are using a secure line, whatever is said will stay between those two people."

"Hmmm, so it's kinda like talking in code. Your words get scrambled as you talk, then unscrambled so the other person can understand you."

"Basically, yeah," Slade told her, smiling at the simple way she put it.

"Cool."

"Yeah. Now, you got any more questions, or can I call Tex?"

Her cheeks flushed, but she said simply, "I'm done...for now."

Slade grinned. He enjoyed her curiosity more than he could say. The fact that she wasn't curled into a ball scared out of her mind said a lot about her inner fortitude. And he liked it.

Slade leaned over and kissed her on the forehead to reassure her before dialing Tex's number. He clicked on the speaker button so Dakota could hear the conversation. He was honest earlier when he'd told her he had nothing to hide from her.

"Hey, Tex."

"Cutter. Where in the hell have you been?" Tex exclaimed grumpily.

"I told you where I was going," Slade told him without rancor. "Unfortunately, I didn't think about the fact there might not be cell service out there in the desert."

"Did you find her? Tell me you found her."

"I found her."

"Thank God."

Something in his tone struck Slade as wrong. "Why? What's wrong?"

"Fourati knows where she is. You need to get on the move. Now."

"We're already on the move, and yeah, we figured he found her when one of his goons broke into the trailer we were occupying. But what I want to know is *how* Fourati found her. Tex, she was in the middle of fucking nowhere. There was no cell service and there are only about fifty people living in Rachel. How in the hell did he track her down? Was it me? Did I lead them there?"

"I'm not sure," Tex told him. "She doesn't have a cell?"

"No."

"Could her car have been tracked?"

"Not likely, she's been there quite a while. They would've been out to snatch her long before now if it was."

"Two-way radio? Using her credit cards? Has she been sending letters to anyone back home?"

Slade felt Dakota shake her head at his shoulder. "She says no."

There was a pause before Tex asked, "She there now?"

"I'm here," Dakota said in a soft voice. "It's nice to meet you, Tex. Slade has nothing but good things to say about you."

"Well, shit, he's lying then," Tex returned immediately with a hint of humor. "You all right, honey?"

Slade's lips twitched. How like Tex to be in the middle of an interrogation, but pause to make sure a woman was good.

"I'm okay. Although I think Slade's Harley is trying to kill me."

Tex chuckled. "Give it time. You'll get your biker legs in no time."

"No offense, but I don't think I *want* biker legs," Dakota told him.

"You stickin' with Cutter?" Tex asked her.

"If Cutter is Slade, then yeah, I'd like to," Dakota said, blushing.

Slade grinned. He loved that she basically just flat-out confessed to Tex that she liked him. It was one thing to admit it to him, it was a whole other thing to tell someone else.

"Cutter is Slade," Tex confirmed, then said, "so you'll be getting your biker legs. Now…you talk to anyone back home while you were hiding out in Rachel, Dakota? Call anyone? Write anyone a letter?"

"Not really. I sent postcards to my dad, but I gave them to tourists and they mailed them for me when they got home."

"It's how I figured out I needed to start in Vegas," Slade interjected. "Two people didn't wait until they got home to mail them."

"Hmmm. Did her dad say anyone else had visited?"

"A couple of people who claimed to be with the government. He sent them all on their way without talking with them though. He was extremely cautious with me and didn't say anything about Dakota until he was sure of who I was."

"So the question is, what information does Fourati have? Were his people in Vegas for months looking for her and somehow made the same connection to Rachel that you did, Cutter? Or did he somehow get to her dad after you were there. Could you have been followed? Maybe one of his people saw you in Vegas and trailed you."

"Damn…we've got too many unknowns," Slade

said with a shake of his head.

The line was silent for a moment as everyone pondered the mystery.

"I honestly don't think he could've known about me," Slade mused. "I'd only gotten the assignment from Lambert recently. There's no reason for him to have me on his radar at all or to link me to Dakota."

"You might not be," Tex countered. "Maybe he's been tracking her somehow this whole time. It's possible he had things he needed to take care of in his organization and wasn't ready to claim her yet. But when those things were done, her time ran out and he sent someone to fetch her."

"Pat and Connie, the owners of the A'Le'Inn, have wi-fi," Dakota said into the silence. "I didn't get on last night because I didn't have access to a computer, but I've been on it before, searching San Diego news sites and stuff for information on the bombing. Could he have found me that way?"

"It's possible," Tex mused. "If he doesn't have a tracker on you, he knows that pretty much the only directions you might've gone from San Diego are north and west. You could've gone into Mexico, but that would've been a long shot. So he probably had his eyes out for use of your credit cards and any suspicious internet activity. I'm guessing your searches could've tipped him off. He could've traced the IP address to

Rachel. It might have simply taken him two months to hit on the searches and pinpoint your location. Which was lucky for us."

"I'm sorry," Dakota whispered. "I honestly didn't think he'd be able to find me if I did searches for general news stories. I knew I'd been there too long, but I wanted to save up a bit more money before fleeing again."

"It's not your fault," Tex said, before Slade could reassure her. "You weren't using your credit cards, and stuck to cash, that was all good."

"I guess I know what not to do next time," she said softly.

"There isn't going to *be* a next time," Slade said fiercely, squeezing her shoulders tighter. He looked down into her eyes and willed her to believe him. To trust him to keep her safe.

"What're your plans, Cutter?" Tex asked, interrupting the emotional moment.

"To get to San Diego as soon as possible," Slade said.

"Dakota, you gonna be able to handle the bike that long?" Tex asked.

Before Dakota could answer, Slade grumbled, "You think I'd push her past what she can handle, Tex?"

"It's okay, I can—"

Tex interrupted. "Just making sure I've read the situation right."

"I got this," Slade told his friend.

"Good. Once you get home, then what?"

Slade could feel Dakota staring at him, but he ignored it for the moment. "I'm going to call Wolf tonight. I'm hoping we can crash in his basement. I don't want to go back to my place in case that fucker *has* clocked me."

"You gonna let Wolf in on what's happening?"

"Yeah. I'm not supposed to, but I don't give a shit. He has a right to know, since I need him to help me look after Dakota," Slade said.

"He'll have your six."

And he would. Slade knew that. It was why he didn't hesitate to consider his place to crash while they figured out how to get to Fourati.

"What about my dad? Is he safe?" Dakota asked.

"I'll talk to Wolf. See if he can get some eyes on him. If needed, we'll hide him until Fourati is out of the picture," Slade told her.

She stared up at him with big eyes. "You'd do that?"

"He's important to you, so of course I would. I'm not going to sit back and let anyone hurt him, because hurting him would hurt *you*. So yeah, Dakota, I'm going to do everything in my power to keep him safe."

"Thanks," she whispered, clearly overwhelmed.

"You'll let me know what you find out?" Slade asked

Tex, but his eyes were still on Dakota.

"Of course. You'll have your phone on tomorrow?"

"Yeah, although since I'm on the bike, I won't be able to answer it."

"I'll leave a message if I need to," Tex reassured him. "Be careful out there. I don't have any information on the guys who showed up to escort Dakota to their boss. I'll see what I can do to find them, but if Fourati is even a little savvy with technology, and it seems he is, it might not be as easy as I'd like."

"I will. Last I knew one is probably on his way to lock up, at least until he bonds out, and any others were stranded in Rachel, but I wouldn't put it past them to steal a car."

"They'll definitely improvise," Tex said dryly. "Dakota, it was great to meet you. And for the record, you couldn't have found a better man. Cutter has saved my life more times than I could tell you. If my wife and children were in trouble, there's no one I'd want looking after them more than him."

"Okay," she whispered.

"Talk to you later," Tex said, then hung up.

Slade clicked off the phone and hugged Dakota. "Don't worry about the wi-fi thing. You've done so many things right over the last couple of months, I'm impressed with just how well you've been able to stay under the radar."

She sighed. "I knew being found was bound to happen sooner or later. I'm just glad it happened when you were there. They would've had me if you weren't."

"Look at me, sweetheart." Slade waited until she met his eyes before continuing. "If for some reason, everything gets FUBAR'd, I want you to—"

"FUBAR'd?" she asked before he could finish.

"Sorry. I keep forgetting you don't know much about the military. Fucked up beyond all repair. FUBAR."

She giggled, but gestured for him to continue.

"If something happens and you somehow end up with Fourati, do not, under any circumstances, give up. I don't care what he does or what happens. You. Do. Not. Give. Up. Don't antagonize him into hurting you. Don't take crazy chances to try to escape. Because I'm coming for you. I'll get the entire US Navy to come for you if that's what it takes. But I need you to hang on and do whatever you need to do to stay alive until I can get there. Okay?"

Dakota bit her lip. "I'm really not brave."

"Bullshit," Slade countered immediately. "You're one of the bravest women I know. You didn't sit at home and wring your hands when the shit hit the fan. You didn't hide out at your dad's house and cry. You didn't stay at your job when you knew the kids could be in danger. Even without having the expertise, you managed to evade capture for a fuck of a long time."

"I ran. That's not brave," Dakota insisted.

"The hell it's not. Sometimes running is the smartest thing you can do. You got out of the situation you were in and bought yourself some time. Where do you think you'd be if you hadn't?"

"Probably chained to a bed in a basement, forced to do whatever that jerkface wanted me to do," Dakota mumbled.

"Exactly." Slade's voice gentled. "I made you a promise to do whatever I could to keep you safe. And I will absolutely uphold that promise. But shit happens. Unfortunately, I know this better than a lot of people. All I'm asking is that if shit happens to *you*, to us, you try to stay calm. Don't antagonize Fourati, but don't be a doormat either. Whatever happens, you hold the fuck on until I can get you out of there. All right?"

"Okay. But you'll…hurry, won't you? I can fake being brave for a while, but eventually I'll break."

"I'll do everything in my power to get to you as soon as I can and not a second later."

Dakota nodded, then looked down at his chest. Her finger made little circles there and she asked, "So…Cutter?"

He grinned and decided to go with the PG version of his name for her. She definitely didn't need to know about his throat-cutting skills. "My last name."

"Ah. That makes sense," she said.

Slade relaxed muscles he didn't realize were tense when he felt her melt into him once more. "I'm going to call Wolf now, that okay?"

"Sure."

He dialed Wolf's number and waited as it rang.

"Hello?"

"Hey, Wolf. It's Cutter."

"When are you coming back?" the other SEAL asked without any other pleasantries.

"Why? You miss me?" Slade teased.

"Fuck yeah. That guy who took your place at work is slow as molasses. I swear to God, I had to show him how to change the margins on a Word document today. How in the hell he ever got a government admin job is beyond me. Please tell me you're coming back. Where the hell are you, anyway? I heard you went to Vegas?"

Slade could feel Dakota smiling against his shoulder. Wolf sounded extremely put out. It was funny as shit. "I'm hoping to be back in town tomorrow night."

"Thank fuck."

"But not at work yet. My plate is still full with the reason I took the leave of absence in the first place."

"Damn."

This time, Dakota giggled.

"This a bad time to talk?" Wolf asked, obviously hearing the quiet giggle.

Knowing the man was trying to be both professional and nosy at the same time made Slade's lips twitch. "Not at all. Dakota, meet Wolf. Wolf, Dakota."

"Hi," Dakota said softly. "It's nice to sorta meet you."

"Same, darlin'," Wolf said. "How come I'm gettin' the feelin' it might be longer before you're back at work than I'd like, Cutter?"

"Need a favor," Slade said without answering his friend's question.

"Name it," Wolf responded immediately.

"I need a place to crash with Dakota for a few days."

"You got it."

"I don't know how long we might be there," Slade warned.

"Basement's yours as long as you need it," Wolf said.

"Thanks. Appreciate it."

"You know I have your back no matter what. But I gotta ask…is whatever you're involved with gonna have blowback on my wife?"

Slade hesitated. He wanted to say no but the bottom line was, it was possible. Until Tex found out more information about how Fourati had tracked Dakota, he wasn't sure. "We can stay at a hotel," Slade told Wolf.

"That's not what I was implying and you know it, Cutter," Wolf said in a low, hard voice, very unlike the easygoing tone he'd been using thus far. "I wouldn't give a shit if Osama Bin Laden was hot on your heels, I'd still open my doors to you with open arms."

"Isn't he dead?" Dakota whispered after Wolf stopped speaking.

Slade didn't even crack a smile even though she was cute as shit.

"Oh my God," Wolf exclaimed. "It's her, isn't it?"

Slade knew what he meant. They'd had a few conversations since they'd known each other about how Wolf had known from the moment Caroline had helped save his life that she was the woman he wanted to spend the rest of his life with, even though he'd tried to deny it. He'd even gone on to say that it didn't matter how old Slade was...he'd know when he saw his own woman.

"Yeah."

"Fuckin' pleased for you, Cutter," Wolf told his friend. "And to answer your question, Dakota, Bin Laden *is* dead, a team of Navy SEALs killed his ass. But even if he was a ghost coming back from the grave to haunt Cutter, I'd still let the man next to you stay in my house. All I need is a head's up."

"That sounds fair," Dakota murmured under her breath. Then said, "I bet Wolf isn't afraid of ghosts. He'd explore the Goldfield Hotel with me."

"Sweetheart, I'm not afraid of ghosts, I'd just rather

not have a brick thrown at my head by one," Slade told her, squeezing her waist at the same time.

He felt her smile against his chest, but cleared his throat and told his friend what was going on. "Remember that LAX bombing? Looks like it wasn't a one-time thing."

"Already know that, Cutter."

"Dakota was there. She can ID Aziz Fourati."

Wolf whistled low and long. "He know where she is?"

"Unknown."

"Okay. I'll talk with the team. We'll set up rotating patrols around the house. I'll send Caroline to Cheyenne's house. She needs some baby Taylor time anyway."

Slade swallowed hard and closed his eyes, trying to get his composure back. Wolf and him had always been friendly. They'd shot the shit about some of the non-top-secret aspects of his missions and Slade had always offered his advice when asked. But for the man to not only readily agree to let them stay at his house as a place for him and Dakota to lie low, but to arrange for his SEAL friends to keep watch over them and send his wife away without even seeming to blink was almost too much. Slade knew he'd missed being a part of a team, but he hadn't realized until right this moment how *much* he'd missed it.

"Thanks, Wolf. If it's any consolation, Tex is on this. I don't expect this to drag on. I'm gonna end it sooner rather than later."

"Anything that gets your ass back in the chair behind that desk, I'm one hundred percent behind," Wolf joked. "I can't stand your temp replacement another day longer than necessary."

"I'll let you know when we're close to home," Slade said.

"Great. I'll give you the code to the alarm when you call."

"Wolf?" Dakota piped up.

"Yeah, hon?"

"Thanks."

"I'm looking forward to meeting you. And when things settle down, I know my wife and her friends will descend upon you en masse. Just a friendly warning."

"Can't wait."

"Heh. You say that now. Take care of Cutter for me. The office can't run without him. Later." And like Tex, Wolf ended the phone call without waiting for Slade to sign off.

"I think your friends like you," Dakota told Slade after he'd leaned over and placed the phone on the table next to the bed.

He shrugged.

"What is it that you do in the office that Wolf can't

seem to get over?"

"Paperwork."

"It's gotta be more than that," Dakota insisted. "He can't stand whoever is there now."

"I'm good at what I do," Slade told her without conceit. "I have a knack for it. Maybe it's because of the years I spent on the teams, or that I don't put up with bullshit from anyone. But I get stuff done. One way or another."

"I can see how that'd be important."

"Yeah. Now, can we stop talking about my job? You need to get some sleep. Tomorrow's gonna be a long day."

"Can I say one more thing?"

Slade sighed in mock exasperation, but gave Dakota a squeeze, making sure she knew he was teasing.

"I like that you've got people who'll have your back."

"You don't have that." It wasn't a question. If she did, Slade knew she'd be with them now.

"Not really. I mean, I'm good friends with the secretary at the school, and some of the teachers and I get together at times for dinner or drinks. But those are more work relationships, if you know what I mean."

"I do know what you mean," Slade told her.

"I guess you and those men tonight are work friends too, but it's different."

And it was. When you put your life in the hands of another, bonds were formed. Unbreakable ones. Throw in several life-or-death situations and friendships for life were the result. "Yeah," he said softly.

"I'm relieved that you found me," Dakota said in a small voice. "I'm glad it was you."

"Me too. Now close your eyes. Sleep," Slade ordered.

"You don't mind me sleeping like this?" she asked, tightening the arm over his belly, indicating her closeness.

"Fuck no. I want you right here. It about killed me to sit next to you in your car this morning and not touch you. You looked so uncomfortable in that seat."

"How long were you sitting there before I noticed?" Dakota asked.

"Two hours."

At that, her head popped off his shoulders and she peered at him in disbelief. "Two hours? How in the world did I sleep though you shutting the car door? And you were there the whole time?"

"You were obviously tired. And yeah, the whole two hours," Slade said.

"What did you do?"

"Watched you sleep." He didn't even pretend not to know what she was talking about. "I sat there for two hours and watched you breathing, wishing I had the right to pull you into my arms. I also devised a plan to keep you safe."

"Wow," she said, and dropped her head back to his shoulder. "I had no idea."

"If I was a threat, you would've known I was there," Slade told her definitively. "But because I wasn't, your body allowed you to stay asleep."

"I think you're giving me way more credit than I deserve," Dakota said. "I'm not that astute. I'd probably sleep through Aziz bombing a hole through a door to get to me."

"Sure you are. You've been on the run for months. You trusted me from the get-go."

"That's true," she agreed.

"Now...will you please shut your eyes and get some sleep?"

"Are you gonna lie here and stare at me if I do?"

Slade grinned. She constantly surprised him with her offbeat humor. "Maybe."

"Whatever. But you have to drive. And maybe shoot at people tomorrow if they find us. You'd better get some sleep too."

He knew she was kidding, but he would absolutely use the pistol he had in his ankle holster to protect her if he had to. "Shhhhh," he murmured, running his hand over the back of her head in a gentle caress. When she sighed in contentment and burrowed farther into his shoulder, he did it again.

"That feels good," she whispered. "No one has touched my hair like that since my mom died."

Her words hurt his heart, so he continued running his hand from the top of her head all the way to the ends of her hair in a rhythmic motion.

Within minutes, she relaxed against him completely. Dead to the world, but safe in his embrace.

Slade lay under Dakota, his hand petting her as he tried to relax enough to sleep. All his senses seemed heightened, just as they were when he'd been on the teams and on a mission. And he *was* on a mission, the most important one of his life.

As if all the times he'd been sent overseas for his country were dress rehearsals for this moment, Slade went over as many scenarios as he could think of for what might happen in the next couple of days. And every single one ended with Aziz Fourati dead, and Dakota free to live her life without fear…with him.

Chapter Nine

"**Y**OU DOIN' OKAY?" Slade asked for what seemed like the hundredth time that day.

Dakota was *not* okay. She'd been on the back of Slade's bike for eight hours and was more than ready to get off the stupid machine. Her cooter was numb and her feet had been tingling for the last hour or so. The only thing that worked in her favor was the weather. It wasn't as cold as it'd been in the higher elevations of Nevada and she was quite comfortable in the leather jacket Slade had gotten for her.

She'd woken up that morning, stiff and sore beyond belief, but also extremely comfortable. She and Slade had shifted in the night, and she'd been on her side in front of him by morning, his large body curled around hers. His arm had been around her waist, and as she'd shifted, she'd felt his very large morning erection pressing into her ass.

"Mornin'," he mumbled, even as his arm tightened and pulled her closer to him.

She didn't say a word, caught in that half-aware state between being asleep and awake. But Slade didn't seem to care that she didn't return his morning greeting. The hand at her waist moved and slipped under her T-shirt. He caressed her belly, which she tried to suck in, but she promptly forgot about any excess weight around her middle when his hand kept moving toward her breasts.

He shifted behind her, propping his head up on his free hand. The morning light made its way through the thin curtains, giving the room a weird orange glow. When Slade's fingers made contact with her bare breast, Dakota inhaled sharply, which pressed her chest into his questing hand.

Taking advantage, his fingers brushed over one of her nipples lightly. Dakota felt it immediately tighten, as if begging for Slade's touch. He didn't disappoint. He tested the weight of her breast in his hand for a moment, then his fingers went back to lazily playing with her now rock-hard nipple.

He continued for several moments, before Dakota finally squeaked, "Slade?"

"Shhhh, don't panic. I'm not going any further than this," he said softly. "I just need to touch you. I'll stop if you're uncomfortable. Just say the word."

Dakota shook her head, not liking the idea of him pulling away from her. "No. I'm okay with this. More than okay with it." She could feel his erection, fully engorged now, pulsing against her ass, and she couldn't help but push back against him when he pinched her nipple. The eroticism of his movements overwhelming.

"You like that," he said, and repeated the action on the other nipple this time.

Dakota nodded, speech beyond her at the moment.

Slade pulled back, and when she was about to open her mouth and complain about losing him, he put pressure on her hip and she turned so she was lying on her back next to him. His face was inches from her own and he murmured, "good morning" again, then bent his head and began what was the most amazing good morning of her life thus far.

He kissed her forehead, then her nose. He skipped her lips and tasted her earlobe. Then he licked the side of her neck and leisurely kissed every inch of skin he could reach. In the meantime, his fingers went back to tormenting her breasts, much more accessible to him now that she was lying on her back.

Dakota wasn't sure what to do with her own hands, so she grabbed the sheet at her hips and held on. It wasn't until Slade moved down her chest and sucked one of her nipples into his mouth through the cotton of her T-shirt that she found her voice.

"Slade, God, that feels so good. It's never felt like this before. Never."

One of her hands came up to rest on the back of his head, and she tried to press him back to her breast when he lifted his head and murmured, "For me either, sweetheart. I swear I could come just from just sucking on these beauties."

"Me too," she told him dazedly, but with a smile.

He kissed her nipple, which was now clearly visible through the damp material of her shirt, then commented, "Slept like a log."

"What?" Dakota's mind was slow catching up to what he was saying. She was still lost in the sensation of his mouth and fingers on her body.

"Haven't slept that good in a very long time. I usually wake up a couple times a night...remembering some of the shit I've seen in my life. Last night, didn't wake up once. Slept like a baby. All night."

His hand was still beneath her shirt and his thumb was gently brushing back and forth on the underside of one of her breasts. The morning had started out erotic, but morphed into a gentle intimacy. She'd never experienced anything like it, and knew she'd crave this from him from this moment forward.

Dakota brought a hand up to his face and lightly brushed her fingertips over his beard. It wasn't long, it wasn't short. It fit him. The thought raced through her mind about what it might feel like against the sensitive skin of her breasts or inner thighs, but she stopped her thoughts before they went any further. The thought of his beard between her legs as he feasted on her was too much for the moment.

"Last night was the first since the bombing I didn't dream of Aziz," she said softly.

"What do you dream?" Slade asked.

"What *don't* I dream?" Dakota countered. "He's raping me, shoving his tongue down my throat, laughing as he shoots a child in front of me; he taunts me, saying that no one will ever find me, that I'll have his babies, which he'll raise to hate women and be killers."

"Jesus," Slade breathed, then lowered his head until his nose nuzzled the skin behind her ear.

"But I didn't dream of *him* last night."

"What did you dream about?" Slade asked, his voice muffled.

"You. Us. This." The three words were simplistic, but had so much deeper meaning, Slade inhaled sharply.

"I want you," he said as he lifted his head. "In my life. In my bed. I want to be the reason you're safe in your dreams."

"It's crazy, but I want that too," Dakota whispered back, scared, but at the same time surer than she'd ever been of anything in her life.

They stared at each other for a long moment and Dakota thought they'd get down to the business of making love, when Slade stated, "We need to go."

She must've made a pathetic noise, because he smiled in resignation. "I know, sweetheart. There's nothing more I want to do right now than pull off your shirt and feast on your beautiful tits. Okay, yeah there is, I want to taste your very essence. Inhale it and let it mark me. You're going to ruin me for any other woman, and I can't fucking wait. I *want* you to ruin me. But we need to get to Wolf's tonight. It's the safest place for you, and I won't do anything that will put you in any more danger than you're already in. Because of that, instead of lying here with you in this bed and planting my cock so deep inside you we don't know where one of us ends and the other begins, I have to get some pain-killers in you and we need to head south."

Dakota liked everything about Slade's words. She could feel how much she liked it, on her inner thighs. She was soaking wet for him and wanted his mouth and fingers on her. She wanted to watch, and feel, as he emptied himself inside her…but he was right. They had no idea where the men were who'd tracked her to Rachel or if Aziz had sent more to try to intercept them.

"Okay, Slade. But can we maybe…" She trailed off, suddenly unsure about what she'd been about to ask. It was too soon.

"What? You can ask me anything. You name it, I'll give it to you," Slade said softly.

"You can say no, or that you'll think about it, but

do you think…once this craziness is done…could we come back up here? Maybe spend some time in Rachel as just us? Come back to Goldfield and do this again, but without the need to make a mad dash home?"

"Absolutely," Slade told her with a small smile. "We'll take a week or two, maybe find some of those geocache things. We'll make love before we go to sleep, and I'll wake you up with my tongue on your clit and we'll start every morning with more than a bit of petting. I'll make sure you're completely satisfied before I get up and find you a peppermint mocha and maple donut."

Dakota stared at him for a moment, the longing for the picture he'd put in her head almost a physical thing. Needing to diffuse not only the lust in her body, but the intimate situation as well, she teased, "Do you think Wolf will give you the time off? I'm not sure he's gonna want you to leave anytime soon after you go back to work."

Slade chuckled. His hand, which had been resting on her breast, slid down her belly and moved to her side, his thumb caressing her hipbone. "Wolf's not my boss, sweetheart. I've got a ton of vacation time saved up." He shrugged. "Never had anywhere I wanted to go to use it."

"Okay then."

"Okay then," he echoed. He leaned down and kissed

her lightly on the lips, then pulled back and said, "I'd give you a proper good-morning kiss, but I've got morning breath. Go shower. I'll see if I can't rustle us up some food. You can eat while I shower and we'll get on the road."

"Sounds good."

"Don't get used to solo showers," he told her sternly, his eyes sparkling. "When we're the 'us' I want us to be, that I hope we'll be soon, I want to start my day with you naked, wet, and writhing in my arms."

Dakota shivered from head to toe at the carnality of his words. Yeah, she wanted that too. She didn't even have the words to respond.

"Go on. Don't forget to take the painkillers before you shower. Unfortunately, you're gonna need 'em by the end of the day." And with that, Slade squeezed her waist and climbed out of the bed.

Dakota stared at him as he walked leisurely to the chair he'd draped his clothes on last night. The muscles in his long legs flexing as he moved. He was wearing a pair of boxer briefs, which did nothing to hide his muscular ass from her eyes.

She continued to stare at Slade as he pulled up his jeans. He turned to her then, his pants unbuttoned, his erection plain to see straining against the denim. "Dakota? We really do need to get moving."

"I'm going, I'm going," she mumbled, not taking

her eyes off him. Slade might be almost fifty, but he was literally the sexiest man she'd ever seen. He was still in shape from his days of being a SEAL. She figured he must still work out because the muscles in his chest and arms looked solid, and rippled when he moved.

He chuckled and bent over to grab his T-shirt. Suppressing a sigh, Dakota watched as he pulled it over his head.

"I'm going. I adore your eyes on me, love, but I'll never get my cock to relax enough to ride if you don't stop eye-fucking me."

Dakota blinked, then blushed. She looked away from him then and said, "Don't mind me. Go on, find me some coffee and sugar. I'll be ready when you return."

She heard him stalking back to the bed, and it dipped as he rested his hands on the mattress and leaned over. "Love this," he declared, and didn't make her ask what. "Love that you can't keep your eyes off me. Never had it. My ex never cared enough about me to look at me the way you do. As if you want to eat me alive. And so you know, the feeling's mutual. The only thing keeping me from fucking you until neither of us can move is the hairs on the back of my neck standing straight up. Those assholes are out there just waiting for me to fuck up. And it's not gonna happen. Shower. I'll be back." Then he gave her a hard, closed-mouth kiss on the lips and stalked out of the room.

The memory of the morning had kept her occupied for most of the ride out of Nevada. Riding on the back of the motorcycle had been scary when they'd hit the traffic of Las Vegas, but Slade had somehow sensed her nervousness and had reached back and patted her thigh and shouted, "I got this, love. Close your eyes and trust me."

And she had.

But the long stretch of interstate between the California border and the small military town of Barstow had been brutal. There wasn't much to look at and Dakota kept imagining Aziz's goons driving up from behind and ramming them.

By the time they were headed down the Cajon Pass and into San Bernardino, Dakota was way over the whole motorcycle thing. All she wanted to do was lie down and stretch out all the kinks in her body. She'd never think that sitting in a massage chair was cool ever again. Her brain felt as if it had been rattling around for days rather than hours.

"Dakota, you doin' okay?" Slade asked when they were passing by the city of Escondido.

She sighed and yelled back, "Fine!" The word came out more irritable than she'd wanted it to, but whatever. She couldn't take it back now.

"Twenty minutes, tops," he told her with a squeeze

to her hands on his belly.

Dakota nodded, even though she knew Slade was totally lying to try to make the last part of the trip easier. She knew Escondido was about thirty miles from San Diego. She rested her helmet-clad head on Slade's back and closed her eyes, letting her mind wander as they covered the remaining miles to Wolf's house.

She should've been nervous to be back in the town where her apartment had burned down and she'd been threatened by Aziz, but at the moment, all she could think about was Slade.

She tried to analyze why she'd fallen for him as quickly as she had. It probably had to do with the fact that she was in danger…although when she'd first seen him, she hadn't *felt* as if she was in danger. She'd been in Rachel for so long she'd become merely cautious, rather than freaked out by the people who entered the small restaurant/bar.

Maybe it was because she hadn't had sex in so long…years. But she didn't think that was why she'd fallen for Slade either. She enjoyed sex, but didn't *need* it. Before everything she owned had turned to ash, she'd had a vibrator in her bedside table that she'd used on a regular basis. It wasn't the same as having the intimacy a man provided, but it worked for her. So yeah, she didn't think she was attracted to Slade simply because he was hot.

There was just something about him that made her feel…grounded. Yes, she felt safe with him. Yes, she wanted him. But it was more. Dakota knew the man wasn't perfect. He'd lived almost half a century; he would certainly have his own quirks, idiosyncrasies, and ways of doing things that would probably drive her crazy, just as she wasn't perfect. But she'd easily over-look his quirks if the contentedness she felt around him continued.

Was she crazy for imagining herself spending the rest of her life with him? For even knowing after two days that she *wanted* to spend the rest of her life with him? Probably. Dakota grinned. But who the hell cared. It wasn't as if she was getting married anytime soon. But she'd been cautious enough in her life. It was time to be spontaneous and go with her heart rather than her head. If she was crazy, so was Slade. And being crazy together sounded a hell of a lot better than being crazy by herself for the rest of her life.

Her thoughts were brought to an abrupt halt when Dakota felt the machine between her legs rumble as it slowed. She opened her eyes and lifted her head to look around. She saw they were in a neighborhood with small, cute houses. Slade eventually pulled into the driveway of a gray house with a small front porch. There were two cars already parked in front. He stopped the Harley and turned off the engine.

Dakota sighed in relief. The next time Slade wanted her to ride this beast, she was at the very least requesting earplugs.

As he'd done every other time they'd stopped, Slade immediately hopped off the motorcycle and turned to her. He'd already unbuckled his helmet and reached for hers. Dakota let him remove it; she'd tried to tell him earlier that she was perfectly able to take care of herself, but he'd only smiled and said, "I know, but it pleases me to do it for you." How could she deny him when he'd said something so sweet?

He unbuckled her helmet and hung it alongside his own on one of the handlebars. Slade gently massaged her head, magically homing in on the places where the plastic had bitten into her skull. He'd tenderly braided her hair again that morning before they'd set off and she decided his fingers felt like magic.

"You ready?"

Dakota knew he meant was she ready to get off the bike. And she wasn't, because she knew it was going to hurt, just like it had every other time he'd stopped and made her walk around. But she simply nodded, trying to hide her discomfort and anxiety from him.

Apparently, she did a shit job, because he sighed and said, "I'm sorry, love. I know you hurt, but you did an amazing job today. I'm proud of you. If I didn't know better, I'd think you've been riding bikes all your life."

"Yeah well, did I forget to mention my dad is a member of the Hell's Angels and I've been riding with the gang since I was a small child? Silly me."

His lips twitched, but he didn't laugh. "Thank you for joking about this and trying to make me feel better. But it won't work. I feel like shit for hurting you."

Dakota could see that Slade really did feel awful. Her heart cracked even more. Besides her parents, no one had cared this much about her...ever. She laid her hand on his arm and said softly, "You didn't hurt me, Slade. I'm fine. Yeah, I'm sore, but it's not like we had a choice. You're helping me, and that's something I'll never forget. Ever."

"I'm not doing this for your gratitude," Slade bit out.

"I know you're not," she returned. "But you need to stop getting all pissed off every time I thank you. I know better than anyone what Aziz has in store for me because he explained it to me in great detail. I can't stop being thankful to you for helping me, so getting upset with me doesn't do either of us any good. But just because I'm grateful, doesn't mean I don't feel more for you. I didn't jump on the back of any other guy's motorcycle who came through Rachel, and believe me, there were plenty. I got on the back of *your* bike. So cool it with the macho bullcrap and if I say thank you, swallow hard and say you're welcome."

She probably wouldn't have snapped at him if she wasn't so tired and sore, but it had been a long two days and Dakota wanted nothing more than to get clean, then sleep. In that order. She wasn't in the mood to deal with Slade's crap.

"You're right. I'm sorry," he said immediately. "And you're welcome."

Dakota blinked. Well. All right then. She'd mentally tallied a strike against the man for not wanting her thanks, but had to erase it when he'd so easily and quickly apologized.

"Good."

"Now...you ready to stand?"

Dakota grimaced. "No." But she threw her leg over the bike and prepared to do it anyway.

As he'd done every other time, Slade's hands went to her waist and held her steady as she stood. It took a few moments for her to get her balance, as usual, and she stayed still in Slade's arms until she felt as if she could walk on her own.

"I'm ready," she told him after several moments went by without him moving back as he usually did.

"Fuck, you're gorgeous," Slade breathed.

Dakota snorted. "I'm sweaty, dirty, windblown, and walking as if I've got something stuck up my butt. I think you need glasses."

"You're sweaty, dirty, windblown, and walking funny, but I can see you clear as day, love. And what I see is an unpretentious woman who is in the middle of a fucked-up situation, doesn't own anything but what's in a beat-up old backpack, but who can still somehow embrace new experiences, be open to a relationship with a retired old Navy fart, and who doesn't complain even once about feeling like shit after an eight-hour bike ride."

"Uh…okay, whatever."

"And *you* need to learn to take a compliment," Slade said, grinning.

His smile did something to her insides. Dakota loved when he grinned. It made her belly do cartwheels, especially knowing he was smiling at *her*.

"Is my retired Navy fart ever going to help me walk inside so I can get that shower?" she asked cheekily.

In response, Slade leaned down and kissed her. It wasn't short, but it wasn't long either. His tongue swiped over her bottom lip and when she opened for him, it ducked inside, caressed her once, then retreated. Dakota swayed toward him when he pulled back, and blinked.

"Come on, love. Let's go meet Wolf—who's been watching us for the last five minutes—and whoever else he's got inside.

"Oh geez, he's been waiting for us to get inside?" Dakota asked, frowning. "How rude of us."

Slade didn't respond, but turned her so she was tucked up against his side, which she was thankful for because she wasn't sure she could walk on her own, and steered them toward a door off to the side of the house.

Ready or not, it looked like she was going to meet Slade's friends. Briefly glancing up at the heavens, Dakota sent a short prayer upwards. *Please let the craziness of my life end soon. I really want to be able to spend time with this man without the threat of a terrorist hanging over my head.*

Chapter Ten

I T WAS AN hour later and Dakota had showered, taken more pain pills, and was currently sitting curled against Slade's side on Wolf's couch as her current situation was discussed.

"So Fourati is American?" Wolf asked.

"Yeah, I'm almost positive," Dakota said.

"Damn," the SEAL swore, running his hand through his hair. "No wonder the government wasn't having any luck finding him. Not if they were looking for a foreigner. This makes tracking him down more difficult."

"I know," Slade agreed.

"And how'd you get involved in this again?" Cookie asked Slade. Cookie was a SEAL on Wolf's team, and who Slade worked with all the time. He'd come over at Wolf's request so they could talk about security for Dakota. The rest of the team would eventually be brought up to speed as well, but for now it was just the three men, and Dakota, talking.

"Can't say," Slade told him. "But the bottom line is that it's a matter of national security to take Fourati down. And not just because he's after Dakota. Though that's my main motivator at the moment."

"How come the papers didn't report on the fact you were the lone survivor of that blast?" Cookie asked, switching topics easily. "Does anyone else find that odd?"

"It's not odd," Dakota piped up. "I was scared, and even though I hoped Aziz was dead, I wasn't sure. I waited a day or two to see a doctor about my arm, just to be safe. And his speech about me being the mother of his future children who he'd train to be terrorists was fresh in my mind. It had been absolute chaos both inside and outside the airport, and I just wanted to go home. I didn't tell anyone I had been in there, so the press simply didn't know."

Slade tightened his hold on Dakota and glared at Cookie. He didn't like that his question had disturbed her.

"That makes sense...but you knew about her being at the bombing, right?" Wolf asked, looking at Slade.

"Yeah, but not until recently. My...contact told me about her. Said recruitment videos online talked about her, and even had a picture of her from that day," Slade informed his friends, hating how Dakota's body tightened further at his words.

"So everyone in his network knows about her," Wolf concluded.

"Seems so," Slade agreed.

"So we need to find this Fourati guy and take him out before this goes any further," Cookie added.

"No," Slade disagreed. "*I* need to find this Fourati guy and take him out. You and your team, Wolf, have nothing to do with this. This is off the record, and you will *not* be involved beyond protecting her while I get things sorted here. I'm retired. It's why I was specifically asked to take care of this."

"That's bullshit and you know it," Wolf growled. "SEALs don't work alone. No fucking way. We're a team."

"This is unsanctioned. I can tell you this much though, the job came from the highest fucking levels of the government. You cannot be involved."

"But we *are* involved," Cookie argued.

"Maybe I should leave," Dakota said. "If you guys could get in trouble, I should just go."

"You're not going anywhere," Wolf said.

At the same time, Slade and Cookie said, "No."

Slade put his finger under Dakota's chin and forced her to look up at him. He hated the look of uncertainty and fear on her face. "I'm going to fix this for you, love. I'll take Fourati down and he won't hurt you again. Soon this'll be just another story we can tell our friends and family when we're old and decrepit. Got it?"

"But—"

"No. No buts about it. You're not going anywhere."

The look of fear was replaced by irritation. "You're annoying."

"I know. But I'm the annoying old Navy fart who is going to make it safe to rebuild and live your life…hopefully with me beside you every step of the way."

"Fine."

"Fine," he echoed. Then he turned to Wolf and Cookie. "Your job in this is to keep your eyes on Dakota when I can't."

"We were gonna do that anyway," Wolf told him. "But you need to—"

"No offense, but no. I don't want to involve any of you more than you already are. If it makes you feel better, however, I've got Tex on this."

"Fuck. Why didn't you say so in the first place?" Cookie asked. "If Tex is on this, Fourati is as good as captured. Me and Fiona will expect you and Dakota to come over for dinner next week." He grinned, the natural cockiness of a man who was that sure of his friend's success showing through loud and clear.

"Done."

Slade could feel Dakota's head whipping back and forth between him and his friends, and it made him smile. SEALs could be crass and uncouth sometimes, but the men in front of him had hearts of gold. "Caroline get settled over at Dude's place?"

Wolf nodded. "Yup."

"And you guys still don't want any kids…even when she's dying to spend time with their daughter?" Slade asked Wolf.

Wolf shook his head. "Caroline loves children, but neither of us really want our own." He shrugged. "It's hard to explain."

"No need," Slade reassured him. "Once upon a time, I wanted a household full of rug rats, but something deep inside me knew Cynthia wasn't the one to have them with." It was his turn to shrug now. "Now I'm too old to even think about it." He mock shuddered. "I'd be almost seventy by the time they got out of high school. Can you imagine?"

Wolf's eyes flicked to the woman at his side, and Slade stiffened. Shit, had he offended her? Did Dakota want kids? They hadn't known each other long enough to even have sex yet, much less talk about babies. Had he fucked up?

He turned to look down at Dakota, and found her staring off into space with a wistful look on her face.

"You okay, sweetheart? I hope I didn't say something that'll make you rethink spending the rest of your life with me," Slade asked somewhat nervously.

One side of her mouth tilted up into a smile. "No, Slade, you're fine. I'm not exactly a spring chicken myself. About twelve years ago, I talked with my mom about this very topic. I was considering in vitro fertilization. I was single, but was at a point in my life where I thought I'd either need to have a kid right then, or never have one." She looked away from him then and continued.

"But after talking with her about all that she went through with me, and hearing what she had to give up, I decided that being a single parent wasn't something I wanted to do. I loved my job and sometimes worked until it was dark out. It wouldn't be fair to a child to work those kinds of long hours, and it wouldn't be fair to slack off on my job so I could be home with a kid. Don't get me wrong, my mom wasn't upset that everything changed after she had me, but it just drove the point home that my life would be completely upended if I had a kid, and I wasn't sure I wanted to do that."

She looked back up at Slade. "So you can relax, you didn't offend me and I'm not going to expect you to be a dad at fifty."

"Thank god," he breathed, and leaned down and kissed her forehead.

"But I wouldn't object to snuggling with other people's babies," she went on, and looked at Wolf. "Your friends have kids?"

"Yup," Wolf told her. "Jessyka will love you forever if you take a shine to hers. She's got a houseful of them and is always looking for a sucker…err…babysitter."

Everyone laughed at Wolf's good-natured teasing.

"On that note…I need to talk to Tex, and Dakota's about done in," Slade told his friends. "You ready to crash, love?"

She nodded. "Definitely."

"Do you mind if I talk with my friends for a bit?" Slade asked. He didn't want to keep secrets from Dakota, but he also didn't want to needlessly worry her. He wanted to talk schedules and let Wolf and Cookie know what his immediate plans were and when he'd be away from the house.

"Of course not," Dakota told him. "You'll be…um," she blushed and blurted, "coming down later…right?"

Slade leaned in and nuzzled the skin behind her ear and whispered, "Yeah, love, I'll be down later. Save me room in bed, okay?"

She nodded and her blush deepened.

Wolf and Cookie were considerate enough to look away from them as they spoke. But since they were both smiling, Slade knew they'd heard the short conversation.

Slade helped Dakota stand, knowing she wouldn't be able to do so gracefully by herself. He'd gotten his stuff from the bike and put it and her backpack in the basement earlier. He needed to stop by his apartment and grab more clothes, and he needed to pick up some stuff at the store as well. But for tonight, they'd get by.

He walked her down the stairs—slowly, because the muscles in her thighs were obviously sore—and kissed her long and hard before heading back up to his friends.

The next hour was spent discussing the logistics of making sure Dakota stayed safe in the house, and what Slade's movements would be the next couple of days. When they were done, Slade tried once again to thank his friends. "I appreciate this. I could drag Dakota around with me, but I think it'd be safer for her if she stayed out of sight. If Fourati doesn't know she's back in town—which is a possibility, though unlikely—it's better for her to lay low."

"You're beginning to piss me off," Wolf stated flatly. "If this was happening to Caroline, Alabama, Fiona, or any of our women, you'd help in a heartbeat."

"Damn straight," Slade confirmed.

"We take care of our own," Cookie chimed in. "You might not've fought on our team, Cutter, but you're as much a part of it as we are."

"Thanks," Slade said. "Seriously."

"Again, no thanks necessary. The sooner we get your ass back in the office, the better," Wolf grumbled.

"The new guy still not working out?" Slade asked.

"He's an idiot. Had no clue how to set up a secure browser today. I walked by his desk and he was using fucking Google to search for something. I thought Hurt was going to lose his shit. Sent him home early and told him not to come back tomorrow if he didn't have his head out of his ass."

Slade smirked. Commander Hurt was pretty easygoing, but when it came to the men on the teams he was in charge of, he wouldn't stand for anything less than perfection. The lives of the SEALs literally depended on it. He knew Greg Lambert probably had the best of intentions, but he'd clearly sent the replacement without knowing how clueless the man was with administrative matters. He'd have to give Lambert shit the next time he talked to him.

Thinking of Wolf's team, or some of the other men he worked with on the base being put in a position of vulnerability because of an incompetent contractor, made Slade's eye twitch. He'd been gone less than a week, but he missed it. It was crazy; who would've ever thought he'd miss a desk job? But he *liked* working behind the scenes to keep the men on the front lines safe. Sometimes it was only a matter of making sure they had fresh batteries before they went on a mission, but even that could literally be life or death.

Yeah, he was old enough and experienced enough to realize the excitement that came with being on the teams was for the young and enthusiastic. He was past that point in his life, and the only thing he wanted was to do his part to keep his fellow SEALs safe and go home to a loving woman. To Dakota.

The thought made him smile.

"And with that, I'm out of here," Cookie said with a smirk. "I'll talk with Abe and the others and let them know what's up."

"Don't forget Dakota's dad. I wouldn't put it past Fourati to try to use him to get to her," Slade said as they all stood.

"On it. If nothing else, maybe Dakota can convince her old man to move in with Benny and Jess. I don't know how he feels about kids, but their brood would keep anyone busy. We give them shit all the time, but those kids are some of the most well-behaved children I've ever met. They'd love to have another adult around to entertain them."

"Sounds good," Slade told Cookie. "If you guys think it's necessary, we'll make it happen. I'll talk to Tex and see if he's heard anything about Mr. James being in danger."

"Good. Later," Cookie said, and after a chin lift, headed toward the kitchen and the side exit of the house.

"You gonna call Tex?" Wolf asked.

"Yeah."

"All right. I'll leave you to it. I'm headed upstairs. I'll turn on the alarm," Wolf told Slade. He'd already shown both him and Dakota how it worked and told them the code.

Slade nodded. "I'm gonna try to sneak out of bed in the morning and get some errands done early. I'd like Dakota to sleep in, but with the way she climbs all over me during the night, I'm not sure I'll succeed," he told Wolf with a grin.

"It's a great problem to have."

"That's for sure," Slade agreed. "I'll see you in the morning?"

"Yup. I got approval to skip PT tomorrow. I'll be hanging around here with your woman until you get back."

Slade sagged in relief. "Thanks."

Wolf waved away his gratitude.

"Oh, one more thing. You got a coffee shop around here? And a donut place?"

"Yeah, about three blocks away. Your woman have a hankering?"

"Oh yeah. Big-time addiction. She's been without her peppermint mochas for a while now. Figured she wouldn't mind a surprise in the morning."

"She's gonna fit in with our women just fine," Wolf told him. "I've tried to tell Ice that she can make coffee here, but she insists that it's just not the same."

The men grinned at each other in commiseration. Then Wolf lifted his chin at his friend and said, "Later."

"Later, Wolf."

As soon as the other man had disappeared up the stairs, Slade called Tex. As he waited for him to pick up, he marveled at how quickly his world had changed. A week ago, he hadn't even known Dakota. Now he was literally imagining how to rearrange his entire life to make her fit. Making plans to get up early just so he could stop by the coffee shop to pick up a peppermint mocha for her. But it was the realization that he was actually excited for what his future would bring that made him sigh in contentment.

He'd been living his life as if on autopilot. He did the same thing every day, ate the same food, saw the same people. No, chasing a terrorist wasn't exactly the shake-up he'd wanted in his life, but Dakota was. He knew without a doubt that every moment with her would be exciting, and he was filled with anticipation for that to begin now. All because of her.

"Cutter," Tex said as he answered the phone.

"Tex," Slade returned.

"You at Wolf's?" Tex asked, not beating around the bush.

"Yeah. Made it here a few hours ago. Cookie just left."

"I'm sending a tracker for Dakota," Tex informed

him.

"I don't think—" Slade began, but Tex cut him off.

"It's necessary. Fiona didn't think she'd be kidnapped by sex slavers. Benny didn't think he'd be conked over the head and his woman would have to give herself to his kidnapper. Melody didn't think—"

"Point made," Slade bit out, stopping Tex's tirade.

"They're earrings. Had a set made for a friend's kid. I think they're pretty kick-ass, myself. I'll also send along a few of the others so they can be placed in her clothes too, just in case. They won't get there for a couple days though."

"No problem. We'll be careful in the meantime. What did you find out about Fourati?"

"Not much. I tried doing a few searches for a blond guy in his twenties who showed interest in terrorist leanings, and came up blank. Either he's completely new to the terrorist business and extremely lucky, or he's incredibly smart."

"What else has been posted about Dakota?" Slade asked.

Tex hesitated, and Slade's stomach cramped. "He's escalating in his determination to find her. There are new pictures being posted almost every hour on the Dark Web. Recruitment posters about how Fourati's woman will be the salvation of Ansar al-Shari'a, and how the babies she'll bring to the cause will be celebrated and revered for years to come."

"What kind of pictures?" Slade bit out, ignoring the last part for the moment. Fourati could say whatever he wanted, it didn't mean it'd come true, but pictures were another thing.

"They look photoshopped to me," Tex said calmly. "Pictures of her wearing a traditional Tunisian outfit, bustier, silk pants, beige shawl. Standing side by side with a man whose face is blacked out. On her knees looking up at a man."

"Okay, so he's getting pictures from the Net and altering them."

"Right, except…" Tex's voice trailed off.

"Except what?" Slade asked impatiently.

"There's one, posted a couple of hours ago, of Dakota on the back of a motorcycle. It's captioned, "If you see this woman, take possession until the Ansar al-Shari'a ruler can claim her."

"Fuck me," Slade said. "Can you tell where it was taken?"

"It's grainy, as if captured from far away," Tex said, not answering the question.

"Maybe it's not Dakota."

"It is, Cutter. It's your bike. I should know, I was there when you bought the damn thing. It's definitely her."

"So he's put out an all-points bulletin on her," Slade

concluded.

"Looks that way," Tex said silently.

"I need to find this Fourati guy and shut down his communication channels." Slade told Tex something he already knew.

"Shutting those down will be easy. All it'll take is me hacking into the main site he's been using to communicate with his followers and posting a cease-and-desist order supposedly from him. I can get creative and word it in a way that any of his potential recruits will think it's Fourati. But he has to be neutralized in order for it to work, otherwise he'll just start a new site. But it's finding *him* that's the tricky part."

"What if I egged him on?" Slade asked.

"Use yourself as bait?" Tex asked.

"Yeah. By now, he has to know she's with me. And if he's even marginally good at searching, he'll figure out who I am. He'll want to get rid of me to be able to get his hands on her easier. Let's face it, if I go off the grid with her, no one will find us unless I want them to. But I really don't want to take Dakota away from her life. She doesn't deserve that. I'd rather take him out now so she can be free of all this bullshit. If I set myself up as an easy target, he'll come after me to get me out of the way, and I can take him down."

"Risky," Tex commented.

"Yeah, but what other choice do I have? I could pass

him on the street and have no idea it was him. If I control the where and how we meet, I've at least got a shot of stopping him and making Dakota safe."

"And preventing another attack on US soil," Tex added.

Slade was silent for a moment before admitting, "It might make me an asshole, Tex, but I couldn't give a shit about that right now. He wants to make Dakota his sex slave. Get her pregnant and take her baby away from her. He wants to use her for whatever his own sick perversions are. That is *not* going to happen."

"You could use her to—"

"No," Slade said before Tex could finish. "She is not going to be bait. She's scared to death of this guy, Tex. I'm not going to put her through that, not even if it means we catch him tomorrow."

"Okay, it was just a suggestion," Tex said calmly.

"A shitty one."

"I'm missing something," Tex said, moving on. "I don't know what, but it's important. Be careful, Slade. I don't like this. My shit's-gonna-hit-the-fan meter is pegged."

"Agreed."

"I know you got shit to do, but don't let her out of your sight if you can help it," Tex told him.

"After I get some stuff done, I wasn't planning on it. A couple of days, max, then I'm connected to her hip.

But work fast, Tex. Help me end this."

"I will. If I figure out what we're missing, I'll call. Later." Tex hung up, obviously more interested in continuing the search for Fourati than being polite.

Slade didn't take offense. He glanced at his watch. It was late, but he had one more call he had to make. It was even later on the East Coast, but he didn't give a fuck.

He dialed the special number he'd been given and waited.

"Lambert."

"It's Cutsinger."

"Have you found Fourati?" the former commander asked, not beating around the bush.

"Not yet. But I found the witness. She's under my protection now."

"Good. She tell you what he looked like?"

Slade proceeded to tell Greg Lambert everything Dakota had said about that day at the airport, including her description of Fourati. When he was done, Greg was silent for a long moment.

"So he's American," he finally said.

"Seems so, Sir."

"You know, I never thought I'd see the day when I'd be fighting to keep citizens of our own country from blowing each other up. Gang wars are one thing. Drugs, guns, emotions running high…they're all one thing. But the likes of people like Timothy McVeigh and Aziz Fourati, if that's even his name, are something else altogether. I'll never understand how someone can decide killing their own fellow citizens is the right and just thing to do."

Slade agreed with him, but didn't respond.

Greg sighed. "Okay. I'll run the description past the experts here. Tell them that I have a source who ferreted out the information. If I find anything new, I'll let you know. In the meantime, you need anything, let *me* know. I'm not going to tell you how to do your job, but it's possible the only way we'll catch this asshole is to use the witness to—"

Slade tuned the man out. Why in the fuck did everyone think the only way to catch Fourati was to put an innocent woman, who had already been through hell, in more danger?

He realized that Lambert had stopped talking and said woodenly, "I'll keep that under advisement, Sir." He didn't know what the fuck the man had proposed but if it involved Dakota, it wasn't happening.

"I expect you to remain professional," Greg warned, obviously picking up on the fact that Slade wasn't happy with his suggestion. "One of the reasons I reached out to you is because you're known to be levelheaded and not fall for every fucking damsel in distress you've been sent to help. I can make your replacement at the base a permanent one if you go off the rails."

"I don't give a fuck if you take me off this assignment," Slade said in a low, deadly voice. "I'm going to catch that motherfucker and end his miserable life if it's the last thing I do. But don't you *ever* threaten me again. You want to get me fired? Go for it. The replacement you arranged sucks. He'll have every SEAL team under Hurt's command killed within the year. But I'll be gone. I'll take Dakota and go so far undercover you'll never find either of us again, and you won't have a shot in hell of finding Fourati. I know about your wife, and I'm as sorry as I can be that you lost her to cancer, but that doesn't give you the right to be a dick when it comes to other innocent lives and any relationship I might have."

"Fuck. You're right, I apologize," Lambert said in a quiet tone. "Do what you need to do. I'm counting on you to get this done, Cutter. The country is. I didn't mean to imply that Ms. James' life is worth less than the hundreds or thousands of people who could die if Fourati follows through with his plans. But I still have nightmares about those killed on 9/11. I see the people jumping from the burning towers every time I close my eyes. I don't want to see it happen again. Not when I'm around to stop it."

"Understood," Slade said in a slightly less edgy voice. "I'll call again if I find out anything else."

"Be careful," Greg said softly.

"Always," Slade returned. "Later."

"Bye."

Slade hung up and forced himself to relax. The urge to see Dakota crawled through him all of a sudden. Done with making phone calls, Slade went to the basement door. He took one last look around the small house. The lights on the alarm system were lit, indicating it was on and armed. Nothing looked or sounded out of place. Satisfied that for the moment they were as safe as they could be, Slade quietly slipped through the door and headed down into the basement. To Dakota.

He stood by the queen-size bed for a long moment, absorbing all that was Dakota. She lay on her side, one arm outstretched as if reaching for him and the other tucked close to her chest. She was once again wearing a T-shirt. Slade couldn't see what else she had on because the covers were pulled up to her waist.

Wanting to be in bed next to her more than he wanted his next breath, Slade quickly stalked toward the bathroom. The sooner he changed and brushed his teeth, the sooner he could be where he needed to be.

Within minutes, Slade was slipping under the covers and snuggling into Dakota's warm body from behind. The minute his legs tangled with hers, he stifled a groan. Her legs were as bare as his. Lifting the sheet and peeking down at her, he saw she wore a shirt and a pair of white cotton panties, and that was it.

His cock immediately surged with blood, ready and willing to do what God intended for it to do. Slade gritted his teeth and ignored the discomfort of his body, concentrating instead on how amazing Dakota felt against him.

The second he wrapped his arm around her waist, she turned sleepily to face him.

"All's okay?" she slurred, obviously more asleep than awake. Her forehead rested against his chest, her arms curled up between them, and her legs tangled once more with his.

He was surrounded by her warmth and scent, and the way she so trustingly curled into him made Slade's heart fill with love.

He loved her. Every inch. He hadn't seen her naked. Hadn't had the privilege of making love with her yet. Didn't know her favorite color or even when her birthday was. But he didn't need all of that to know she was now the most important thing in his life. More important than his job, his home, his siblings, his friends. She was his everything.

"Shhhh," he whispered. "All's good. Sleep."

"'Kay," she mumbled, and he felt every muscle in her body sag in her sleep.

His erection was nestled between them, hard against her belly, but Slade hardly noticed. All he could think about was how right Dakota felt in his arms.

Chapter Eleven

TWO DAYS LATER, Dakota thought she was going to go stir crazy. She hadn't been out of the house since she'd arrived with Slade and she was beginning to feel as if she were a prisoner. The thought made her feel guilty, as she knew Slade and Wolf were only trying to protect her, but it was driving her insane.

Slade had left that morning to do some super-secret SEAL thing. He wouldn't tell her what, had only kissed her on the forehead and told her he'd be back soon. Not only was she feeling claustrophobic being locked up for her protection, she was about to self-combust from horniness.

For two mornings in a row, she'd woken up with Slade's hands on her body. This morning she'd practically been orgasming before she'd fully woken up. Slade's hand was down the front of her panties and his fingers had been coated with her juices.

All it had taken was one look into his lust-filled dark eyes as he'd deliberately and expertly flicked her clit and she'd exploded. The second her thighs had started to tremble and she'd arched up in ecstasy, he'd prolonged her pleasure by easing one long finger inside her body and groaning at the way her muscles gripped him. Seeing his excitement and feeling the insistent stroking of his finger against her G-spot, she'd come again, wishing it was his cock deep inside her instead.

Then he'd blown her mind even more when he'd removed his hand from between her legs and immediately sucked the finger he'd had inside her into his mouth. His eyes had rolled back into his head and he'd groaned at her taste.

He'd met her gaze, said, "Fucking fantastic," and kissed her until she didn't know her name anymore. Between her own musky flavor on his tongue and the feel of his beard against her face, she'd almost come again. When he pulled back, she'd tried to return the favor, wanting to see him up close and personal, but he'd stopped her hand when it trailed down his stomach toward the erection she could feel against her leg, kissed her palm and told her that he had to go, but he'd take her up on her offer later. He'd promised that he had to wrap up one last thing and when he returned, he'd be able to spend more time with her. He would still be hunting Fourati, but could do that with Tex's help and not have to leave her alone as much. Then he'd left her in bed, sated and sleepy, and ordered her back to sleep.

As expected, Slade had been gone when she'd finally roused enough to get up, shower and wander up to the kitchen. But surprisingly, Caroline was there. She'd met the woman the night before when Wolf had stopped by with her in tow. Apparently, she'd convinced her husband that she'd be safe in her own house as long as he or one of the men on his team was with her.

And now this morning, Caroline was in the kitchen when she wandered upstairs, with another SEAL, whose name was Benny.

After warming up the peppermint mocha Slade had left for her, Benny informed her over a breakfast of cheese omelets and bacon that, if needed, her dad would be moving into his house with him and his wife. They'd make sure he was safe, comfortable, and entertained.

Dakota had almost burst into tears of relief and gratitude, but managed to hold them back. While her life had been turned upside down, she'd done her best to keep her dad out of it. But with Fourati still on the loose, Slade wasn't taking any chances that the terrorist would use him to get to her.

"What do you want to do today?" Caroline asked from across the table. They'd been getting to know each other over breakfast and Dakota liked the other woman. She was down-to-earth, not pretentious at all, and they'd really clicked. It was nice to talk to a woman about something other than teachers, Common Core, and testing for once.

Dakota shrugged. "No clue. I'm about TV'd out, board games aren't my thing, and I'm not much of a cook. I'm open to any ideas you guys have."

"We could play a prank on Wolf," Benny suggested, a grin on his face.

Caroline rolled her eyes. "I can't believe you guys are still on this practical joke kick. What's the latest?"

The smile on Benny's face didn't dim as he looked down at his phone and searched for something.

Dakota couldn't help but be entertained by Benny. There were times that morning when he'd seemed like an immature little boy, but when he'd answered his phone and spoke with Wolf, she saw another side of him. The dangerous side. Apparently, Slade had been concerned because Tex had called and said Fourati had posted on his recruiting Dark Web site that his wife would soon be giving her own speech to their followers, and Wolf had called to give Benny a head's up.

Dakota didn't like the sound of that, because if Aziz was talking about her, then he'd have to *have* her in order for her to give a speech. But Benny had reassured Wolf that Dakota was safe and they had no plans to leave the house.

The determination on Benny's face was easy to see. And it wiped the playful boy right off his persona. It made her relax a bit and understand that while he might joke and kid around about some things, he was still a badass Navy SEAL.

But now he was back to being the entertaining host, trying to find something to make her smile and not feel as if she were a prisoner in the house. Benny turned his phone toward Caroline first and explained through chuckles what she was seeing. "So you know the new guy sucks, right?"

Caroline nodded. "Uh, yeah, Wolf hasn't stopped bitching about him since Slade took his leave of absence."

"Right, well the guy might be a good mathematician, but he sucks at computers. Time and time again, we've had to explain shit to him that he should already know. It's gotten really old. So, Mozart and Cookie distracted him this morning, asking if he'd come help them with something in another office, and Dude and Abe sabotaged his computer. They hooked up smoke bombs to certain keys on his keyboard. Apparently, Dude had seen this done before but hadn't had a chance to try it out. He prepped one at home and switched it out with Zach's while he was being distracted."

"What am I looking at, Benny?" Caroline asked, tilting her head to the side as if that would help her understand the picture in front of her. Benny leaned forward and pointed to the screen as he spoke.

"Zach came back from the other room, mumbling

about what assholes Mozart and Cookie were, and sat down and began to type. Smoke immediately started pouring out of his keyboard. He panicked and pushed more keys, which made more smoke come out! Instead of doing the smart thing, and getting a fire extinguisher or calling for help, he began to smack at the keyboard like a little kid instead. This picture is of the entire area around his desk filled with smoke," Benny informed Caroline.

He scrolled through a few more pictures, still chuckling. "See? It just kept getting worse. We were all laughing so hard we couldn't even tell him to stop. I could barely hold my phone steady enough to get pictures. It got so bad, Hurt came out of his office, mumbling about how juvenile we all were, and grabbed the keyboard away from Zach, hauled it into the hallway still smoking and slammed the office door. It. Was. Hilarious."

"It doesn't look like Zach found it funny," Caroline observed, her lips twitching.

"That's 'cause he's an ass," Benny declared, then turned toward Dakota. "And a big baby. He glared at us all, said we were pathetic, and left the office in a huff. When I left to come over here and relieve Wolf, he still hadn't returned. I hate people who can't take a joke. Look, Dakota, tell me this isn't funny as shit."

Dakota took the phone Benny offered and grinned,

excited to see the results of the prank. It sounded hilarious to her.

The first picture was of the back of a man sitting at a desk, smoke rising from the keyboard in front of him.

For some reason, the hair on the back of Dakota's neck stood up.

She used her finger to quickly scroll to the next picture. The smoke was thicker in that one, but the camera was closer to the man sitting at the desk. She scrolled again—and her breath caught in her throat as she stared at it.

"Hilarious, isn't it?" Benny asked, misconstruing her reaction.

"T-this is Zach?" Dakota asked. "The guy who took Slade's place in the office?"

"Yup. Doesn't look like an admin guy, does he?" Benny asked rhetorically. "He was transferred over from another office, not sure which one, but he's completely hopeless. Hurt is about ready to boot his ass out, and the hell with whoever it was who pulled strings and got him the job. Before the smoke-bomb incident, the commander begged Cutter to come in this morning and show the guy how to do some simple shit. Of course your man agreed. He's such a perfectionist when it comes to his shit, and he was afraid Zach was fucking it up ten ways to Sunday."

Benny got up to refill his coffee cup, missing the

stricken look on Dakota's face.

Dakota tried to school her features. The last thing she wanted was to look panicked in front of Benny and Caroline. She was ninety percent sure that this Zach person and Aziz were one and the same, but she didn't want to jump the gun until she was positive.

She looked down at the pictures in front of her once again.

There was a lot of smoke obscuring the features of "Zach," but when she studied them again, she knew without a doubt the man who was doing Slade's job was none other than Aziz.

The man they'd been looking for had been right under their noses all along.

"Did you talk about me in the office? Say anything about why Slade was on a leave of absence?" Dakota asked Benny shakily.

"What do you mean?" he asked. His voice abruptly changed, from the happy-go-lucky tone he'd been using when talking about the joke they'd played on Zach to one of intense scrutiny.

Dakota had no doubt the SEALs were close-lipped about the missions they were sent on, but were they about other things? She knew how the employees had been in her office, they gossiped about lots of things, even sometimes confidential information they shouldn't be discussing.

"Hurt got us all together and told us Cutter was taking a leave of absence, but not why. We never discuss anything about our missions where we can be overheard by anyone without a need to know," Benny said, his tone serious now, his eyes watchful.

"Did anyone mention V-Vegas?" Dakota stammered.

Benny sat back down and leaned toward her, all business now, and looked into her eyes. "No. We might gossip like girls around each other, but we'd never share anything inappropriately. Our lives depend on secrecy What's wrong, Dakota? Talk to me."

Dakota had heard Slade talking with Tex enough to know they thought Aziz had to be somewhat good at technology, in order to track her to Rachel via her web searches, but what if that's not how he'd found her? What if he'd somehow been able to track *Slade*? They hadn't talked about the possibility of Slade's motorcycle having a tracker on it, or his supposedly secure phone, but Slade or Tex would've checked for that…right?

She shook her head and tried to control the panic trying to consume her. According to Wolf, Benny, and the other SEALs, they thought this Zach person knew nothing about computers. Either Aziz had help posting his anti-American and pro-terrorist stuff online, or he was one hell of an actor when he was at the base.

"Zach is Aziz," she whispered.

To give Benny credit, he didn't tell her she didn't know what she was talking about, that she was mistaken. He stared at her for a long moment, eyes narrowed, his jaw ticking, then looked down at the phone in his hand.

Just as he began to dial, the window over the kitchen sink shattered.

The security alarm immediately began shrieking, the sound ear piercing and painful.

As if in slow motion, Dakota saw Benny slump bonelessly onto the table, his phone falling face up with only three numbers keyed in.

Dakota noticed Caroline's mouth open and assumed she screamed, although she couldn't hear it over the noise of the alarm, and she saw her new friend whip her head toward the now-broken window.

Dakota never heard the man who broke into the house by kicking in a window in the other room. Never heard him approach as he came up behind her.

She'd just stood, her chair falling over with the force of her leap upward, when an arm wrapped around her neck, holding her tightly against a rock-hard body, and a hand with a chloroform-soaked rag covered her nose and mouth.

The last thing Dakota saw before losing consciousness was Caroline desperately struggling with a masked man who was dragging her into the other room.

Chapter Twelve

SLADE LOOKED AROUND his apartment, wanting to make sure he didn't need to come back for the foreseeable future. He'd grabbed enough clothes to last him for the time he needed to be gone. As long as he had a chance to do laundry, he'd be good. He picked up his extra pistol and ammo and even grabbed a couple of his knives.

When he'd been on the teams, he'd been known for his expertise with the latter. Both throwing and using them in hand-to-hand combat. It had been a while since he'd needed to use them, working a desk job wasn't exactly dangerous, but something told him that he should grab them today.

It was partly because he wanted to be prepared, but it was more than that. Tex's report of the video Fourati had posted about his "wife" making a statement soon wasn't sitting well. He knew Benny and Caroline were at the house with Dakota, but he still wouldn't be satisfied until he joined them and could see for himself that all was well.

His eyes swept over his living room, the weight of the knives in holsters at his ankles, small of his back, and at his waist comforting. Slade could see the waves lazily crashing against the shore as children played and their parents soaked in the sun. There were a few surfers in the water, crazy motherfuckers...it was damn cold outside, and he knew from experience the water was downright frigid.

He'd emptied his fridge and pantry of anything that would spoil and set the timers on a couple of lights to make it look like there was someone occupying the space. He didn't have a newspaper delivered, and he'd had his mail forwarded to Wolf's house. The other man said he'd make sure bills were paid and any important mail was taken care of if he needed to bug out with Dakota at any point.

Taking a deep breath, Slade took one last look around. He wanted Dakota *here*. In his space. In his kitchen. In his bed. She didn't have an apartment to go back to when the threat of Fourati was over, so he hoped he could convince her to move in with him. It was insane, their relationship was extremely new, but deep down, Slade didn't give a fuck. He wanted her with him.

Nodding, and telling himself to stop fucking around, Slade abruptly turned and left without a backward glance. Wolf was already headed home and said he'd meet him there. He locked his door and double-timed it to his Harley. He couldn't wait to see Dakota.

DAKOTA CAME AWAKE slowly. She groaned and turned her head. Her eyes opened into slits and she stared groggily at the sight before her. Caroline was lying on the concrete floor beside her. She was wearing a long black robe that covered her from her neck to her toes.

Seeing her new friend wearing such an odd piece of clothing was all it took for Dakota to remember exactly what had happened. She sat up and winced. Her head felt weird, probably a residual effect of whatever had been used to knock her out.

She looked down at herself and gasped in shock. She wasn't wearing a long black robe like Caroline; instead, she was dressed in what looked like some sort of traditional Middle Eastern dress. No, not really a dress.

She slowly stood, keeping one hand on the wall for balance, and glanced down at herself again. She was wearing a pair of beige silk baggy pants. So baggy it almost looked like she was wearing a skirt. Dakota fingered the material. It was soft and luxurious, and creepy as all get out. Covering her breasts—her naked breasts, she realized—was a bustier. It was elaborately embroidered with red and gold thread and had different kinds of gold sovereigns sewn into the pattern. A matching necklace with over a dozen of the small coins was around her neck and when she turned her head, Dakota could tell she had in a pair of earrings as well.

In addition to the necklace and earrings, each arm had at least six bracelets of varying widths and metals, and when she shifted where she stood, Dakota could feel the heavy weight of more adornments around her ankles. She was barefoot, and the concrete was cold against her toes. There was a beige bolt of silk on the floor next to where she'd been lying as well.

Dakota shivered. This could not be good.

Caroline hadn't moved, and Dakota shuffled across the small space to her, each step making the metal on her body clink together melodically. She kneeled down next to her friend and gently shook her. Caroline didn't respond.

Dakota looked around the room again. There was no furniture. It was simply a small room, concrete floors, and a rectangular window. The walls were white and, even as she strained to hear something, completely silent.

There was nothing to use as a weapon. Nothing that would help them escape. Nothing at all. Beginning to panic now, Dakota shook Caroline again, harder this time.

"Come on, wake up," Dakota begged in a whisper. "I'm scared."

As if her words were all the other woman had been waiting for, her eyes popped open as though she'd been faking sleep the entire time. Dakota could see recognition in Caroline's eyes, and was more relieved than she could remember being in a really long time when Caroline pushed up to a sitting position, put a hand to her head as if it hurt, and asked, "What happened?"

"I'm not sure. I think someone shot Benny, then they must've drugged us. The guys will be looking for us, right?"

"Fuck. Benny? God, I hope he's okay. Jessyka is gonna freak. But yes, I know the guys are looking for us," Caroline said confidentially. "Not only that, they'll be here sooner rather than later because…" Her voice trailed off as if she realized something vitally important.

"What? Why?"

"Where are my clothes?" Caroline asked.

"I don't know. When I woke up, I was dressed in this," Dakota said, gesturing to her elaborate and fancy outfit. "And you were in that robe."

"I'm completely naked under this," Caroline told Dakota. She fingered her earlobes. "And they took my jewelry."

Dakota didn't want to be a bitch, but worrying about some earrings and stuff was the least of their problems at the moment. "Me too," she told the other woman. "I mean, I'm wearing earrings now, but not the diamond studs I had on when we were taken."

"No, you don't understand," Caroline said gravely. "I had trackers on. I always wear those earrings because there are location trackers in them. In my bra, too."

"What? Why?" Dakota asked in shock.

"Because being the wife of a Navy SEAL isn't all fun and games. Me and my friends have had way too many close calls, and our guys had Tex make them for us. That way, if we're ever in trouble, we can be found."

She hadn't really understood *wanting* to wear a tracker, until right this second. "So no one knows where we are. They aren't coming."

"They are," Caroline countered. "But it's going to take longer than I thought because none of our clothes or jewelry are here. If they didn't change our clothes here, the trackers won't help our guys find us."

"Oh crap. Caroline, why are we dressed so differently?" Dakota asked, suddenly not liking her outfit at all.

"I don't know, but I'm thinking it can't be good." Caroline said exactly what Dakota had been thinking.

"Nothing about this is good," Dakota agreed. "What are we going to do?"

"What we *aren't* going to do is sit around like helpless females," Caroline said sternly and stood, shaking out the long black robe as she did. The garment swam on her frame. It didn't have a hood, but no skin other than her neck, face, and hands could be seen. "Look, as shitty as it is, I've been in this kind of situation before."

Dakota stared at Caroline in disbelief. "You have?"

"Yeah. And one thing I learned—okay, two things I learned are that we gotta be brave, and we have to do what we can to help ourselves."

"But there's nothing in this room. Nothing at all," Dakota countered.

"I see that," Caroline groused, wrinkling her nose as she looked around. Her eyes came back to Dakota's. "But *we're* in this room. We have to be ready for anything. I'm assuming Aziz is behind our little vacation."

Dakota nodded. "I'm so sorry. He's obsessed with me." A thought occurred to her. "Oh no."

"What?"

"He wants me to be his wife, to get me pregnant so I have a baby he can raise to be a terrorist."

"Fuck," Caroline whispered. "Are you wearing a wedding outfit?"

Dakota gulped and confirmed, "I think so."

Caroline grabbed her arm and leaned in, urgency clear in her tone. "Do you know my story?"

Not understanding, Dakota merely shook her head.

"Okay, we don't have a lot of time, but suffice it to say, I went through a lot of shit, but I got out of it, and we will both get out of this. Matthew and Slade will be coming for us. We have to hang on for them, and we have to be smart and help them find us if given the opportunity."

"I don't understand."

"One thing I learned is that assholes like to taunt our men. They like to show off the fact that they got one over on the SEALs. I don't know what's going to happen, but if Aziz dressed you up like that, he's probably going to want to record your so-called wedding for his followers. And that means a video. And that means he'll probably put it online so he can show you off."

Dakota shivered. She didn't want to be on film and she *definitely* didn't want to marry Aziz. She closed her eyes in despair for a moment, then squared her shoulders. If Caroline wasn't panicking, she wouldn't either. "What's the plan?"

Not knowing how long they had until someone came to get them, Caroline spoke quickly. Giving Dakota a brief history of what had happened to her and what she'd done to try to help Wolf find her. Neither of the women knew what Aziz's plan was, but they wanted to be ready for anything.

By the time the door opened and two men entered, they had a plan...of sorts. They'd been able to look out the window and make some observations about where they might be. They might not have a physical weapon, but they had their brains. Neither knew what curve balls would be thrown their way, but Dakota felt better knowing she wasn't going to simply cower in a corner and cry. She might not make it out alive, but she certainly wouldn't go down without a fight either.

SLADE PULLED UP to Wolf's house, and the hair on the back of his neck immediately stood up. He whipped off his helmet and ran to the kitchen door. Wolf was in the middle of his kitchen crouched by Benny, who was lying on his back on the tan tile, unmoving.

"What the fuck?" Slade bit out, joining Wolf at his teammate's side.

"Dart," Wolf told him, motioning to the needle lying next to the unconscious SEAL.

Without a word, Slade stood and left the room. He searched Wolf's house from top to bottom, calling out for both Caroline and Dakota. He had hoped the women were hiding somewhere, but by the time he got back to the kitchen, he knew his greatest fear had been realized.

"How in the fuck did this happen?" he asked, running a hand through his hair in agitation. He'd failed Dakota. He'd told her nothing would happen to her. That she'd be safe. That Fourati wouldn't get his hands on her. And he'd been wrong on all counts.

"Window over the sink is broken. My guess is that whoever shot Benny, did so through it. His phone was lying on the table, the first three numbers of my cell punched in."

"Why didn't the alarm go off?" Slade asked, pissed off.

"It did," Wolf replied in a tone that said he was barely keeping his shit together. "But my motherfucking override code was punched in. It's why I wasn't notified."

"Who knows your code?"

"The team. Caroline. And you and Dakota. That's it."

"There has to be someone else," Slade insisted.

"There isn't," Wolf told him.

"What about the neighbors?" Slade asked. "Wouldn't they have called the cops?"

"Not necessarily. Sometimes Caroline doesn't get to the code fast enough to shut it off. The neighbors used to call the cops when it first happened, but they've learned not to by now."

"Fuck," Slade swore.

"Whatever happened, the women were incapacitated quickly. I've taught Ice self-defense. She wouldn't go quietly. She knows better. I'm calling Tex." Wolf clicked some buttons on his cell and brought it up to his ear.

Something Slade had seen when he'd been frantically searching the house clicked in his brain, and he rushed out of the kitchen to the front hallway.

There on the floor were two piles of clothes and accessories.

He recognized the jeans and T-shirt he'd bought Dakota the day before. She'd been so pleased with his choices of clothing for her. Slade heard Wolf come up behind him and say, "God *damn* it. Pick up, Tex. Dammit, pick up."

Slade looked down at the clothes the woman he loved had most likely put on that morning and felt his heart encase in ice. They'd stripped her. Taken all her clothes off and left them on the floor. They had plenty of time to do it too, especially since apparently, no one had alerted the cops. He had no idea why they'd removed her clothes. To rape her? To taunt him? Any semblance of the man he'd become after getting out of the teams, any softness he'd built up as a result of being away from the death and destruction men could do to one another, disappeared. All that was left was the highly trained killer the Navy had created.

Slade knew Dakota was probably hurt. Not only that, but Fourati had touched what was his, he knew that without a doubt. He'd been determined to kill the man before, but now the outcome of their meeting was a certainty. Fourati would fucking die. The pile of clothing before him was the catalyst.

"Tex? Wolf. Track Caroline now," the other man ordered tersely.

Seconds passed, but they seemed like hours to both men.

Slade's jaw ticked as he continued to stare at the piles of clothes on the floor. He tried to block out the thoughts of what Dakota was going through, but couldn't. Slade had seen too many broken women after they'd been in the hands of terrorists. He'd see too many rape victims staring into space, shells of their former selves. The thought of his Dakota being that way was abhorrent. The hate in his soul bubbled and festered.

"She's there in the house," Tex said through the phone speaker.

"No, she's not. We checked," Wolf bit out.

"All of the trackers are showing her location right there," Tex insisted. "What the fuck is going on?"

Without answering his friend, Wolf kneeled next to his wife's clothing and, using only his index finger, separated each item. Shirt, pants, underwear, bra...and on the bottom were her wedding ring set, a necklace she always wore, and a pair of earrings.

"They're here," Wolf said, standing up but still looking down at his wife's belongings. "All her trackers are here. How in the fuck did they know about them?" Wolf asked in an eerie tone. It was almost calm, but Slade and Tex could hear the absolute fury behind it.

Instead of answering, Tex asked Slade, "You get Dakota's trackers yet, Cutter?"

"No. But it wouldn't fucking matter if I did, because those fuckers took off not only every piece of clothing, but her jewelry as well. In case we're not making this clear, they stripped our women of every fucking thing they were wearing before they left this house. You need to get on your computer, hack into every fucking satellite, computer, and phone in a sixty-mile radius and fucking find them. Now!" His voice had risen with each progressive word until he was shouting the last.

"Fuck, I need to call Lambert," Slade added. "I know this job was supposed to be unsanctioned, but I swear to Christ if he doesn't get the VP and president involved, he'll be sorry."

"I'm on this," Tex reassured Slade. "*I'll* call Lambert."

"This isn't your job," Slade told his friend.

"Maybe, maybe not. But I gave your name to Lambert in the first place. I'll call and fill him in on what's going on and make sure you have all the assistance you need to find Caroline and Dakota."

"Fuck," Slade repeated, not sure he could come up

with anything more coherent at the moment.

"If it makes you feel any better, Fourati doesn't want to kill Dakota," Tex tried to reassure his friend.

"Yeah," Slade said bitterly. "He only wants to rape her over and over until she's pregnant."

"And he might not want to hurt Dakota, but he doesn't give a shit about Ice. Why did he take her too?" Wolf added.

Both men could hear Tex's fingers clicking on the keys of his computer in the background. The sound was usually comforting, but at the moment it was anything but. Not when their women were in the wind.

"Call me back the second you have anything," Wolf ordered. "I gotta check on Benny. I've already called for an ambulance."

"What happened to Benny?" Tex barked. "God-damn. What the *fuck* is going on?"

"That's what *we* want to know," Wolf said, then relented. "I found Benny facedown on my kitchen table, a dart in his neck."

"I'll be in contact," Tex said, and ended the connection.

Wolf and Slade looked at each other for a long moment. As if they'd worked together for years, the men turned at the same time and headed back through the living room to the kitchen.

They both noticed the broken window, obviously

where entry was made into the house, but ignored it; not that it mattered now. They needed to get medical help for Benny and they needed to gather the team.

Slade thought about how Lambert had said the mission was to be a solo one and frowned. He'd definitely blown that to hell and back.

Screw it. He'd already told Wolf and some of the other guys most of the story. He needed as much help as he could get right now. Besides, it wasn't just Dakota on the line. Caroline was involved up to her neck right now too. There was no way Wolf's men would sit back and do nothing.

Slade didn't care if Lambert refused to pay him a dime. Nothing mattered but Dakota. He'd end the threat of Aziz Fourati to the American public, but more important, he'd end the threat to his woman.

Slade fingered the knife strapped to his waist absently as he kneeled down next to Benny. Fourati was going to get an up close and personal lesson on why Slade's nickname was Cutter. His knife would be the last thing the man ever thought about…as it severed his carotid artery and his blood spilled on the ground.

Chapter Thirteen

D AKOTA STOOD SILENT and still, eyes full of tears she refused to shed, and prayed for all she was worth.

Two men had come to collect her and Caroline, and they hadn't been gentle about it. Both women had struggled and strained against their captors' holds, with no luck. When Caroline had kneed one guy in the balls, her effort hampered by the voluminous folds of the robe she was wearing, he'd backhanded her so hard she'd stumbled backward and fell on her ass.

Seeing her new friend fall, Dakota lost it and fought for all *she* was worth, trying to gouge out the eyes of the man holding her. But he'd avoided her fingers and had turned, ramming her forehead against the nearest wall. She'd seen stars and had lost any advantage she might've had.

Both she and Caroline had been brought into another room, where Dakota saw Aziz for the first time since that awful day at the airport.

The man she knew as Aziz Fourati was definitely the same person the SEALs knew as Zach, she'd recognized him immediately in Benny's pictures. She had no idea how in the world he'd gotten a job as a contractor for the Navy, or passed the background checks, but ultimately it didn't matter. He had, and now she was back in his clutches.

Dakota shivered in fear. All of her nightmares were coming true, but she wasn't dreaming this time. Slade wasn't there to kiss her awake, to hold her tightly and tell her everything would be okay. Thoughts of Slade bolstered her. She remembered what Caroline had said. She had to keep it together so she could help Slade and his friends find her. That was the ultimate goal.

"Ah, beautiful Dakota, it's so good to see you again. Your wedding outfit is absolutely stunning," Aziz said. The man holding her stopped in front of Aziz so she had no choice but to look at him.

"I wish I could say it's good to see *you* again," she retorted snarkily.

He made a tsking noise, as if she were a recalcitrant child rather than a grown woman. "I was so hoping you'd come to your senses. I gave you time to think about what your destiny was and to come to terms with it. I'm disappointed that you're still fighting it, fighting me. You *will* become my wife today. You *will* have my children. And you *will* stop defying me. Those three things I guarantee you."

Dakota fought down the urge to throw up. She raised her chin and spat at him. The spittle didn't quite make its mark, but the feelings behind it definitely did.

The amused look on his face disappeared and Dakota got a glimpse of the killer she'd seen in the airport all those weeks ago.

"Your intended doesn't have many manners," someone said from behind her.

Aziz curled his lip in derision at her. "She will. Take a seat, my bride," he ordered in a gruff tone.

Dakota had no intention of doing anything he said, but she didn't have a choice. The man behind her manhandled her over to a chair and forced her to sit. He then held her down while two other men quickly zip-tied her ankles to the legs.

Her heart beat overtime in her chest. She really didn't like the feeling of being tied and helpless in Aziz's presence. At least if she was sitting, he couldn't rape her...could he? She glanced to her right and saw Caroline being held between two men. Each had hold of an arm and had wrenched it upward so she was standing awkwardly on her tiptoes. Dakota could see a bruise forming on her cheek where she'd been hit, and the small mark made her stomach clench in concern. They'd stuffed a piece of fabric into her mouth and taped her lips together. The noises she was making were muffled and weak.

Seeing Caroline helpless and in pain, hurt. She had to remember that it wasn't just her in this situation. No matter how often Slade had told her she was brave, at that moment, Dakota didn't feel brave. But strangely, having Caroline there with her made her feel better. If she'd been by herself, she would've been completely freaking out. She was scared shitless, there was no doubt about that, but she made a vow that she wasn't going to calmly do whatever Aziz said. She couldn't. The longer she could drag whatever this was out, the longer Slade and his friends had to find her and Caroline. She could take what he dished out.

"Here's what's going to happen," Aziz said, his calm demeanor once more at the forefront. "We're going to have a wedding ceremony. You'll sit there calmly and answer affirmatively when prompted. If you say or do *anything* that gives the impression you don't want to become my bride, you'll regret it."

"I won't marry you," Dakota said with less force than she wanted, tugging at her arms which were being held down by the two men who had restrained her ankles to the chair. "This is insane. *You're* insane."

Aziz didn't respond to her comment, but shook his head as if disappointed. "You don't want to make me angry, my bride."

"Why not? What are you going to do? Hit me? Blow

up the building? Rape me? You're going to do the last anyway. Go ahead. Do it. If you wanted a docile wife, you picked the wrong woman."

"I was kind of hoping you'd be this way," Aziz said strangely. "I knew you had passion and spunk when I saw you in the airport. I watched you for a while, you know," he said conversationally. "I decided you were there at the exact time I was for a reason. To be mine. I followed you, making sure I didn't make a move until you were in my web. You tried to think of something to do that would stop the inevitable. It was brave of you, but too little too late, I'm afraid."

Dakota looked at him in horror. He'd followed her in the airport? He'd waited to take hostages until he knew he could take her too?

Wanting to think about anything but what he was saying, Dakota looked around. The men in the room with them were a mixture of American and Middle Eastern. They obviously knew Aziz wasn't Tunisian, but didn't care. They all looked to be in their late teens or twenties. Aziz was wearing what looked like something a traditional Tunisian would wear. Some sort of long shirt which went all the way down to his knees. It had a deep vee in front and he had on a maroon silk shirt under it. His pants were also maroon. If she wasn't mistaken, the same embroidery pattern on his long shirt was on her own clothing. He wore a pair of pointed leather slippers and a close-fitting red cap on his head made of what looked like felt, with a black tassel hanging from it.

Dakota's breaths came short and fast. Aziz also looked like he was dressed for a wedding. It wasn't that she'd thought he was bluffing earlier, but now that she'd had a moment to think about what he'd said and take in what he was wearing, it was obvious he really did want to marry her right this minute. Aziz wouldn't ever pass for a Middle Eastern man, no matter what he was wearing. The government had simply assumed he was, based on his website and posts. She flinched when he began speaking again.

"There will be a time when I'll encourage your passion. A time when I'll crave your fingernails in my skin. It'll only make my taking of you all the more…exciting. But, alas, today is not that day. Today I need you to be a proper Arabic wife. It's important to show my recruits that I am in charge of all things, including the woman who will be my wife." He stepped closer and knelt at her feet. His hands went to her thighs and he slowly but surely pushed them apart.

Dakota tried with all her strength to keep her legs together, but she was no match for Aziz's strength. His hands squeezed her thighs with enough pressure to make her wince, but she controlled it and didn't give him any outward sign that he was hurting her.

He smiled, a scary, wide expression that made Dakota shiver in revulsion.

"Your name is now Anoushka," he informed her. "It means lovely or gracious. From here on out, that is what I will call you and that is what you will call yourself. You will never answer to your heathen American name again. Your new life starts right now, Anoushka. You will be the revered wife of the leader of Ansar al-Shari'a. You will learn how to please and serve me. Everyone and everything you've known is now a thing of the past."

"I will never serve you," Dakota told him. "You can rape me, beat me, and lock me up, but when you least expect it, I'll stab you in the back. You'll never be able to drop your guard because I'll do anything possible to take *you* down."

"Such a pity," Aziz said without a trace of worry in his tone. "I mean, do you really think you, a mere woman, can take down a chosen one such as myself?"

"I'm not scared of you," Dakota said. "And you're no more a chosen one than I am."

"Will you cooperate for our wedding ceremony?" Aziz asked as if she hadn't spoken.

"Never," she vowed.

"Pity," Aziz repeated, shrugging. He squeezed her legs once more, hard enough that Dakota did wince that time, and smiled. He stood and motioned to one of the men standing against the wall.

"Not even if you're beaten?" he asked.

As soon as the last word left his mouth, the man he'd gestured to turned sideways and kicked out at her with the bottom of his foot. It made contact with her knee and Dakota shrieked in pain. It felt as if he'd broken something, or at the very least tore a tendon. She'd never felt such pain before in her life. For a moment, all she could think about was the radiating waves of agony from her leg. She forgot where she was and forgot Aziz had even asked her a question.

"Will you cooperate for our wedding ceremony? Aziz asked again.

The tears Dakota had been holding back fell down her cheeks, but she shook her head at him in defiance.

Aziz nodded at the man again, and he once again kicked her in the knee. The same knee.

Black spots crept into her vision and Dakota thought she was going to pass out. Welcomed the black void in fact. Aziz reached forward and grabbed hold of one of her nipples through the bustier, and twisted. Dakota struggled against the men who were holding her arms and tried to turn away from Aziz. His fingers pinched harder as he leaned toward her and put his face inches from her own.

"I can do this all night until you agree," he warned.

Even though the pain was worse than anything she'd ever experienced in her life, Dakota glared up at Aziz and panted, "I can take whatever you dish out. I will never marry you!" She hoped she sounded brave and strong rather than desperate and on the verge of giving in to whatever he wanted.

At her words, Aziz abruptly let go of her nipple. He stood in front of her, his hands clasped behind his back. One side of his mouth quirked up into a lopsided grin and he said, "That's what I thought you'd say. My woman is strong."

Dakota kept her eyes on his and refused to look down at her chest to see if her nipple was still attached. It was throbbing and literally felt as if he'd ripped it off. She breathed through the pain and tried to remember to be brave. Caroline had said she needed to be strong, and dammit, she was trying.

Aziz gestured behind him again—and this time the men who had been holding a squirming Caroline came forward with her between them.

Dakota's eyes widened. What was Aziz planning now?

"Since I knew you would endure whatever I did to you, I made sure to have a plan B," Aziz said. He walked over to a small table Dakota hadn't noticed before now. He stood in front of it so she couldn't see what lie on top. His back was to her, contemplating whatever was on the table top, and asked once more, "Will you cooperate for our wedding ceremony?"

"No," Dakota whispered, truly afraid now.

Without another word, Aziz picked something up from the table and turned. But instead of heading for her, he went to Caroline.

In horror, Dakota watched as he grabbed the hair at the back of Caroline's head and tilted it backward. She tried to kick and lash out, but a fourth man knelt behind her and wrapped both his arms around her knees, effectively hobbling her.

Holding the knife he'd picked up from the table, Aziz put it against Caroline's throat. He turned to stare straight at Dakota while slowly drawing the knife downward. The robe the other woman was wearing slit as easily as if Aziz was cutting a piece of aged and tender beef.

When he was done, Caroline stood exposed from her neck to her knees. She was completely naked under the garment and her body was now on full display for everyone in the room.

Dakota strained against both the hold of the men and the bindings around her ankles. Suddenly her knee didn't hurt at all anymore. He was going to hurt Caroline because of her. "Stop it!" she ordered breathlessly.

"I can't wait to sink inside your lush body, Anoushka. You will provide me with many hours of enjoyment. However, I am not a greedy leader. Once you carry the heir to Ansar al-Shari'a, I am willing to allow my most trusted and brave warriors to share in the bounty I have been given." Aziz's beady blue eyes met her own. "I see you understand. I like to share, my bride. I have no problem watching as each and every man who vows loyalty to me and our cause takes a turn with you."

"No," Dakota said in a voice barely audible. His words were too much to bear.

"Yes, Anoushka. Your only job from here on out is to please and obey me. In all things. You will go to your knees in my presence, you will allow me to take you whenever and wherever I want. You will spread your legs for anyone I give you to, willingly. You will not struggle when I want to film myself filling your body with the gift of life. And if you don't? I think I'll keep this one around to make sure you understand what will happen if you disobey me."

Aziz let go of Caroline's hair and ran the tip of the knife between her breasts once more, a slim line of blood welling up in its wake.

"No. Stop it!" Dakota ordered, once again struggling to escape the grasp of the men next to her. "This is insane!"

"Will you cooperate for our wedding ceremony?" Aziz asked once again.

Dakota knew Aziz wasn't kidding. He knew she'd continue to refuse him no matter what he did to *her*. She'd rather die than marry him. But there was no way

she'd be able to sit there and watch him torture someone else. He would keep Caroline around if only as a
means to an end...namely, Dakota doing whatever
depraved thing he wanted.

Apparently deciding she hadn't answered soon
enough, Aziz went back to the table and put down the
knife and picked up something else. He took the few
steps back to Caroline.

"Wait, please stop!" Dakota begged.

Aziz ignored her and held up a small pair of needle-
nose pliers. He grinned a sadistic grin then turned to
Caroline once more.

"I'll cooperate," Dakota yelled desperately. "I'll marry you! I'll say whatever you want me to, just leave her
alone!" she went on, trying to make him step away from
Caroline. The other woman had already been through
too much at the hands of another evil man. There was
no way Dakota was going to make her go through
anything like that ever again. Not if she could prevent it.

Without moving away from Caroline, Aziz turned
his head toward her. "Ah, Anoushka, those are the
words I want to hear. But how do I know you mean
them?" He moved the pliers toward Caroline once more
and her screech of fright was easy to hear through the
gag.

"You knew I wouldn't let you hurt anyone else on
my behalf. Let her go and let's get this over with,"

Dakota said as calmly as she could. She couldn't look at Caroline's face anymore, but out of the corner of her eye she saw the other woman shaking her head desperately. Dakota didn't know if she was saying no to the pain Aziz wanted to inflict on her or to her words. But it didn't matter. Aziz would torture Caroline until Dakota did what he wanted anyway. She would spare her friend the pain.

Dakota knew good and well Aziz wasn't going to let Caroline go after he married her. He'd flat-out told her he was going to keep the other woman around to use as incentive if he wanted her to do something. And she'd do whatever he said. She could handle pain, but she couldn't handle him hurting Caroline because of her refusals.

Aziz let go of Caroline and stepped back. He handed the pliers to one of his cronies and walked back to Dakota.

She held his eyes, hating him with everything she had.

"You've made me a very happy man, Anoushka," Aziz told her in what could've been a tender tone. "A word of warning, just to make sure you understand, if you do *anything* to bring dishonor to our wedding ceremony, I won't hesitate to pause and show little Ice over there what pain truly is."

"I understand," Dakota told him, not even questioning how he knew Caroline's nickname. He knew everything else about her and the SEALs, why wouldn't he know that too? She might have to marry Aziz, but she hadn't lost hope that Slade and his friends would find them. She just wished they'd do so before her wedding night. They had to.

If Aziz violated her, Dakota knew she'd never be the same again. Oh sure, she'd survive it, but something inside her would die. She'd never feel clean again and would forever lose her chance to belong to Slade.

I'm trying to be strong, she silently told the man who meant everything to her, *but I don't know if I can do this. Please, come get me.*

Chapter Fourteen

S LADE PACED BACK and forth in Wolf's living room as they waited for Tex to get back to them. Benny was at the hospital. He'd still been completely out when he'd been taken away by the ambulance. His heartbeat was strong and the paramedics seemed to think he'd been drugged, not poisoned, as a result. They'd have to wait for whatever had been used to knock him out to wear off before they could get any information about what had happened right before the women were taken.

The other men on Wolf's team had assembled. Abe, Cookie, and Dude were in the kitchen. Mozart, the sixth man on the team, was holed up with the women and children. None of the men were going to risk anyone else being put into the line of fire. Even though Slade knew Mozart wanted to be with them, helping to rescue Caroline and Dakota and catch whoever had shot Benny, they all knew the other women and kids were just as important right now. The last thing they wanted was Fourati getting ahold of them too.

Commander Hurt was dealing with the police and keeping the authorities away so the SEALs could plan. He was a good man, one who knew when to bend the rules and to look the other way.

Slade didn't give a shit who was involved at this point. As far as he was concerned, the more the merrier. These men had been through this too many times to count. Their women had been in danger one too many times. Slade needed their expertise as warriors, and husbands, to help get Dakota back. If he got in trouble with Greg Lambert, so be it. He was just so frustrated with the entire situation. All he wanted was Dakota, and Caroline, back safe and unhurt.

His phone rang and Slade answered immediately, putting it on speaker so everyone could hear the conversation.

"Cutsinger."

"It's Tex." He didn't wait for acknowledgement. "There's a new video being streamed. It's live."

Slade gestured wildly at Wolf and the man ran into another room and came back with a laptop.

"I've sent everyone a link to the URL. I'm not sure how stable or secure the site is, but for as long as it's up, I'm recording it."

Slade didn't respond, just watched impatiently as Wolf brought up his email, then clicked on the link Tex sent.

The room fell silent as what they were seeing sank in.

Dakota was sitting in a chair, some sort of beige silk shawl around her shoulders and head. Sitting in front of her, with his back to the camera, was a man. He also had a shawl over his head and shoulders. Not one inch of his skin or hair was visible to the camera.

Dude commented, "He's being very careful to keep his identity a secret."

"There's no way to tell what he looks like from this angle," Abe agreed.

Slade ground his teeth together and clenched his fists at his side. He didn't give a shit about Fourati at the moment. All his attention was on Dakota. She looked at the face of the man sitting in front of her, her back ramrod straight, and didn't move a muscle. Someone in the background was speaking, probably in Arabic, but Slade didn't hear any of it. He tried to figure out what Dakota was thinking instead.

She looked scared...and pissed. Seeing how angry she was made him relax a fraction. If she was upset, then she wasn't broken...yet.

"Where's Caroline?" Wolf asked no one in particular as the video continued. The camera didn't waver, as if it was on a tripod or some other sturdy surface.

Slade had no idea what a traditional Tunisian wedding ceremony was like, but when someone off camera began to speak in English, he figured it wasn't this.

"Do you, Anoushka, take Aziz Fourati as your husband? Do you promise to obey and follow his every command? Will you defend him over all others, even give your life for him and the cause of Ansar Al-Shari'a?"

"Yes," Dakota said immediately.

Slade frowned. Why had she agreed so easily? What had Fourati done to her to make her so compliant?

The voice off camera continued. "Do you promise your womb to the Ansar al-Shari'a cause? Will you freely and willingly take your husband's sacred fluid into your body to create the next supreme ruler?"

"Yes," Dakota said again.

Slade saw her flinch this time, but she kept eye contact with the man in front of her.

"Aziz, the woman in front of you is now yours to do with what you want. Yours to punish, yours to praise, yours to worship. She will give the cause their next leader and we will praise this day for years to come. This is the beginning of Ansar al-Shari'a's reign of supremacy. So it shall be."

The man sitting in front of Dakota bowed his head, then kneeled on the floor in front of Dakota. He did something they couldn't see because of the angle of the camera, and Slade wanted to reach through the computer screen and snatch Dakota away from him when her lip curled in disgust at whatever he was doing.

The voice off camera then began to speak in Arabic once more. The man Dakota had apparently just married moved sideways out of range without once turning his face to the camera.

The person speaking in the background went silent and the camera zoomed in on Dakota. She glanced to her left, winced again, then looked back at the camera. Then she began to speak. Her voice was flat and had no intonation whatsoever. It was obvious she was reading something held up in front of her, off camera, word for word.

My name is Anoushka Fourati. My husband, Aziz Fourati, is the leader, chosen by God, of Ansar al-Shari'a. I am honored to have been chosen to carry his offspring, the future of our movement. God willing, this child will be born to all of us in due haste. In the meantime, carry on the fight. Do not let the heathens of this country lead you astray. Our time is coming. We need more soldiers. I am willing to die for my husband, for my God, and for Ansar al-Shari'a. Are you? Will you ascend to heaven to be with our God, or will you spend the rest of eternity in the pits of hell with the other citizens of this country who don't believe? Stay tuned for more instructions. Long live Aziz Fourati.

Dakota remained seated, her legs apart, her hands

gripping the arms of the chair she was sitting in. Her face blank of all emotion. The last thing Slade saw before the screen went blank was Dakota's eyes looking off to the left of the camera once more, her head nodding once.

"What the ever-loving fuck?" Wolf exclaimed. "Where's Ice? Did we just watch Cutter's woman marry that asshole Fourati? Tex, you better have something," he finished in a cold, hard voice.

"I'm sending a copy of the video to all of you now," Tex answered.

"And?" Slade asked. "Where are they? Did you trace the feed?"

"It's untraceable," Tex said reluctantly. "They've got a really good tech person."

"Tex, *you're* a really fucking good tech person," Cookie said. "I can't believe you can't get a lead on this guy."

"Tex," Slade said softly with desperation in his tone. "We've got nothing. No tracker. Fourati made sure of that. We don't even have a picture of this guy. All we know is that he's blond and American. We need more. You *have* to find him."

"I'm trying," Tex told his old friend. "Swear to Christ, I'm trying."

"She just married him," Slade whispered. "He's going to rape her. I don't know how he's controlling her, but if we don't get there, fucking soon, he's going to hurt the woman I love. She won't be the same if he gets his hands on her."

"I don't have a definitive trace," Tex said, all business, "but I do know it's coming from your area. The signal is bouncing around like crazy, but it's pinging off all local towers and servers. He's not far. One, he didn't have time to get that far away, and two, he has to have an inside connection to you guys. He wouldn't have known about the trackers if he didn't."

Relieved now that Tex seemed to have his head back in the game, Slade sat back and listened as he spoke with Wolf and the rest of the guys.

"He'd need to use local power to be able to broadcast. The kind of thing he's doing can't be done with a simple modem. The camera set up they have is more sophisticated than a simple cell phone and broadcasting via Facebook Live. And wherever they are, it's not in the middle of nowhere," Tex said, talking more to himself than anyone else.

"The room they were in was concrete," Cookie added.

"And what about her clothes? Those aren't exactly found in the local Walmart. Maybe they were special ordered," Abe suggested.

"Yeah," Tex nodded enthusiastically. "I'll do a search for online orders of traditional Tunisian clothing."

"The camera equipment isn't shit either," Wolf noted. "The video almost sounded and looked professional."

"Got it," Tex said. "I'll look for purchases of video stuff too. Maybe we'll get lucky."

"We don't have a choice," Slade said. "We *have* to get lucky."

"Tex, we're going to review the footage. See if anything stands out. Can you take out the voices and see if there's any background noise that will help point us to their location? Vehicles, boats, planes, fucking birds, *anything*," Wolf said.

"Will do," Tex agreed. "I'll see if I can pick up anyone else talking behind the scenes as well. Sometimes people whisper behind the camera, thinking they can't be heard. I'll also see if I can pinpoint who else was watching the feed. Maybe some of his recruits have information and we can backtrack to Fourati through them. Later."

Slade clicked off the phone.

Wolf immediately sat on the couch with his laptop. "You guys remember when Ice gave us a huge hint as to where she was being held when the asshole who took her filmed a beating he gave her? She might've talked to Dakota and it's possible she did the same."

"Yeah, Caroline talked about gulls and boats, which

led us to look near the coast. Dakota is smart, she could've done that too," Dude said softly.

The men gathered around the laptop, eager to watch and listen to the video again to see what clues they could find in Dakota's speech. At this point, it was all they had to go on.

Thirty minutes later, and twenty-two replays of the footage, Slade couldn't take it any longer. He'd been holding on to his composure by the skin of his teeth, but if he heard his Dakota call herself Anoushka Fourati one more time, he was gonna fucking lose it.

He pushed up from the couch and paced in agitation. "There's nothing there. She was reading word for word from a script. She was too scared to say anything outside of whatever he wrote down for her," Slade said in frustration, resisting the urge to punch the wall…barely.

"There has to be something. Did you see how she looked to the left immediately before she spoke and again before the tape cut off? Who or what was she looking at?" Dude asked.

"She could've been looking at one of Fourati's flunkies who was holding a gun on her, making sure he approved of her speech," Abe said with a shrug.

"Or she could've just been desperate to look anywhere but at the camera," Cookie suggested.

Slade tuned the men out. Wolf started the video for

the twenty-third time. Slade knew the man was as desperate as he was to find something, *anything*. His wife was out there somewhere, just as Dakota was. At least Slade had seen with his own eyes that Dakota was physically okay for the moment. Wolf didn't even have that. They didn't even know for sure that Caroline was still alive. With every minute that passed, the women seemed to be slipping away.

Slade stood behind the couch and stared at the computer screen over the heads of the other SEALs. He couldn't quite hear what Dakota was saying, but it didn't matter because he had her fucking speech memorized by now anyway.

For a moment, something registered in his mind as he watched her, but the fleeting thought was gone almost as soon as it appeared.

He tilted his head and concentrated on the computer screen harder.

Dakota sat with her back ramrod straight in the chair. The beige shawl draped over her forehead rustled in a small breeze in whatever room she was in. He could see a faint blue mark on her head, the beginnings of a bruise. *Fucker put his hands on her. Hurt her. He'll pay for that along with everything else.*

Dakota's hands were in constant motion as she spoke, as if the hand gestures would help get her point across to the fuckers who were watching. It was odd.

Slade hadn't noticed that she used her hands when she'd talked to him over the last few days. She was more likely to clasp her hands together when she told him something important, not wave them around distractedly.

That was it.

"Start it over," Slade ordered.

"But—" Wolf began to protest.

"I said, start it over," Slade repeated. "And turn off the fucking sound."

Without another word, Wolf did as Slade requested. The video began to play once more and Slade concentrated on Dakota's hand movements, staring at her with intense concentration.

"What are we looking for?" Dude asked into the now silent room.

"I don't know for sure," Slade said when the video finished. "It's just a hunch. Again, Wolf."

The other SEAL did as Slade asked and started the video over again.

Slade narrowed his eyes. He was missing something. "But what?"

"Holy fuck," Cookie whispered. He turned to Slade. "Does Dakota know sign language?"

Slade shrugged. "I have no idea. Fuck, I don't know much about her at all. Don't know where she grew up, how old she was when she lost her virginity, what foods she doesn't like and what she does, if she—"

"I'm pretty sure she's signing," Cookie interrupted before Slade could go off on a tangent. "We've only had a couple of classes with Cooper, but I would swear what Dakota is doing with her hands looks an awful lot like Kiera and Coop when they're signing to each other."

"Holy shit, I think you're right," Slade said, wishing fervently they'd had time to have Cooper give them more classes in sign language now.

The five men turned back to the screen and watched with intense concentration.

"Fuck me," Wolf breathed. "She *is*. She's talking to us with her hands, not words."

Slade pulled out his phone and dialed.

"Hurt."

"I need Coop's number."

"On it," the commander said immediately. "What's up?"

"I'm watching a video of my woman, who just married fucking Aziz Fourati, and she sent me a message, but I need someone who knows sign language to tell me what the fuck she's saying."

"Hang on, I'm settin' up a group call," Hurt said, and the phone went silent.

Within a minute, the commander was back. "I'm here, and I have Coop and Kiera," he said.

"I need your secure email," Slade demanded of Cooper. The man might be retired, and spending his time with kids at the deaf school his girlfriend worked at rather than killing bad guys, but he hadn't lost any of his edge, if the immediate acquiescence was any indication.

Slade gestured to Wolf, and the other man slid the laptop over. Slade punched in the email Cooper had given him. "I'm sending a video," Slade told the soft-spoken woman and the retired SEAL. "Don't bother with the sound. It's irrelevant. She's using sign language. I need you to tell me what Dakota is trying to tell us."

"What happened, did—" Kiera started to ask, but was interrupted by Slade.

"I don't have time to answer your questions, and I'm sorry I'm being so abrupt. But while you pull up the video, I can tell you that we're dealing with a life-or-death situation. A terrorist kidnapped Caroline Steel. My woman was with her and was just forced to marry a really fuckin' bad man, but we have no idea where they are. I can get them back if you help me figure out what she's trying to tell me. Can you *please* help me?"

"Of course we will," Kiera said immediately. "Cooper is bringing up the video now."

The men in Wolf's living room heard keys clicking through the phone speaker and they waited as Kiera and Cooper watched the film.

"Well?" Slade asked when an appropriate amount of time had gone by for the video to have played all the way through.

"I'm learning quickly, but I think this is outside my expertise. I'll let Kiera take the lead on this one," Cooper told the men.

"Holy crap," Kiera breathed.

"What?"

"Wait, give me a second?" Kiera asked, sounding uncertain. "Let me watch it again to be sure. Some of the signs are slurred."

"How can a hand signal be slurred?" Abe asked quietly.

"She's not being precise with them. That's one of the first things interpreters are taught. Signs should be crisp and unmistakable. Think of it as annunciating when you speak. She's not annunciating because she's trying to be sly and hide the signs in her wild gestures, they're not clear," Kiera explained.

"Deep breath, baby," the men heard Cooper say quietly. "You can do this."

After several moments went by, Kiera finally said, "It looks to me as if she's spelling something in the beginning when she first starts speaking."

"What?" Wolf blurted, his tone communicating how urgent the situation was.

"Z-A-K is what I think she's signing in the first part. Three letters. She does it at least twice."

No one said a word for a long moment, and Kiera

continued. "I don't know what she's trying to tell you though, sorry."

"Wait!" Cookie exclaimed, and sprang up from the couch and ran into the kitchen. He came back holding Benny's cell phone. He typed in the code—all the guys had the same password on their phones for cases just such as this—and closed the keypad to reveal the last thing Benny had been looking at before being shot with the dart.

He showed the picture to the group.

"Yeah, we know someone named Zach," Wolf told the woman on the other end of the line tersely. "What else?"

Slade clenched his teeth and tried to control the need to break something. He stared at the picture of Zach on Benny's phone. The man had been pissed off at the practical joke that morning and had left. Had their actions put the man over the edge? Fuck.

Before he could continue beating himself up, Kiera began to speak again. "The rest of what I think she's saying is confusing to me. It looks like she signed four things, other than Z-A-K, as far as I can tell. Three of them are the number eight, beach, and basement."

"Eight men?" Wolf asked, focused now.

"A number of a license plate or address?" Dude asked.

"I'm sorry, I don't know," Kiera said softly.

"They're just talking it out, baby, they're not asking you to tell them what she means behind her signs," Cooper told Kiera quietly.

"Beach is easy. She's somewhere near the ocean," Cookie said.

"Which means shit, as half of San Diego is near the fucking ocean," Abe grumbled.

"Yeah, but beach house narrows it down," Dude countered.

"What else?" Slade asked Kiera, not hiding the impatience in his voice. He felt bad. Taking out his frustrations on Kiera, who was only trying to help, wasn't cool, but he couldn't stop it.

"There was basement," Kiera reminded them.

"Which could mean they're underground or under a building, not necessarily in a house," Cookie pointed out.

"Or that they're in a fucking basement," Wolf bit out, his patience also obviously gone.

"The last sign I'm not a hundred percent sure about," Kiera said reluctantly. "It doesn't really make sense."

"What?" Slade asked.

"Tornado."

"What the fuck does that mean?" Abe asked no one in particular.

"I know, it doesn't make sense. But from what I can

tell, she definitely made the sign for a tornado. But..."
Kiera's voice trailed off. Then she said, "Hang on a
second."

Slade impatiently waited for whatever Kiera was
checking. Every second that went by grated on his
nerves.

"I...I don't know. But it looks to me like she made
the letter C, then made the sign for tornado. She did it
twice, and each time looked the same. I don't think that
C was an accident."

"A tornado and the letter C? I don't get it," Wolf
said, running his hand through his hair in frustration.
"C for Caroline? C for coast? C for fucking come and
get me? It could mean almost anything."

Slade closed his eyes and tried to think. He vaguely
heard the other men discussing what Dakota could've
meant, but tuned them out. Tornado. C. C. Tornado.
Beach, basement, eight and C.

It came to him then. It was as clear as if Dakota had
screamed the word at him. "Coronado. Tornado was
probably the closest spelling she could get to Coronado
without finger-spelling it out. The fucker's right fucking
here."

"It makes sense," Wolf said slowly. "Zach worked at
the base. He's probably given himself access to the
super-computers there. If he's as good at tech shit as Tex
thinks he is, he probably hacked right into the main-

frame. He could bounce the signal around to almost anywhere."

"There are quite a few houses on the beaches over there. Especially on the south side," Abe observed.

"I'll be in touch," Slade told Kiera, Coop, and Hurt, and didn't even feel the slightest bit bad when he hung up in the middle of whatever the commander was saying. He immediately dialed again and got Greg Lambert.

"Lambert here."

"He fucking worked beside the team when I took my leave of absence," Slade said in lieu of a greeting.

"What? Who?" Greg asked.

"Zach Johnson. The guy you had work in my place. We just watched a video of Zach, otherwise known as *Aziz Fourati*, forcing my woman to marry him. She used sign language to talk to us. She spelled his name. Zach is fucking Aziz!"

"Fuck me," Greg said softly. Then louder said, "His name was at the top of the list of trustworthy employees when I checked for your replacement. I didn't even question it. He was already there at the base, it seemed to be an easy decision."

"Fuck, we bought right into his 'I don't understand computers' act," Abe bit out.

"Something wasn't right when I was trying to help him this morning," Slade commented. "I couldn't put my finger on it at the time, but now it makes sense. It was as if he was trying too hard to look like an idiot when it came to the computer. Clicking on stupid shit anyone who has been alive in the last twenty fucking years would know not to click on."

"So he's actually a techie…how'd he get one step ahead of us? How'd he track Dakota down?" Dude asked.

"He didn't seem to be a real threat to her until Lambert asked me to take on the case," Slade said.

"So you're the key," Wolf surmised. "How?"

"My computer?" Slade asked.

Wolf shook his head. "Our computers are secure."

"He could've hacked into it once he had access," Dude said.

"Possible, but there's no way he would've found out some of the information about Dakota from there. My computer was clean. I don't use it to email anything remotely personal," Slade informed the group.

"What about the phones?" Abe asked.

Slade shook his head. "The only time I used the office phone was when Lambert called that first time…before Zach or Aziz or whatever the fuck we're calling him, took over my job."

"How about your cell?" Lambert asked.

Everyone was silent for a second.

"It's Navy issued," Slade said slowly.

"That phone is supposed to be secure." Cookie told the group something they all knew.

"Fuck me. Yeah well, Cookie, I'm guessing it isn't as secure as we thought," Slade said, shaking his head. "I've been using it the whole time. Updating Tex on my progress. Telling him where I was, where I was going. He talked about sending Dakota trackers like the ones the other women had. Hell, Wolf even gave me his security code when we were on the way to his house. Fourati most likely listened to every fucking one of those conversations. Could be listening right now. All he had to do was follow along. I delivered Dakota to him on a silver fucking platter."

"I'll get as much information as I can on Zachary Johnson," Greg told the now extremely pissed-off group of men. "I'll get all known addresses for him and anyone remotely connected to him. Parents, siblings, a fucking UPS man who happened to deliver a package. I'll get them all. I never meant for this to happen," Greg told Slade. "When I asked you to take this mission, I never expected this."

"I never expected Dakota either," Slade said softly. "And this isn't your fault. None of it. Just get us the info, like fucking yesterday."

"I'll be in touch," Greg said, then hung up.

Slade clicked off the connection and motioned to Wolf for his phone, dropping his own on the table as if it were poison. He glanced at the window and noticed how fast time seemed to be passing. Fuck, they were taking too long. He needed information and he needed it now.

With a grimace, Wolf understood and threw it to him.

"Don't have a choice, I'm takin' a chance that your phone is clean," Slade said, before punching in a number.

"You got Tex."

"Tex, it's Cutter. I need houses on the beach on Coronado. Someplace that has a basement, or something similar that's underground. That could be a long shot though."

"Fuck me, how'd you get that intel? Did Dakota say all that in her speech?" Tex asked even as he was clicking keys on his computer.

"I'll tell you later," Slade reassured his friend.

Wolf and the other men were already on the move, headed for the door. Slade followed along behind them, the adrenaline coursing through his body. He was more than ready to get this shit done. It had been way too long since that video had played. Who knew what Fourati was doing to Dakota.

"Okay, I pulled up the MLS listings of all the houses on Coronado. Um…right, okay it looks like there are thirty-three houses with basements near a beach."

"Is there unusual electricity usage for any of them? What about cars in driveways or parked nearby? Any boat docks? Any with an eight in the address?"

Tex's fingers were moving nonstop, and Slade could hear his friend muttering under his breath as he did the searches.

"Nothing stands out, Cutter."

"Fuck, Tex. There has to be something. Fourati is Zach. The guy who replaced me."

"What? I thought that guy was a fuckup."

"Obviously he wasn't as much of a fuckup as everyone thought," Slade said dryly. He got into the backseat of Cookie's SUV and held on to the oh-shit handle as the man backed out of Wolf's driveway as if the hounds of hell were after him. Slade approved. As long as they didn't catch the attention of a ticket-happy cop, he didn't care what it took, they needed to get to Coronado. "My phone was compromised. I'm using Wolf's. Bastard listened to every one of my conversations. Followed me right to Rachel and back to San Diego. He knows everything about Wolf's team...and me. I led him right to Dakota. We need this info, buddy."

"Fuck," Tex swore. "Okay, hang on. That puts a completely different spin on this then. If that fucker hacked into your phone, he had to have left a trail. No one is that good. The Navy doesn't—oh yeah, there you are, you asshole..."

Slade listened impatiently as Tex did what Tex did best, use his computer knowledge to track terrorists…and find missing women.

"Got him. There's a house with a beach view owned by Dolores and Richard Johnson. You'll never guess what their son's name is."

"Address, Tex," Slade said impatiently. He'd worry about Zach's parents later.

"Right, after you go over the bridge, take a left on Orange Avenue. There's a housing development at the end of the street. The houses are centered around a park. Address is 418 Ocean Boulevard."

"You're sure?" Slade asked.

"Fucking positive. Fucker's not as smart as he thinks he is," Tex said.

"There's an eight in the address," Wolf commented, but Slade tuned him out. He didn't care *what* Dakota was trying to tell him. Address, license plate, eighty-eight fucking bad guys. He'd kill them fucking all if they did anything to hurt her.

"Thanks, Tex. We're already on the move," Slade said.

"I'm shutting his website down. He won't be able to post anything else."

"Good."

"And I'll be talking with the admiral out there at the base and letting him know there was a breach, and that he'd better fucking get on that or there'll be hell to pay," Tex swore.

Slade didn't give a fuck about that. His only concern at the moment was for Dakota.

"Call me when your woman's safe," Tex ordered.

"Will do," Slade told him, and clicked off the phone. He gave it back to Wolf and tried to concentrate on the upcoming rescue. All his focus was on retrieving Dakota and Caroline and putting an end to Zach—and anyone else who got in his way.

"What's the plan?" he asked the other men in the vehicle as they flew toward Coronado, racing the setting sun.

Chapter Fifteen

D AKOTA HUDDLED ON the floor with Caroline. The two women had their arms around each other as they spoke quietly.

"Are you okay?" Dakota asked.

"Yeah. I'm good."

"I'm so sorry, I didn't—"

"This isn't your fault," Caroline said fiercely. "*He* did this, not you."

"But he hurt you," Dakota said sadly.

"Yeah. But you stopped him before he did something awful. Besides, I've been hurt worse."

"Are you still bleeding?" Dakota reached out and put her hand over Caroline's breastbone. At the other woman's inhalation, she realized what she'd done.

"Jesus, I'm sorry," Dakota told her, yanking her hand back. "I didn't mean to...I mean, we don't even really know each other, I shouldn't be touching you like that, and—"

Caroline reached out and grabbed Dakota's hand.

She placed it back between her breasts and held it there. The two women sat like that for a long moment, drawing strength from each other, connecting in a personal and empathetic way.

"I'm okay," Caroline reassured Dakota. Her lips quirked up in a semblance of a grin as she said, "It's only a scratch, and thanks to you, he didn't hurt me worse. We need to figure something out before he comes back though." Caroline dropped her hand to her lap and Dakota grabbed it and held on tightly.

"I swear I'll do whatever he wants so he won't hurt you again," Dakota vowed. "I could probably hold out if he hurt *me*, but I can't stand to see him do anything to you."

"I'd like to tell you that it doesn't matter, but I can't," Caroline said in a soft voice. "One of us needs to get out of here. Get help."

Dakota motioned to her knee, which was swelling enough that an unusual bump could be seen even though she was wearing silk pants. "I can barely walk, much less run. That asshole really did a number on my knee. It's going to have to be you. It's probably better anyway; if you're out of here, Aziz can't hurt you to make me compliant."

Thinking about the terrorist she'd just married, Dakota shivered in revulsion. As soon as she'd finished the speech she'd been forced to make earlier, Aziz had motioned for two of the men in the room to cut the zip-ties holding her ankles to the chair. He'd hauled her up, putting his arm around her waist so she wouldn't fall to the ground when she put weight on her injured knee. "You did wonderful, my bride. Unfortunately, the consummation of our wedding will be delayed. Our marriage is big news and I have recruits I need to talk to. If you promise to be good, I'll let you stay with your friend."

He'd looked at her expectantly then, and Dakota had nodded and said softly, "I'll be good."

"I'm glad to hear that, Anoushka. I'd hate to have to hurt your friend. I do *so* hate the sight of blood."

Dakota had resisted the urge to roll her eyes, and stayed silent as she was helped into another small room with Caroline. This one had a dirty mattress on the floor and a wooden chair in the corner. There was no other furniture.

"Here you are, my bride."

"It's not exactly comfortable," Dakota said dryly.

"The more you show me that you can obey your wedding vows, the better your accommodations will be," Aziz said smugly. "Since I don't trust you yet though, no matter what you swore to God in our wedding ceremony, we will consummate our marriage here. Your friend Caroline will be in that chair over there," he pointed to it with his chin, "and will be accompanied by two of my most trusted followers. If you refuse me in any way, *she* will pay the price. Understand?"

Dakota had nodded immediately, horrified by what the evening would bring.

"Good. Get comfortable. I'll be back once I've secured the major funding I've been working toward." He kissed her gently on the forehead, as if he really was a loving new husband. "Our wedding was the one thing my backer was waiting on. Now that he knows I have done my duty, he will pay. And we'll be that much closer to our ultimate goal."

"Of?" Dakota asked, afraid to hear the answer.

"To make the LAX bombing look like small potatoes," Aziz answered readily. "Take a nap, relax." He leaned into her, grabbing her chin with a cruel grip and forced her face up to his. "I will be back. I will fuck you into submission, and when I'm done, I might just let my loyal followers take a turn as well. To reward them, you know. I honestly don't give a shit who gets you pregnant. It doesn't matter. In fact, it'd probably be better if the brat had dark hair anyway."

Then he ground his mouth down onto hers. Dakota had refused to open her mouth, but he bit her bottom lip until she gasped at the pain and his tongue swept inside her mouth.

After a moment, he pulled back but didn't let go of

her. "You'll have to do better than that, my bride, if you want your friend to remain unmolested." Then he laughed. "On second thought, don't. I'd love to take a shot at her as well." And with that, Aziz had left them alone in the room.

Dakota shook her head, trying to remove the memories. "I'm not sure we'll even get a chance to make a break for it," she told Caroline in despair. "I don't think there's anything we *can* do."

"Bullshit," the other woman said, determination clear in her tone. "You sent the message like we talked about, right?"

"Yeah, but I don't know if Slade will understand it. I don't know much about him at all, other than he's got a Harley and is sexy as hell."

Caroline shook her head and squeezed Dakota's hand almost to the point of pain. "One of the guys will understand."

"Does Wolf or any of his teammates know sign language?"

"They're in the process of trying to learn it, but I don't know how fluent they are yet. But they have their own nonverbal signals they use all the time. Because of what I did when I was captured, they're going to know to look for a message of some sort," Caroline reassured her. "I know it."

"I hope so. It's been a while since I've signed, I hope

I didn't screw it up."

"I know my husband and the others are on their way, but we can't sit around waiting on them. We need to help ourselves." Caroline pushed herself to her feet, swaying slightly before locking her knees and walking around the room.

Caroline explored their prison, even though there wasn't much to see. The window was nailed shut and wouldn't budge so they couldn't get out that way. The chair was impossible for them to break apart to make a weapon. There wasn't anything on either of their outfits that would pass for a weapon, and the barrettes in Dakota's hair were useless as a defensive tool.

Even with the odds against them, neither woman was willing to give up. Caroline sat back down on the mattress next to Dakota and they plotted and planned. With Dakota's bum knee and Caroline's robe—which was slit up the middle, exposing her if she wasn't holding it closed—they were somewhat handicapped, not to mention outnumbered, but both made a vow not to give up, especially after Caroline told Dakota her entire story. How she'd literally been on the edge of death in the ocean when Cookie had shown up with lifesaving oxygen.

"Don't ever give up," Caroline said. "Even when you think all is lost, hang on for one more second."

Dakota nodded. "You too."

"We can get through this. Our men will come for us," Caroline said firmly.

Dakota could see the absolute certainty in the other woman's eyes. She had no doubt whatsoever that her husband was on his way. "How long do you think it's been?"

"I have no idea. It's getting dark though, so several hours," Caroline said.

Dakota closed her eyes and leaned against the wall behind her. She and Caroline once more had their arms around each other as they waited for whatever was going to happen to happen.

I can do this, Dakota told herself. *Slade is coming. I know it. We might have just met, but he's coming.* The last week flashed through her memories. Slade sitting in the passenger seat of her car, watching her sleep. Slade holding her in the trailer of the motel in Rachel. Riding on the back of his bike as she held on tightly to him. Looking up at the stars before they'd gone into the hotel room in Goldfield. He'd taken her in his arms and they'd silently gazed upwards before Slade had kissed the top of her head and led her inside. Slade smiling at her as they ate pizza in Goldfield. And how good his hands felt on her body.

Yeah, Slade was coming for her. Her only job was to hold on until he got there.

THE FIVE MEN silently exited the SUV a block away from where they believed Zach was holed up with the women. The darkening sky aiding in their cover. They weren't sure how many followers he had with him, but assumed it was anywhere up to a dozen. Twelve against five didn't seem like great odds, but not only were the men silently stalking toward the house on the beach highly trained killers, the mission was personal.

"I contacted Hurt," Wolf told the others quietly. "He called in that new SEAL team under his command to back us up and watch over the coastline. I wouldn't put it past this asshole to be ready for anything."

"Are you talking about Gumby, Rocco, and their team?" Cookie asked. "The guys who helped us over in Turkey?"

"That's them," Wolf affirmed.

"Fuck yeah," Abe whispered.

Slade didn't give a shit who was covering what. All his focus was on the house and finding Dakota before it was too late.

"Abe, Cutter and I will go around the left. Dude and Cookie, take the right," Wolf ordered, taking command of the small group. "Take out any tangos you run into...silently. We don't want to give Zach any head's up we're here."

They'd been calling Fourati "Zach" since they'd found out who he was. The fact that the man had duped not only the Navy, but all of them, had pissed them off to no end. Besides, Aziz Fourati was simply a name he'd been using, it wasn't who he was. No matter how much he might want to be an international terrorist, he wasn't.

Zach was a spoiled rich kid who, for whatever reason, had decided to become a terrorist. Slade didn't give a shit how and why the man had became what he did. He was sure the man's entire history would come out after the women were rescued, but ultimately it didn't matter. He was a dead man for touching Dakota.

THE DOOR TO the room opened with a crash and both Dakota and Caroline jumped in surprise. They'd become more and more wary and stressed as the time had gone by and neither Aziz, nor any of his followers, had returned.

The men moved fast once they burst into the room. Two men in black robes grabbed Caroline and another two yanked Dakota to her feet before they could do more than weakly protest.

Dakota struggled in the grip of the two men who'd restrained her earlier. Her knee throbbed and was excruciating to stand on, but she refused to go down without a fight.

"Looks like they still have some spunk in them, Aziz," one of the men drawled, clearly amused by their struggles.

Dakota glanced at Caroline and saw her doing her best to slip out of the grip of the men holding her, too.

"Tsk, tsk, tsk, Anoushka," Aziz murmured as he came up to stand in front of her, now dressed in a black robe like the other men around them. "I was so hoping you would've spent your time waiting for me more constructively." He leaned in and took her chin in his hand in a brutal grip. "I like it when my woman fights me," he said with a gleam in his eye. "It turns me on."

"Fuck you," Dakota bit out, wrenching her head out of his grip.

Aziz motioned with his head to another man standing in the doorway. "It appears if I want to beat any sense into you, I need to do so before you're pregnant. I don't give a shit about you, but I wouldn't want to hurt the future leader."

The man Aziz had signaled moved toward Dakota and, without a word, drew back his fist and hit her in the face.

The men holding her let go, and she fell like a stone to the concrete floor. Her hand went to her face and she tried to hold back the moans of pain that were in her throat.

Before she recovered from the strike, the man's boot hit her stomach. Dakota curled into a ball, trying to protect herself. He simply moved, kicking whatever he could reach as she tried to get away from him.

"Dakota!" Caroline cried. "Oh my God. Stop it, you're going to kill her!"

"Ah, maybe you think I should pay attention to you, huh?" Aziz asked as if he didn't have a care in the world. And with a tilt of Aziz's head, the man who'd been kicking Dakota turned to Caroline.

As if in a daze, Dakota watched as he reached for her friend. Then her vision was blocked by Aziz. He'd kneeled down in front of her and was speaking softly.

"You will learn that defiance earns you nothing but pain. I might like a little fight in my woman, but I do have limits. Don't worry, you'll learn how far you can push me, Anoushka. You'll submit to me sooner or later. But for now, I think you might need a little help relaxing, hmmmm?"

Not knowing what he was talking about, Dakota did her best to keep her eyes open. It hurt to breathe and her knee was screaming in pain, but she still managed to glare at the man in front of her. "I will…" She took a deep breath, and even though it hurt, it felt good to be defying Aziz. Her eyes narrowed as she finished her thought. "*Never* submit. You'll never be able to turn your back on me. You'll never be able to leave me alone. I'll spend the rest of my life doing whatever I can to escape."

Aziz grinned then. A nasty, evil grin that Dakota

knew she'd see in her nightmares for years to come. "Oh, you'll submit to me, beautiful Anoushka. You're my wife. It's my right to discipline you as I see fit. It says so right in the Quran. But for now, I'm going to take the edge off of that passion and fight. We have to travel, and I'd rather not worry about you drawing unwanted attention to us. As a bonus, some men like their women to be completely unconscious when they take them, but me? I want you to know it's me, your husband, taking you. I want you to remember how you could do nothing but take whatever it was I give you. I will fill you with my seed until it overflows from your nether lips. Then I'll do it again, and again. I'll fuck you whenever I feel like it. You'll be pregnant before the month is out, even if I have to keep you drugged the entire time. Oh yes, Anoushka, you are mine. Forever...or until I tire of you. But..." He ran his knuckles down her bruised cheek, smearing the blood from her nose and bleeding lip as he went. "Mark my words, my bride. You will never escape me. Ever."

Dakota tried to push herself away from Aziz, but the men who'd held her earlier were there to hold her still. She struggled weakly as another man came toward her with a syringe. She shrieked in pain as her arm was roughly stretched out and held down on the floor. The man injected her with whatever drug was in the needle.

She glanced over at Caroline and saw another man

inserting a needle into her arm as well. Dakota panted in pain and terror as she felt an unnatural lassitude take over her body. She sagged on the floor, almost boneless.

"There. That's much better," Aziz said with a smirk. "You are conscious. You know what I'm saying and what's happening, but you're too out of it to fight back. Exactly how I like my women." He turned to the others. "It's time to go. There are some Ansar al-Shari'a supporters waiting for us just over the border. We'll use the boats. Go get them ready."

Without a word, most of the men left the room to do Aziz's bidding, now that she and Caroline weren't a threat. Dakota felt as if she were floating. The good thing about whatever Aziz had injected her with was that she didn't hurt anymore. The pain in her knee was now a dull throb and she couldn't even really feel the injuries on her face and torso from the beating she'd been given.

Aziz was busy talking to a man over by the door, probably planning how they were going to leave undetected. Earlier, when she'd looked out the window, Caroline had said she could see the ocean and a beach, and that it seemed to her as if they were in a residential house.

Dakota rolled her head to the side and saw Caroline lying on the floor near her. Her robe was open and her body was on display, but she made no move to cover herself. Their eyes met and both women blinked. Caroline rolled her head away and stared straight up at the ceiling. Then she brought her hands up to her chest and made the sign for run. Then she patted her chest twice.

Dakota got it. The other woman was telling her that she was still going to make a run for it. She wanted to believe her. Wanted to believe that Caroline would be able to make a break for freedom when they were brought out to the boats, but she wasn't sure she could. Even though it should be dark outside by now, she didn't know if Caroline could do it. With the way she felt, Dakota wasn't convinced Caroline would be able to move any better than she could, much less break free from whoever would certainly be holding her and run away.

Feeling as if she were looking down at herself from high above the room, Dakota closed her eyes and let the feeling from the drug take over her body. At the moment, she didn't care what happened to her; as long as she didn't have to go back to the pain she'd been feeling five minutes ago, she was good. Everything was just super.

THE SEALS MOVED silently as they parted and surrounded the large, beautiful house. Wolf paused near a window and held up his hand for Slade to stop moving. As they were waiting and listening, a commotion caught their attention.

Both men watched in disbelief as a group of men in oversized black robes exited through a door almost hidden under a large wooden deck at the back of the house. They began to walk in a huddle toward the beach. Slade didn't know where they were going, but was pleased they'd have fewer men to worry about when they entered the house to find Caroline and Dakota.

Just then, shouts went up and a figure dressed in a long black robe broke free from the group and began to stumble down the beach into the dark night.

A feminine voice Slade would recognize anywhere yelled, "Go, go go!"

He looked at Wolf, and without hesitation, all five SEALs shifted to Plan B and took off running toward the group at the same time.

Spotting the SEALs running pell-mell toward them, one of the men yelled, "Leave her! Get in the boats!" As a unit, the group of men began to sprint toward the beach, where Slade could now see four rubber boats waiting.

"Fuck, we have to stop them!" Slade bit out, and pushed himself to run faster.

The figure who'd broken away from the group fell onto her hands and knees, but immediately got up and began to make her way down the beach once more. But this time Slade could see that whoever it was—most likely Caroline, if Dakota yelling "go" was any indication—was weaving and moving as if drunk. She looked back toward the group who'd left the house, and what she was wearing clicked in his brain for the first time.

It was definitely a woman. And definitely Caroline. She was nearly naked, the robe she was wearing huge and flapping around her body as she ran. It was open down the middle, and her pale body was easy to see in the moonlight as she tried to flee.

"Fuck, Wolf," Slade exclaimed.

"I see her! It's Ice," the other SEAL returned.

"Go." Slade needed the man's help, but if it had been Dakota running away, half naked, panicked and in obvious distress, nothing would've kept him from going after her.

Without a word, Wolf turned left and sprinted toward his wife.

Slade turned his eyes back to the group of men and cursed. They weren't going to make it to them before they cast off from the beach. They were entering the four boats now and pushing them away from the beach at the same time. His eyes roved over each one, trying to see which held Zach.

In one of the middle boats, Slade saw the man's blond hair, easily recognizable amongst his dark-haired friends and followers.

Dude and Cookie reached the edge of the ocean at the same time Slade and Abe did.

"They've got one of the women," Cookie said, not even breathing hard.

"You sure?" Slade asked.

"Yeah, I saw one of them toss her over his shoulder and throw her into a boat."

"Where are they going?" Slade asked, not taking his eyes off the boats, which were quickly putting distance between the beach and themselves.

"Mexico?" Abe guessed. "Where else would they go?"

"We need to stop them," Slade bit out in frustration.

Cookie had his phone to his ear and said, "Rocco and his team are two minutes away. Two boats will come and pick us up and two others will make chase and give us coordinates."

Slade nodded and paced impatiently along the sandy shoreline.

"Where's Wolf?" Dude asked.

"Caroline's the one who got away and took off. He's on her," Slade told the other SEAL succinctly.

"Thank fuck," Cookie breathed.

"Yeah," Slade said between clenched teeth.

"I didn't mean—"

Slade held up his hand, stopping his friend's words. He knew Cookie didn't mean anything by being happy Caroline was free from the terrorists. But *his* woman was not.

Within a minute and a half, the four men saw two boats coming at them at a high speed. Slowing only enough not to ram the boat halfway up the beach, the SEALs driving the high-speed vessels were backing out even as Abe, Cookie, Dude, and Slade were jumping inside.

As if they'd worked together on missions like this for their entire career, the men from three different SEAL teams moved in a kind of deadly harmony. Their focus was on catching up to and eliminating the threats from the other boats.

DAKOTA LIE ON the bottom of the boat she'd been tossed into and tried to understand what was happening. She'd seen Caroline break away from the group. She had no idea where she'd found the strength, but was impressed. No one had been paying much attention to her because they assumed she was too far out of it to be able to defy them. But instead of running after her, the men had bolted toward the boats they'd obviously gotten ready earlier.

She was thrown over someone's shoulder and she'd

bounced bonelessly as they'd raced toward the surf. The water was cold as it splashed onto her face, making her only slightly more aware of what was going on. She was unceremoniously thrown into the boat, and Aziz began to yell to the drivers of the others.

"Once we're away from shore, separate. They must not know which boat I am in. The leader must escape! We'll meet up across the border. Long live Ansar al-Shari'a!"

"Long live Ansar al-Shari'a!" was shouted back, then the voices were drowned out by the motors being revved.

Dakota had a momentary thought that Aziz was the biggest coward she'd ever met. He'd basically ordered the others to do whatever it took to make sure *he* escaped. What a douche.

Her limp body was thrown against the back of the boat as the driver gunned the engine and raced away from the shore. She concentrated on trying to see who was at the wheel, but the farther they got from Coronado, the harder it was to see anything. The two men in the boat hadn't turned on any lights and the only thing she could see clearly were the stars twinkling over her head.

As her mind floated, Dakota stared up at those stars. She could see the Big Dipper and North Star. She recalled standing in Slade's arms and seeing the same stars in Goldfield. How long ago had that been? Yesterday? No...yesterday she was at Wolf and Caroline's house. Her brow wrinkled as she struggled to remember. After a long moment, she decided it didn't matter and closed her eyes.

The bottom of the boat hitting a wave jostled her back to reality as pain tore through her body, and she blinked. Dakota slowly pushed herself up to a sitting position and looked around in a daze. She saw the lights of Coronado twinkling as they raced southward.

"He'll never find me," Aziz yelled back to her as he stood at the front of the boat. "I've got new identities for both of us, Anoushka. I was right under his nose and he had no idea it was me he was looking for." He cackled, long and loud, and Dakota winced.

"I've got everything I need to grow my flock, and within a year I'll have organized the biggest and deadliest terrorist incident on US soil they've ever seen. And you were my inspiration," Aziz told her. He took a step toward the back of the boat where she was sitting, but a large wave made him lose his footing and he had to grab the railing to keep his balance.

Obviously changing his mind about coming to the back of the boat where she was, he said, "Rest, my bride. And don't worry. I'll have you inside a warm home, safe in my bed, where we can consummate our marriage in no time. Close your eyes, Anoushka, sleep."

Dakota closed her eyes as he ordered, more out of frustration and terror than obedience. She couldn't allow Aziz to get her out of the country. She'd be even more helpless than she was right this moment. It would be twice as difficult for Slade to find her then.

It was thoughts of Slade that gave her the strength and determination to both defy Aziz and overcome the pull of the drug coursing through her veins.

Seeing that her captor and the other man were busy trying to see where they were going by looking at the instruments softly glowing on the panel, Dakota slowly forced her uncooperative body up until her belly rested on the edge of the rubber boat. The lights onshore were swirling dizzyingly, but she didn't let that stop her. The noise of the engine and the waves crashing on the underside of the boat worked in her favor. As did the fact that Aziz thought she was incapacitated by whatever he'd given her.

Without a sound, Dakota held her breath and leaned over the edge of the boat, sliding headfirst into the frigid waters of the Pacific Ocean. The small splash her body made as it knifed into the water was indistinguishable from the other sounds the vessel made as it raced toward Mexico.

Chapter Sixteen

S LADE STOOD WITH his feet braced apart, not even feeling the spray of the cold water on his face as the Zodiac's powerful engine pushed them closer and closer to their objective. The four boats that had left the beach had scattered in four different directions.

He and Cookie were in a boat with another SEAL named Rex. He was wearing a tactical headset and was communicating with his teammates on the other Zodiacs, then relaying the information to the others on his boat.

"Phantom and Gumby neutralized the tango headed north."

"Was Dakota or Zach with them?" Slade shouted to be heard over the engine and water.

"Negative," Rex said as he shook his head.

One down, three more to go.

"Rocco and your men, Abe and Dude, are coming up on another…they're in a firefight, but it looks to only be two men, and not any women onboard."

"Come on, come on," Slade pleaded in a soft voice as they continued to gain on the boat in front of them. *Please be the one Zach is on. I want to be the one to kill that fucker.*

"Second boat down," Rex informed them.

"Update on the third?" Cookie shouted.

"Ace and Bubba are closing in," Rex informed him.

Slade didn't take his eyes off the boat in front of them. It had no lights on, but Rex and Cookie were wearing night-vision specs, and he had on a pair of thermal-vision goggles, allowing him to clearly see the bright red and pink traces of warm air from both the boat and the people onboard.

He could only see two shapes, near the front of the vessel, but that didn't mean Dakota wasn't there. He didn't have a clear view of the bottom of the boat. If they were following Zach, it was likely that Dakota was there too. The alternative was unthinkable.

"Bubba says the female target is not in the third vessel. Repeat, she is not in the third boat."

Which meant they were following Zach, and Dakota *had* to be there.

Slade could see one of the two men look behind him several times, but he otherwise didn't move away from the controls. He had no idea if the terrorists could hear them coming or not, but it didn't matter. The men were as good as dead.

Rex shouted, "Hold on," as he steered the rubber Zodiac straight for the boat in front of them. He pulled up alongside the other craft and without hesitation, rammed it, both figures at the front flying off their feet at the collision.

Slade and Cookie were moving even as Rex gunned the vessel and pulled up alongside the boat again. They'd removed their goggles and jumped into the other boat as both continued to careen forward at a high rate of speed.

Cookie was on the driver before either of the men knew they'd been boarded. He'd reached around and slit his throat so quickly, he didn't have a chance to fight back.

Zach wouldn't be so lucky.

Slade grabbed the man and threw him to the bottom of the boat so hard, he gasped, trying to get air into his lungs. Slade was on him in an instant, crouched over him, his KA-BAR knife at his throat. Cookie slowed then stopped the boat, but Slade's attention was elsewhere.

Keeping the knife on Zach's jugular vein, he turned to look at the back of the boat.

Empty.

Dakota wasn't there. She wasn't *fucking* there! How could she *not* be there?

For the first time that evening, his heart rate increased. He'd been focused and stoic until now. Cold, ready, and willing to do whatever it took to end the threat to Dakota. But she wasn't in the boat. She was supposed to be there. Where the ever-loving fuck was she?

Shifting so that one of his knees pressed into Zach's breastbone, he snarled at the terrorist, "Where is she?"

An ugly sneer slid across Zach's face. "Who? My wife, Anoushka Fourati? Hidden where you'll never find her."

"Bullshit," Slade said putting more pressure on the knife, not caring that a line of blood welled at the man's throat. "Where is she?"

The pain was getting to Zach. He winced and tried to pull away from the knife at his throat, with no luck. "She was a great fuck. I love it when bitches fight," Zach unwisely boasted.

Slade was done. He wanted the man under him to die slowly and painfully, but Dakota needed him. He didn't have time to kill Zach the way he wanted. He leaned down until he was right in Zach's face and said softly, "You're nothing but a coward."

"Maybe so, but my name will be remembered forever. Like Timothy McVeigh and the Unabomber, my actions will live on in infinity," Zach choked out.

"Wrong. I'm going to make it my goal in life to make sure not one news outlet knows your name. Not one." And with that, Slade drew his knife across Zach's neck slowly and methodically, not even attempting to be merciful.

He was turning away from the man even as he gurgled and bled out at the bottom of the boat.

Rex's voice speaking to the men on the other boats sounded as though it were coming from a great distance. "Target not here. Repeat, target not here. Anyone got eyes on Dakota?"

Slade turned back to Zach's body, his blood spilling into the boat in a slow but steady pace, the man's hands at his neck not doing anything to staunch the flow from his jugular. He leaned down and took hold of the man's blond hair, lifted his head up high, and proceeded to slice his throat again. Then a third time, before dropping the man with disgust. "I killed you too quickly, motherfucker," Slade said in a cold, deadly tone.

Then he looked up at Cookie. "Where's my woman?"

"I don't know. But we're gonna find her, Cutter. We're gonna fucking find her."

DAKOTA FLOATED ON her back, arms stretched out, legs spread, and gazed up into the night sky. The stars were as clear out here as they were in Nevada. She'd never seen so many in all her life.

When she'd first hit the water, her breath had left her at the freezing temperature. The water was frigid. It was enough to jolt her out of her drugged stupor for a while. She'd treaded water for a long moment, watching as the boat she'd been on raced away from her. Stupid Aziz hadn't even realized she was gone. Idiot.

Then she'd begun to swim toward the shore. She had no idea how far away it was, but it was most likely a couple miles. Distances were skewed at night, especially in her confused state. After a while, she stopped being so cold and realized she was tired. Really tired.

Happy for her natural buoyancy, and the fact that she'd been a competitive water polo player all through high school and college, thus learning how to swim and float better than the average person, Dakota turned on her back to rest.

She bobbed up and down in the water bonelessly. She'd just rest for a while, then she'd start swimming again. The night really was beautiful, serene. With her ears under the water she couldn't hear anything but the whoosh of the waves as they gently lifted her body up and down, and her own slow heartbeat.

As she stared up at the sky, a shooting star went sailing past her line of vision. Dakota smiled. It had been forever since she'd seen one. A wish. She had to make a wish. Closing her eyes and feeling more comfortable than she'd been in hours, Dakota made her wish.

"WE KNOW SHE was on one of the boats," Rex said into the headset. "We saw someone throw her into the bottom of one of them. She *has* to be out here somewhere. They might've thrown her overboard when they knew we were on their tails."

Slade blocked out the chatter from the SEAL at the front of the boat. He was kneeling on the side of the rubber boat, one hand fisted in the rope at the side to keep his balance, his eyes fixed on the blackness in front of him.

Cookie was wearing night-vision goggles, which gave him the ability to see about twenty feet in front of him, but Slade had put the thermals back on. He could clearly see birds soaring on the thermals in the night sky, and even a couple of flying fish as they jumped out of the water. But what he was looking for was Dakota. He knew the water was cold, which would quickly sap the warmth from her body, but it hadn't been that long. He should still be able to distinguish her body in the water. She had to be out here somewhere.

He refused to think about what Caroline had gone through all those years ago, when her captors had weighted her body down with chains before throwing *her* into the ocean. He refused to think about Dakota sinking to the bottom, struggling with her bindings before running out of air and instinctively taking a huge breath, which would fill her lungs with water instead of life-saving air.

No. He would not lose her now. No way. It had been less than a week since she'd come into his life, and it wasn't enough. It wasn't nearly enough. He wanted to know everything about her. Where she'd learned sign language. What her favorite color was. What she was like as a young child.

The tears came to Slade's eyes unbidden, and he forced them back. He had no time to lose it. He needed his vision to be clear. He needed to be able to find Dakota. She was out here and time was ticking away.

"Come on, where are you, love?" he asked softly, even as his eyes continued to scan the horizon for anything out of place. Any spec of pink that might indicate the warmth from her body. It was like looking for a needle in a haystack...no, a needle in a needle stack. Impossible, but he wasn't going to give up. No way. He would find her.

"Our boat had Zach, it's most likely she's in this area," Rex was telling the other boats. "Converge on our position and begin a grid search. We don't know when she might've been...err...put out of the boat. She could be anywhere between us and the beach."

Again, Slade tuned the man out. The hair on the back of his neck stood straight up as he scanned the waters.

"See anything?" Cookie asked from his left.

"Not yet," Slade said. "But she's here. We're close. I can feel it."

"Yeah, me too," Cookie said. Neither man looked away from the vast ocean in front of them, but Cookie went on. "I've got the same feeling I had the first time I met my wife. I was two steps away from leaving that shithole of a hut in the middle of fucking nowhere, Mexico, when something made me turn back. I shouldn't have. I had Julie and we needed to get the fuck out of there before the sex traffickers came back, but I hesitated, took one last look around and before I knew what I was doing, I was walking toward the back of that hut. Sure I was missing something."

"Fiona," Slade said with certainty.

"Yeah. I've got that same feeling right now."

"Come on, love. Help me find you," Slade whispered as he scanned the waves.

DAKOTA WAS DYING. She knew it. Had no idea why she was still alive as it was. She couldn't feel her extremities and knew there was no way she would make it to land. Aziz was long gone, and she didn't want to get picked back up by him or any of his followers anyway.

The stars twinkled merrily above her head as she floated, and she felt sad. Not for herself; once she was gone, she wouldn't be in any pain. She wouldn't miss her loved ones. She firmly believed her soul would fly free and know nothing but cocooned happiness until it was determined she was to reincarnate and come back to Earth.

She wondered for a moment what Slade thought about death. Was he religious? Did he believe in God? It was one more thing she'd never know about him.

Remembering why she felt sad, Dakota sighed. Her dad would take her death hard. After her mom died, it had taken him a long time to get back to a semblance of his old self. And Caroline? Did she make it to safety? Would she forgive herself if Dakota died? Would she spend the rest of her life wishing she'd done something differently?

And Slade. She'd known the man less than a week, but her soul had recognized his. She didn't talk about her beliefs with that many people, but the second she saw him, she knew they had to have known each other in another life. Knew they were meant to find each other in this one. And they'd had less than a week together. Less than a darn week.

Lifting her arm, not even noticing how much it shook, Dakota reached up to one of the stars. She wanted to touch it. To bring it down to Earth. To share it with Slade. But it remained out of reach. It looked like she was touching it, but when she closed her fist, she was left with nothing but air.

Dropping her arm in frustration, not feeling the water splash onto her numb cheeks, Dakota closed her eyes. She was so comfortable. The water wasn't even cold anymore.

"DID YOU SEE that?" Slade asked Cookie urgently.

"What? Where?"

"Eleven o'clock. It was a flash of pink in my goggles."

Rex was steering the boat in that direction without having to be told. Slade and Cookie repositioned themselves in the boat and aimed their gazes ahead of the Zodiac.

Cookie and Rex didn't even ask if Slade was sure. They didn't second-guess him. If Slade said he thought he saw something, they'd go and investigate. They were all aware of how much time was going by. Precious time that, if Dakota was alive, she didn't have.

Rex informed the other search boats that Slade thought he saw something and to hold for more intel.

As they got closer and closer to whatever it was Slade saw, he held his breath.

Please be Dakota. Please be Dakota. I need her. I can't lose her.

"Fuck me, it's her," Cookie murmured.

At the same time, Rex said into the headset, "We found her!"

Slade had already whipped off his thermals, not needing them to know what he was looking at. Dakota was lying on her back. The beige shawl she'd been wearing in the video was somehow still attached to her and floating around her in a mass of fluff. The silky pants were completely see-through and looked almost ethereal. Her hair around her head formed what appeared like a halo.

Her eyes were closed and her arms and legs outstretched. She looked as if she was taking a nap, except her lips were blue and her skin was an alarming shade of white. Whatever she'd done to catch his attention had probably taken the last of her strength.

Without thought, Slade ripped off his boots and slipped into the water, careful not to make any waves that would wash over her and possibly choke her. A part of him realized that Cookie was right there next to him in the water, but he didn't spare a glance for the other man, all his attention was on Dakota. Was she breathing? Was she alive? It certainly didn't look like it.

He was at her side with two hard strokes. He put one hand on the back of her neck, holding her still and making sure her head didn't slip underwater, and the other went under her, resting on her shoulder blades.

Slade knew Cookie went to her other side and put

his hands under her spine and butt, but he couldn't take his eyes off of Dakota's face. She'd been beaten, badly. Her lip was split and there was still blood oozing from one of her nostrils. Both eyes were swollen and she had several visible cuts on her face. He couldn't see the rest of her body to check for injuries, but he had no doubt they were there.

But she had a half smile on her face and she looked serene. It was unbelievable, but Slade almost didn't want to disturb her. Almost.

"Dakota? Can you hear me?"

Not expecting any response, Slade was shocked when her eyes popped open into slits and she looked at him.

"Slade?"

"Yeah, love. It's me." It was an inane conversation to have in the middle of the fucking ocean after he'd just killed the terrorist who'd married her live on video, but he didn't care.

"You came." The two words were said with absolutely certainty. Not wonder or surprise.

The tears he'd held back earlier filled his eyes and spilled over. Not once in his entire SEAL career had he ever cried over a rescue. Not once. But this was no ordinary rescue.

"You think you're ready to go home?" Cookie asked from the other side of her.

Dakota's eyes moved from Slade's face to Cookie's, and now she did look surprised. "You have a thing for rescuing women from the ocean."

The other SEAL laughed. "I see you and Ice had time to chat, huh?"

"Yeah. She okay?"

"Why don't we get back in the boat and see?" Slade suggested calmly. He had no idea what had happened to Caroline, but figured she was probably good since Wolf had taken off after her and Rex hadn't said otherwise. He and Cookie moved in unison, shifting Dakota closer to the Zodiac. By that time, two other boats had converged on the area to assist. They made a triangle around the trio in the water, protecting them from rogue waves.

Dakota closed her eyes and nodded.

"Keep your eyes open," Slade ordered.

Obediently they opened.

"That's it, love. Keep looking at me. I've got you."

Throughout the entire production of hauling her out of the water, stripping her clothes off, Slade removing his as well, and the other SEALs wrapping them both up together in an emergency blanket, she never looked away from him once.

Slade lie in the bottom of the Zodiac as it raced back to Coronado and the Naval base, where Commander Hurt had medical personnel standing by waiting for them, and marveled at the feeling of having Dakota back in his arms. It was literally a miracle that they'd been able to find her. People fell overboard all the time and were never heard from again.

"Are you injured anywhere besides your face?" he asked into her ear as they raced across the water.

She nodded.

"Where?"

Slade put his ear to her lips as she quietly spoke.

"My knee. My side. My hips."

"Do they hurt?"

"I can't feel anything. I'm not even cold. Maybe it's the drugs?"

"What drugs?" Slade asked urgently, motioning to Cookie with his head. The other SEAL leaned down so he could hear Dakota.

"He did something to me. Gave me something. Caroline too. He wanted us conscious, but not able to fight him."

"Did he rape you, love?" Slade reluctantly asked. He needed to know. Not for his sake, but for hers. If she'd been violated, he'd get her whatever help she needed in order to get past it. She was his, and nothing would keep him from her side. Literally nothing. He didn't care if she was pregnant. He hadn't planned on ever having children, not at his age, but if by some fluke, Zach had been able to go through with consummating his fucked-up idea of marriage and get her pregnant, he'd raise her baby as if it was his own. A child who would be half hers, and he loved Dakota with all his heart. Any baby of hers would never know hate. Would know nothing but love from both its parents.

"No."

Slade wanted to believe her, but wasn't sure he could.

He leaned down and put his lips right near her ear, making sure she could hear him loud and clear. "Nothing that happened will make me leave your side, love. Nothing. You understand?"

She nodded and he pulled back. Her skin was like ice against his. He was shivering nonstop, quaking with it, but she lay over him unmoving and still. It wasn't a good sign.

"He was waiting until we got to Mexico. Wanted to take his time. Give me more drugs. He wanted me to be inpacasitated...incamasitated...unable to do anything while he and his buddies raped me. I swear he didn't touch me that way, Slade. I wouldn't lie about it."

He breathed out a huge sigh of relief, closed his eyes, and rested his forehead against hers. "Thank fuck," he said, his lips brushing hers as he did.

Dakota struggled over him for a moment, and Slade loosened his grip so she could free her arms from between them. She wrapped them around him and buried her nose into the space between his neck and shoulder. Cookie was there to tuck the silver emergency blanket closer around her, making sure she was completely covered after she'd shifted.

Slade put one arm around her waist and the other on the back of her head.

"Did you kill him?" she mumbled into his skin.

"Yeah."

"Good."

And that was that. She didn't ask how. She didn't ask if Slade was sure Zach was dead. She merely relaxed against him. Her entire body going lax as she lay still in his embrace.

Slade looked up at the stars as they raced toward shore, marveling at how bright and clear they seemed. He'd seen the sky from remote places before, but it had never seemed as beautiful as right at that moment.

As he held Dakota in his arms and stared upward, a shooting star flew across his line of vision. It had been ages since he'd seen one. Slade closed his eyes and wished on that star as if he were a little boy instead of a hardened former Navy SEAL.

Please let her live.

Epilogue

"ARE YOU LOOKING forward to our trip?" Slade asked Dakota. They were walking along the beach near his apartment. He had his arm around her waist, letting her lean on him as her knee wasn't one hundred percent healed yet.

"More than you know," she said, looking up at him, the love easy to see in her eyes. "I can't believe Patrick is letting you leave so soon."

"It's been three months, love, it's not that soon," Slade protested.

She gave him a skeptical look, her eyebrows raised.

"Okay, yeah, having a homegrown terrorist working right under your nose would make anyone leery to let someone new in to take my place again, even temporarily," Slade agreed. He leaned down and kissed the tip of her nose as they resumed their walk. The physical therapist had said she needed to continue to take walks to build up the strength in her knee. She'd had surgery to repair the patellar tendon, which had torn when she'd been kicked by one of Zach's followers.

"Who did he finally approve?"

"It's another retired SEAL. Hurt said he will never work with another contractor who *hasn't* been a SEAL ever again." Slade shrugged. "Can't say I blame him. Not sure he can actually control that, but I wouldn't put it past him. Your dad okay with us taking off?"

Dakota nodded. "Yeah. He wasn't happy with everything that happened to me, but he's one of the strongest people I know. I'm so glad Jessyka went and got him and brought him to the hospital so he could be there with me. I know she was freaked out about Benny, but she took the time to go and get him. Your friends' wives are amazing."

"They are, aren't they?" Slade asked with a small smile. "But love, you're just as amazing."

As he thought she'd do, she shook her head. "No, I'm nothing like them."

Slade bought their slow stroll to a halt. "Please tell me you're not still blaming yourself for what happened to Caroline."

Dakota slowly shook her head. "No." When he continued to look at her skeptically, she sighed and shrugged. "I know she doesn't blame me, and neither does Wolf. But thinking about how pissed he must have been when he realized she was practically naked and all of Zach's men saw her like that...I can't help it."

Slade took her face in his hands and kissed her briefly on the lips. "She got off much easier than you, love. Wolf got to her and she was fine. Bruised and out of it from the drugs, but fine."

"You swear Wolf doesn't hate me?" Dakota asked softly. "Or the other guys? I know they say they don't, but I can't help but think that if it wasn't for me, she never would've been in that position."

"They love you. They're in awe of you. No one blames you. You need to let it go."

She sighed. "I'll try. Promise."

"Speaking of the guys, Benny wants to know when you're going over to his place again. His kids had such a great time with you, and you managed them all so well, I think you're in trouble."

"They're great kids. I'm glad Benny is okay. I was so scared when he slumped over the table that day."

"Zach had it well planned. They darted him through the kitchen window, then it was an easy thing to break one in the other room and enter the house. I told you how he'd decrypted my phone and listened to all my conversations. He had the code for the alarm, and punched it in while two other men took care of incapacitating you and Caroline."

She shivered. "I'm glad I don't remember anything after that."

Slade thought about how Zach and his men must've

stripped the two women, and silently agreed with her. He was glad she didn't remember either. "You might be interested to know that I found out the Johnson house was recently sold."

"That sucks."

"Sucks?"

"Not that the house was sold, but that Zach killed his parents. I mean, who *does* that? He chopped them up and kept them in a freezer. That's just sick."

"Love, this was the same man who laughed about that bomb at LAX and was planning on duplicating it all over the country."

"I know, but they were his *parents*. How could he do that?"

Slade kissed Dakota's temple and continued to walk with her. "Some people are just wired wrong."

"I guess. But saying they went on a cruise around the world was really smart. No one missed them and he was free to set up his terrorist shop right there on the beach." She bit her lip then said, "I'm kinda glad they weren't around to find out what a horrible person their son was." Then Dakota looked up at Slade. "And someone bought the house? I can't imagine living there. Talk about seeing ghosts!" she shivered.

"The city of Coronado bought it to tear it down and make it into a parking lot for the public beach nearby," Slade told her.

"Well, whew!" Dakota pantomimed wiping sweat off her brow. But then sobered. "It's still sad."

"You, my love, are simply incredible. I'm in awe of you. You have compassion for everyone you meet. Not only that, but you survived something that even today the doctors are still talking about. Your body temperature was ninety-one degrees, and that's by the time you got to the hospital. Most people lose consciousness at that point. They usually can't reason and are extremely confused. You defied all the odds. You not only weren't that confused, you were completely conscious and talking when we found you."

"It was the drugs," Dakota protested. "I have no idea how Zach knew about conscious sedation or where he got the Propofol, but it was certainly effective. I was helpless to protect myself from him, and he could've done whatever he wanted to me. I would've known he was doing it, but I couldn't have stopped him."

"No, love. It was you. You knew I was coming and you held on. For me."

"That's true," she conceded. "Caroline told me time and time again that you guys would be coming. She swore that you'd figure out my message and were on your way."

"She was right," Slade said. "But be that as it may, Caroline being kidnapped again wasn't your fault."

Dakota sighed and rested her head on Slade's chest,

burrowing into his warm strength. "What happened to the bodies of Zach and his buddies?"

Used to her topic changes, Slade went with it. "Rex's teammates, Phantom, Gumby, Ace, Rocco, and Bubba, secured the boats and their bodies were taken care of."

"And?"

"And you don't need to know anything more than that," Slade told her.

"They're really all dead though, right? They're not sitting in Guantanamo Bay plotting revenge against us? You wouldn't lie to me about that to try and make me not worry, would you?"

"They're all dead. You have nothing to worry about," Slade said in a hard tone. He felt Dakota's arms squeeze him, but she didn't move out of his embrace.

"Do you think...that storm the next morning seemed to move in out of nowhere," she said. "It was supposed to be a beautiful day. Maybe it was a higher power cleansing the entire area, getting rid of the evil vibes that remained or something."

"Hmmm." Slade made the noncommittal noise deep in his throat.

"Whatever. I'm glad he's gone."

"Me too, love. And you don't have to worry about anyone from Ansar al-Shari'a coming after you again. Tex posted a note on the same underground site Zach had been using to say that you both had been killed.

The movement pretty much died after that because there wasn't anyone around to pick up the cause. I'm not saying they won't regroup, but if they do, it'll probably be with a real Tunisian, not an American impersonating one."

They walked for a while, both lost in their thoughts before Slade spoke again. "Can I ask you something?"

"Of course," Dakota said, looking up at him.

"Are you really okay with not going back to work? You've been there a long time. The school board said they'd take you back in a heartbeat if you wanted."

She shrugged. "I know, but...it's hard to explain."

"Try."

"Bossy," Dakota said, but she was smiling when she did. "Slade, I've spent my whole life working. I quit for a valid reason, but I found that working at the A'le'Inn was a whole new kind of satisfaction. I didn't need a degree, it wasn't that stimulating but it was freeing. I didn't have to worry about paperwork after my shift. Once I was done working, I was done. No meetings, no pleasing parents, no worrying about test scores or politics. I met a ton of really neat people. And I enjoyed the freedom of doing what I wanted, when I wanted." She shrugged. "It probably makes me a bad person, but I like not working."

"It doesn't make you a bad person, love. It makes you human."

"I guess." Then she smiled up at him and put her hand on his bearded cheek. Her thumb caressed him as she said, "I hate lemons, but I love lemonade."

Slade filed away the random fact about her, just as he had all the others he'd learned over the months. "In a box at my mom's house is the very first uniform I ever bought when I joined the Navy. She wouldn't let me throw it away."

They smiled at each other for a long moment before Slade turned her in his arms and they slowly started back toward his apartment. They'd begun sharing small facts about themselves shortly after she woke up after her knee surgery and was coherent.

They both realized how little they knew about each other and set about fixing that as soon as possible. She'd learned sign language because one of the kids in her school was deaf. She'd wanted to be able to communicate directly with the child instead of going through her interpreter. If he'd known that about her, they could've figured out her message sooner and gotten to both women before the terrorists had left for the boats.

"If I had a choice between watching only Disney movies for the rest of my life or action/adventure, I'd choose Disney every time," Dakota said as they walked.

"Why?"

"Because there's always a happy ever after with Disney."

"You wouldn't get sick of the cartoons? Or the singing?" Slade asked, smiling.

"Nope. You know how much I love to sing in the shower."

He did. The first time she'd been allowed to shower without the home health care nurse with her, he'd heard a god-awful noise coming from his bathroom. He'd raced upstairs and burst into the room, a knife in his hand, ready to kill whoever was hurting his woman, and had realized the screeching he'd heard was actually Dakota singing. Or trying to. They'd shared a good laugh and he'd made her promise not to scare the shit out of him like that ever again.

Surprisingly enough, as much as he'd been reluctant to rush it, their love life was amazing. Even with her recovery and bum knee, they'd found ways to be intimate. Last month, she'd finally convinced him she wasn't in any pain and was ready to become his in every way.

He'd taken his time, learned every inch of her body with both his fingers and mouth, before slowly sinking into her hot depths. It had been an amazing experience for them both. They hadn't rushed, had taken their time, savoring the feeling of being one for the very first time.

Tomorrow they were taking off on a three-week trip through Vegas, up to Rachel, where they were spending a whole week, then down highway ninety-five, where they'd take their time and visit every haunted hotel and mine they could find. He had a bottle of peppermint syrup already packed in his bag. It wouldn't make her morning coffee taste like the specialty ones she liked, but it'd come close...he hoped. He'd bought one of those fancy coffee makers so she could have a cup of her favorite peppermint coffee every morning.

He'd made plans for them to stay at one of the super-expensive suites in Vegas toward the end of their trip, although Dakota didn't know about that yet.

Slade smiled when he thought about the ring he'd bought for her. It was at the bottom of his bag, and he was going to propose to her one night when they were in Rachel. It seemed appropriate that he ask her to spend the rest of her life with him in the same place they met for the first time. He planned to propose while they lay on top of his car watching for shooting stars. He couldn't ever look up at the night sky and not think of her.

Then he was going to see if he couldn't convince her to marry him in Vegas on their way home. He'd already made arrangements for her dad to fly out so he could be there if she agreed. There was no way she'd want to get married without her dad present, and Slade would never ask it of her.

But he wasn't willing to wait for anyone else. It was

unfair of him, and selfish; she probably wanted the whole white-wedding-in-a-church thing, but he didn't want to wait. He wanted his ring on her finger and his name after hers. If she wanted a big shindig, he'd give that to her when they got home. In fact, Wolf and the rest of the guys would probably demand it, but he wanted to officially make her his as soon as possible.

"I'm sad we can't take your Harley," Dakota told him as they reached his apartment complex.

"I know, but we'll go out another time," Slade reassured her. There was no way she'd be able to ride the bike for long distances with her knee still recovering. He'd bought her a brand-new Subaru Outback to replace the car Fourati's goons had stolen from Rachel. When they'd figured out that their friend had been compromised, they'd left him there to fend for himself with the cops. It hadn't been hard for them to steal Dakota's Impreza since her keys were in the ignition. At least they hadn't killed anyone in the small town.

They hadn't had to rush after them though, because, thanks to the conversations Zach had overheard, Slade's plan to go back to San Diego and Wolf's house wasn't exactly a secret.

Later that night, after Slade had made them a delicious meal of steak and veggies, they showered together and slipped into his king-size bed.

Dakota lay on top of him, naked from head to toe,

SUSAN STOKER

and played with his beard.

"When I was out there—you know, in the ocean—I thought about us," she told him quietly.

Slade was hard and more than ready to slip inside her hot, wet body, but he waited patiently as she worked through what she wanted to tell him.

"We'd only known each other for a short time, but I felt as if I'd known you forever."

"You know I feel the same way. From the first time I saw your photo, I knew I had to find you."

"Do you think...no, it's silly."

"What, love? Nothing you think is silly."

"It's just that...do you think we were lovers in a past life? That we somehow knew each other?"

Slade's heart stopped for a beat, then continued with its regular rhythm, albeit a bit faster. He hadn't really thought about it before, but it made sense. All his life he'd felt as if he was missing something. None of the women he'd been with had made him yearn for them as Dakota did. He'd thought he'd loved his ex-wife, but now that he'd met Dakota and realized what love really was, he realized that he'd liked Cynthia, but had never truly loved her like she deserved to be loved.

"I think anything is possible," he told Dakota.

"There's really no reason I should've survived," she continued, oblivious to the impact her words were having on the man lying under her. "I mean, with the beating, the drugs he gave me, being able to escape the boat without Zach knowing, and then being so cold…it's just not feasible I was that lucky. You know what I think?" she asked softly, leaning down and kissing Slade on the lips.

"What, love?"

"I think we were meant to be together. And even though it took us forever to find each other, whoever is in charge of souls decided we were gypped and it wasn't fair to break us up so soon. We'd found each other, but didn't have time to truly enjoy it. So we got a break, a second chance."

Slade was quiet as he considered her words.

"I told you it was silly," she said with a wrinkle of her nose. "Don't listen to me."

"It wasn't silly," Slade insisted. "I've had some close calls in my career. Times when I knew I should've been killed, but somehow wasn't. I was sitting right next to Tex when that IED hit. He lost his leg, and I came out with not even a scratch. I never understood why. Until now. It's because I hadn't met you."

"Slade," Dakota whispered, her eyes filling with tears.

It was his turn to frame her face with his hands now. "Call it God, call it the keeper of the souls, call it whatever you want. But I'll believe until we're old and gray that it's Fate. We were meant to find each other.

Meant to spend our lives together. And you know what else?"

"What?" she asked.

"I think we'll find each other in our next lives too. And the next, and the next. A love like ours can't be confined to only one lifetime."

"I hope so."

"I know so," he countered. And with that he kissed her. A long kiss that quickly turned carnal. Slade carefully flipped them until Dakota was under him. Her legs spread and his hips notched into hers. One hand went from her face, down her body, stopping to play with her nipples along the way. When they both needed to take a breath, he moved his lips from her mouth down to her chest.

He licked and sucked at her nipples, as his hand continued to move south. He caressed her folds as he bit and nipped at her taut buds. She'd come a long way since the first time they'd been together after her ordeal. The first time he'd touched her chest, she'd freaked out. Slade had held her close as she'd told him about what Zach had done to her.

But now she was eager for his mouth, and she not only enjoyed, but craved a harder touch on her nipples. Loved it when he pinched her hard peaks as he played with her. Wanting to taste her, Slade moved down her body, settling himself on his stomach between her legs.

He pushed them up until they rested on his shoulders.

"Comfortable?" he asked. Ever aware of her knee, he waited to continue until she nodded.

Once she reassured him, he dipped his head and lightly licked her distended bud, which was already peeking out from its protective hood. Using one fingertip, he teased her opening as he licked and sucked on her bundle of nerves.

It wasn't until she was shifting under him, pressing her hips up toward his face, begging for him to stop messing around, that he slowly eased his finger inside her. He'd never get tired of how hot and tight she was. It was as if her body was made for him and only him. He smiled at the feel of her copious juices easing the way. She knew what she wanted and wasn't ashamed of the way her body wept for him.

He licked harder at her clit as he curled his index finger inside her and found her G-spot. Dakota was the most responsive woman he'd ever been with, and he knew it was because they were meant to belong to each other. He smiled as she clenched against him and moaned as he set up a rhythmic stroking of that special spot inside her.

Able to read her body as well as his own, he loved the way Dakota's thighs began to shake and her hips pressed upward. She was close, and he couldn't wait to feel her explode. He didn't need to be inside her to glory in her orgasm.

He concentrated on licking hard and fast over her clit while at the same time increasing the speed of his finger against her G-spot. Within seconds, she was shaking uncontrollably and Slade felt a surge of wetness against his palm as she came.

He continued to lap at her clit until he felt her flinch away from his touch. He brought the finger that had been inside her up to his mouth and licked it clean. Then he crawled up her boneless body and kneeled over her. His cock was dripping precome and he couldn't wait to be inside the woman he loved.

"I love you," he told her.

"I love you too," Dakota responded immediately. Her eyes moved over his face, from his beard, which was soaked in her juices, to his lips, which he licked as she watched. He felt her shiver under him with increased desire.

"I need you," she told him without an ounce of shyness.

"I'll *always* need you," Slade returned. Then reached down and grasped his rock-hard cock and ran it up and down her soaked slit. She tilted her hips up as he got to where she wanted him and pressed her hands into his ass cheeks.

Moving slowly, Slade sank into her body. "Every time feels like the first," he said in awe. "Your body grabs mine and sucks me in."

"I love the feel of you inside me," Dakota told him.

"And I love the feel of me inside you," Slade said with a smile. It was a running joke between them, a ritual of sorts. He pressed inside her until he couldn't go any more, then put one hand under her ass, lifted, and was able to gain another precious few millimeters. When he felt his balls flush against her ass, she used her inner muscles to squeeze him.

Slade took a deep breath and squeezed her butt in response. "So greedy," he said with a smile.

"Always. I want all you can give me."

He pulled out slowly, looking down between them, watching as his cock emerged from her body, covered in her excitement. "I'll never get tired of this," he told her, not taking his eyes away from where they were joined as he sank back inside. "I love seeing you all over my cock."

Then he brought his eyes back up to hers, propped himself up with both hands on the mattress at her sides and began to make love to her.

In and out.

In and out.

He pressed in slowly, then pulled out quickly.

He gave her a few fast strokes, then slowed and moved inside her leisurely, making love as if he could last all night.

But Dakota wasn't in the mood for slow tonight. She bent both knees and wrapped her thighs high around his lower back. "Fuck me, Slade. I need it. I need you."

Knowing he was losing the precious control he'd been holding on to for all he was worth, Slade partially sat up and took hold of her ankles in his hands. He gently placed them on his shoulders, then leaned over her again.

Dakota was now almost folded in half and completely at his mercy. She moved one hand up to her head and grabbed a pillow from next to her. Slade helped her stuff it under her ass, then she raised both arms above her and held on to the slats of his bed.

She looked him in the eye and said softly, "Fuck me, Slade. Fuck me hard."

Her words released his iron control. He slammed into her, hard, knowing from the moan she let out that she loved it. He did it again. Then again. Each time she gripped him and thrust her pelvis up toward him.

Slade knew he wasn't going to last. With every thrust, it felt as if he could feel himself bottom out inside her. She was so tight, and so wet, the noises his cock made as it tunneled inside her were almost obscene. But he didn't care, and apparently neither did Dakota.

"Come inside me, Slade. Fill me up."

After another talk about children, Slade had undergone a vasectomy. He'd wanted the freedom to come inside Dakota and didn't want her to have to fill her body with hormones to prevent an accidental pregnancy. It was the best decision he'd ever made, because now he could fuck her without anything between them. It was messy, sure, but also intimate and exciting.

As if her words were all his balls had been waiting for, they let loose a monster load of come. He reached between them and thumbed Dakota's clit hard as he came. He felt her come a second time as he did. They jerked and thrust against each other, lost in the joy and pleasure of their bodies and being together.

Slade came back to himself before Dakota did, and he gently removed her legs from his shoulders, kissing each calf before carefully placing them back on the mattress, making sure not to jostle her still-healing knee. He kept himself lodged inside her, knowing he'd eventually slip out, and turned them until Dakota was once more lying on top of him.

"Mmmmm," she murmured, stretching against him like a contented kitten.

"You okay? Nothing hurts?" Slade asked.

"No. I'm great. Awesome," she said sleepily.

"I love you," Slade told her.

"Love you too."

A short moment passed, then Dakota said, "My second toe is longer than my big toe."

Slade smiled. He'd never, ever get tired of hearing her give him silly facts about her. "I don't have any tattoos because I'm scared of needles."

She lifted her head at that and looked at him incredulously. "Really?"

"Really."

"Hmmm. I felt awful when I was taken that I didn't know more about you, but I just realized that I knew the most important thing. Everything else is just fluff. Fluff I like, don't get me wrong, but we could go for the rest of our lives and still not know everything there is to know about each other."

"What was the most important thing, love?" Slade asked.

"I knew down to my very soul that you would do whatever you had to do to find me."

"Damn straight," Slade said, and kissed her hard. It was wet, and long, and he hoped it conveyed all that he was feeling.

It did.

"I love you," Dakota said as she lay her head on his chest and snuggled in for the night.

"And I love you, sweetheart."

GREG LAMBERT COULDN'T sleep. He'd re-read through

the final report that Slade Cutsinger had sent him. It had been thorough and complete and he couldn't help but feel a twinge of pride that he'd had a hand in removing a terrorist threat that would've crippled the United States if it had been left unchecked.

But that didn't mean there weren't more threats looming. Slade and his friends might've ended one, but there were still plenty more.

The pressure of knowing there were more terrorists out there, plotting and planning to kill innocent American citizens, made it hard for Greg to sleep. Sitting up and throwing his feet over the side of his mattress, he decided that since he wasn't sleeping, he might as well get up and plan the next takedown.

He shuffled into his home office. Kissing his fingers and pressing them to the glass of the frame that held a picture of his late wife, Greg settled into the chair behind his desk. He pulled out the list of former Navy SEALs who'd been identified as candidates for the solo missions and tried to decide who to call, and which terrorist to take down next.

Running his finger down the page, he stopped at one name. Bingo. He'd researched this man and knew without a doubt he would succeed in what Greg was going to ask of him. The former commander glanced at his watch. It was too early to call right now, but in the meantime, he'd make notes.

One terrorist might've been taken down, but there was always more waiting in the wings.

Greg picked up the cold cup of tea he'd been drinking earlier and added a splash of whiskey. Then he held it up in a silent toast. *To Slade...and Dakota. May you live the rest of your lives free from the worries of terrorism. Love each other like there's no tomorrow, because you never know when there might not be.*

And with that, Greg slammed back the strong concoction and took a deep breath. Time to get back to work.

The End

To sign up for Susan's Newsletter go to:
www.stokeraces.com/contact-1.html

Or text: STOKER to 24587 for text alerts on your mobile device

Discover other titles
by Susan Stoker

Delta Force Heroes

Rescuing Rayne

Assisting Aimee – Loosely related to Delta Force

Rescuing Emily

Rescuing Harley

Marrying Emily

Rescuing Kassie

Rescuing Bryn

Rescuing Casey (Jan 2018)

Rescuing Sadie (April 2018)

Rescuing Wendy (May 2018)

Rescuing Mary (Nov 2018)

Badge of Honor: Texas Heroes

Justice for Mackenzie

Justice for Mickie

Justice for Corrie

Justice for Laine

Shelter for Elizabeth

Justice for Boone

Shelter for Adeline

Shelter for Sophie

Justice for Erin (Nov 2017)

Justice for Milena (Mar 2018)

Shelter for Blythe (July 2018)

Connect with Susan Online

Susan's Facebook Profile and Page:
www.facebook.com/authorsstoker
www.facebook.com/authorsusanstoker

Follow Susan on Twitter:
www.twitter.com/Susan_Stoker

Find Susan's Books on Goodreads:
www.goodreads.com/SusanStoker

Email: Susan@StokerAces.com

Website: www.StokerAces.com

To sign up for Susan's Newsletter go to:
www.stokeraces.com/contact-1.html

Or text: STOKER to 24587 for text alerts on your mobile device

About the Author

New York Times, *USA Today*, and *Wall Street Journal* Bestselling Author Susan Stoker has a heart as big as the state of Texas, where she lives, but this all-American girl has also spent the last fourteen years living in Missouri, California, Colorado, and Indiana. She's married to a retired Army man who now gets to follow *her* around the country.

She debuted her first series in 2014 and quickly followed that up with the SEAL of Protection Series, which solidified her love of writing and creating stories readers can get lost in.

If you enjoyed this book, or any book, please consider leaving a review. It's appreciated by authors more than you'll know.

Made in the USA
San Bernardino, CA
26 November 2017